THE FINGERLESS GLOVES

SECONDS OUT

GARY TULLEY

Matador
9 Priory Business Park,
Wistow Road, Kibworth Beauchamp,
Leicestershire. LE8 0RX
Tel: 0116 279 2299
Email: books@troubador.co.uk
Web: www.troubador.co.uk/matador
Twitter: @matadorbooks

ISBN 978 1785891 038

British Library Cataloguing in Publication Data.
A catalogue record for this book is available from the British Library.

Printed and bound in the UK by TJ International, Padstow, Cornwall
Typeset in 11pt Aldine401 BT by Troubador Publishing Ltd, Leicester, UK

Matador is an imprint of Troubador Publishing Ltd

I'd like to dedicate this book to my brother, Brian.
Thanks, mate, you never gave up on me.

FOREWORD

Expectations were on a high; forecasts were being realized. Like many coastal towns, Stonewater was benefiting from the effects of stable weather and tourism. 'No vacancy' signs appeared to be prolific, dispelling any pessimism, synonymous to the trade. Unlike its counterparts, Stonewater appeared to have that much more to offer, notoriety being no exception. Over the years, the town had attracted many nationalities, all eager to gain a foothold on the framework of opportunity. A 'passport to happiness' brought only misery for some.

Disillusioned, they moved on; the more ambitious chose to stay. Pocket ghettos now existed, in many districts of the town, catering for Irish to Asian. Many of these people were now third-generation families, readily accepted by the locals and classed as 'being one of yer own'. As a result of its cosmopolitan atmosphere, an 'underworld' had emerged. This, in turn, drew its resources from the more ambitious of the fraternity.

For years now, it had long been a backdoor haven for out-of-town villains. In the past, many such types had made the move. Indeed, an hour's run on the motorway became all too convenient for the hop down from London. Add to this the flamboyant circle of media personalities that resided within the community and you have the ingredients of the inevitable melting pot.

CHAPTER 1

GETTING THERE

It was late June. The tranquil coolness of the evening air offered a sense of relief to one particular jogger on the lower esplanade. Overhead whispers of sea mist hung down like gossamer shrouds, as if suspended in time, leaving predatory gulls to wheel and to screech defiantly at the incoming spring tide. Meanwhile, at ground level, the mist began to thicken, while creating diverse shadows from a ceiling of overhead neon lights.

Rapt in his own importance, the jogger appeared to be divorced from the impending crowds and traffic that were now beginning to converge on the nearby Queensway. Head down, chest pumping, he headed towards the direction of the derelict west pier. Momentarily, he shortened his stride pattern to check his watch. He noted that it was fast approaching 6.30 pm. Muttering aimlessly under his breath, he decided to increase his speed.

By now, the vast majority of Beano coaches had long left. Although a few late arrivals still remained, intending to mock the resident curfew. Any other night, they wouldn't have had the prevailing mist as an ally. For their part, it didn't enter the equation. Holidaymakers and locals alike seemed oblivious to its presence. That certain 'buzz' chose to rise above. 'Game on' never sounded so good.

As for the lone jogger, bodies in numbers now represented

1

a threat. Cursing under his breath, he was forced to sidestep a group of hell-raisers bent on seeking sanctuary in one of the many bars and clubs that formed the periphery of the town. His immediate reaction had in turn become personal.

'Ruddy piss artists,' he yelled back at them over his shoulder. His efforts were wasted, as the mist swallowed them up. Before long, the strains of funfair music drifted within earshot, carried on the night air, telling him the pier was now fast approaching. Because of the impending crowd situation, he made a last-minute decision to take advantage of the Kingswalk subway as a means of diversion.

Briefly, his features took on a serious mode, as he reproached himself for the earlier confrontation. It would seem that the strict self-discipline ruling his exclusive way of life had by design come under scrutiny. Any further thoughts died a death, as the welcoming light thrown out by the subway became visible through the fog. Increasing his stride pattern soon brought him to the exit. Like a magnet, the swirling mist drew him inside. His breathing slowed, as he came to a stop, and, hands on hips, he gazed around, squinting to adjust his eyes to the 'plastic' lighting. In the past, he'd always allowed himself a moment of respite, prior to getting to his intended destination, in this case, the boxing gymnasium that he managed in town.

It had become a privilege that went with age. Here was a man, well into his fifties, although his well-honed body could well have graced a man ten years his junior.

'Can't let the bleeders think I'm past it,' would have been his reply had it been questionable. A look of distaste carpeted his face, as his eyesight adjusted to the gloom. He couldn't help but notice the rubbish, the graffiti, and the odd used condom littering the subway floor. He glanced intently at one particular section of graffiti that had caught his eye, forcing him to smile at 'GOD IS A WOMAN!' while below, not to be undone, another joker had added, 'MAYBE... BUT OLD NICK STILL RULES THE WORLD!'

Nearby, he could just make out two resident winos haggling over the dregs contained in a bottle of cider. His facial features changed to one of disgust, as the cold dank night air brought him back to reality.

'Better be on the move,' he reminded himself, and adjusted the towel from around his neck. Moments later, in a show of fantasy, the jogger began acting out his thoughts to an audience of one. Steeling himself, his whole body took on a fresh new meaning, allowing a surge of egotism to take over. Between paces, he began to throw combination punches at shoulder level, as he assumed an imaginary target. It would appear that self-esteem had clouded his judgment by allowing his mind to temporarily wander. 'I reckon I've still got what it takes!' he assured himself.

By now the adrenalin had begun to flow. In a split second, he'd managed to turn the clock back some thirty years. Locked in his own private world, his mind continued to meander.

'Timing still good, reflexes sharp.' He continued to act out the charade.

'Callaghan!' Somewhere from outside of his bubble, an alien voice endeavoured to make itself heard. There was no doubting that the incursion was made intentionally for his ears only. As it was, it made little or no impact on him whatsoever, even though it was his name's sake. From out of the gloom of the subway, an alien figure had begun to bear down on him, backed up with a similar request, this time around with added force.

'Ronnie... Ronnie Callaghan?!'

The sound of the voice slammed into his subconscious, and stopped him in mid-punch. The voice also belonged in the past and Ronnie swiftly questioned his sanity. Any doubts he may have held were unfounded. That particular voice had undoubtedly struck a nerve. To his way of thinking, an altercation could well be on the cards. And right now, that was the last thing he needed.

'I don't believe this, any other face,' he growled under his breath. Tensing himself, he cleared his head, and tentatively approached the shadowy figure. The subdued lighting gave way to realization, forcing him to pull up short. There were strangers, and there were strangers. This particular one just happened to be an 18ct loser, and what's more, he happened to be standing in Ronnie's way! And the figure resembled grief! The minutes were slowly ticking down, and he had a gym to open.

Glaring intently, he decided to take the initiative, and made as if to pass by. For a second, he wasn't about to go anywhere fast. An unexpected outstretched arm made a play for him, the intention being to block his path. Acting on blind instinct, Ronnie parried to one side, causing his tormentor to topple forwards, fully exposing his face. His thoughts were fully justified, and he was far from being impressed.

'Shit! What the hell d'ye think yer playing at?' he questioned, and raised his loose arm, as if to strike back.

'Relax, take it easy, Ronnie. It's me... Paul Rossetti.' Lowering his arm, he eased the situation, but still felt totally bogged down. 'Don't tell me,' continued Rossetti, 'you're off to the gym... right?' It wasn't even a question, and stank of sarcasm. Plainly, it was fodder for a verbal showdown.

Patronising bastard, Ronnie told himself, and didn't allow himself to rise to the bait. With time on his hands, Rossetti had nothing to lose. The circumstances surrounding their altercation, whether it be by chance or otherwise, would serve as a dress rehearsal for the months to follow, although he wasn't prepared to let it drop that quickly. He was eager to push his luck one more time. The corners of his mouth widened into a forced smile.

'I couldn't help but notice—'

'Do yerself a favour.'

Ronnie's intervention fell way short as Rossetti persisted.

'...how sharp yer looking these days.'

Once again, Ronnie turned a deaf ear. Inwardly, his mind, body, and soul were elsewhere. Through no fault of his own, he was facing a situation of his own esteem. It seemed that yet again his colourful past had caught up with him. As a prodigious ex-pro fighter turned trainer, he'd become a personality on the 'manor'. At his peak, the champions' crown had eluded him. The term 'gutsy journeyman' had been the press of his day. Long after his retirement, 'Joe Public' had taken him to their hearts. His genuineness for the leather game was flawless; what he couldn't handle started with the artificial hype that went with the mantle.

As for Rossetti, intimidation was only one facet of his makeup, which he tended to use at every advantage available. From an early age, his dubious track record had come back to haunt him on many an occasion. As a kid living on the street, he revelled in the company of the so-called 'bully boys'. Living as they did a street apart, it was inevitable that a run-in with Callaghan would be on the cards. When it finally happened, credibility was cheap. On a one-to-one-basis, Rossetti appeared to be out of his depth. Ronnie had given him more than a bloody good hiding. From then on, the seeds of eternal hate were sown.

An onlooker who had witnessed Rossetti's downfall had been quick to note Callaghan's prowess. He'd been quoted as stating, 'That kid's gonna be useful when he grows up.' Little did the guy know at the time that was to become Ronnie's hallmark in later life. A wiser man would have learnt by it; not so Rossetti. Over the years that followed, the hate that he'd consumed for Callaghan now resembled a cancer that slowly ate away at his stubborn pride. The exclusive blood that flowed through his veins bore testament only to his psychopathic personality. In the past, other incidents had arisen. The name 'loser' had been bandied around by everyone excluding the firm that stood for him. They lived by their set of rules; the well-worn adage 'You don't fuck your own up!' was well underlined. On a par, Ronnie's version would run with 'If yer out of order, you get a slap!' That became the gospel according to his way of life.

The situation that he now found himself in had become intolerable. He'd heard and seen enough. He threw a hurried glance at his watch; time was running at a loss.

'Shit!' he exclaimed. 'I'm out of 'ere.' Quickly sidestepping, he made for the stairs forming the exit to the subway, pausing suddenly to shout a sarcastic, 'Be lucky,' over his shoulder.

Fists clenched tightly, his face now contorted with anger, Rossetti was left to reflect on what might have been. A nearby empty beer can took the brunt of his frustration; it did little to aid his woeful cause. Staring long and hard into the night, he made a vain effort to collect his shattered thoughts. Eventually, with trembling hands, he removed a packet of cigarettes from within the inside of his jacket pocket. A futile effort to strike a match failed miserably. A second attempt proved to be no better. Cursing the world at large, he threw the box on the ground, methodically crushing it underfoot with his shoe.

Once again, it seemed that the loser syndrome had come back to haunt him. Callaghan hadn't been suckered in, and he didn't like it. Spinning round on his heel, he made for the exit. His mind was on overtime. The chill in the air had affected the prevailing mist. Fog had now started to form, and visibility centred on low.

Apart from constant weaving his way through the now crowded Kings Drive, Ronnie felt good within himself. He allowed a wry smile to carpet his face, as he reflected on Rossetti's pathetic attempt to put him down. 'The asshole done himself up like a kipper!' would have been one way of putting it, he mused, and continued to smile in his own exclusive manner.

Bodies, he noted, were appearing from everywhere. And he found himself forced to make his way through a crowd waiting for a disco hall to open. Once clear, he stopped to tighten his tracksuit top. There was no doubting the coldness in the air. In spite of this, beads of sweat forced their own individual way through his leather-clad skin. The prominent scar tissue over his eyes offered little or no resistance by allowing minute rivulets to form on his brow. With a controlled shake of his head, he managed to disperse the offending drops. The gym felt like it was a million miles away due to his broken schedule.

*

Meanwhile, in the opposite direction, a lone figure with bowed head could be seen approaching a large chauffeur-driven, red saloon car that happened to be parked in a convenient bay. After wrenching the back passenger door open, the figure got in, and spread himself seat wise.

'Where to, guv?' As if in anticipation, the driver made no effort to turn round and acknowledge a reply.

'Miami Club, via the pier!' His request was emphatic and spoken with deliberation. Turning the key, the engine burst into life, and slowly the car slid away from out of the bay.

*

To make up for lost time, Ronnie had decided to ignore a controlled crossing, and instead, forced a path through to the kerb. The fog at this point had really thickened by now, causing him to strain his eyes into making use of the lighting thrown from the adjacent hotels. More bodies seemed to be out in force, and did nothing to aid his concern. Caught up in the never ending sea of people briefly clouded his judgment. In his haste, he decided to cross when a welcome break in the traffic suddenly appeared. The added safety aspect of an island on the camber of the road appealed to him, and spurred his ego on.

Unfortunately, it wasn't to be. For some unknown reason, he suddenly stopped short, as a sixth sense cut in. From out the corner of his eye, he spotted a large menacing red shape looming up towards him.

'What the bloody hell!' was the best he could manage, leaving him to freeze in his tracks. To all intentions he was hospital fodder, all options barred. In a split second, his whole world had turned full circle. Every situation, every corner he had fought his way out of, instantly converged. His heart was thumping, head pounding; the ultimate word 'survival' screamed at him from somewhere inside his obsolete brain. As so many times before, the 'down and out' didn't fit into the equation. As far as Callaghan was concerned, he still had a hell of a lot of living to do yet! Digging deep into his physical resources, self-preservation took on a fresh slant, enabling his reflexes to form a mind of their own. Instinctively, he threw himself backwards, arms outstretched, hoping to break his fall. There was a loud screeching of tyres, and the stench of burning rubber filled his nostrils, as he attempted to regain distant senses. Struggling to focus, his immediate attention fell on a large stationary object that had come to a stop a few yards away from where he had been previously standing. His eyes were forced into a double take; there was no question in his mind. He was now looking at a red Mercedes saloon car, something he wasn't about to forget in a hurry. Continuing to stare at the car, an ice-cold shiver overtook his frame, causing him to involuntarily shudder at the thought of what might have been.

Slowly, the rear passenger window slid down, and interrupted his thinking. The blood drained from Ronnie's face knowing that his first conclusion was the right one. From the open window of the car, the leering face of Rossetti appeared. He gazed downwards at the crumpled form of Ronnie lying outstretched in the gutter. A look of sheer contempt etched his face; for a second he milked the memory. He'd felt good on past occasions, but this was something to savour, especially at Callaghan's expense.

'You got lucky this time around, Ronnie, but you ain't always gonna be a winner!' Rossetti had spelt it out in no uncertain terms, so it came over as a meaningful threat, as opposed to a gesture of sympathy. A half-hearted attempt was wasted. The car lurched forwards, leaving Ronnie to choke once again in the wake of the exhaust fumes. Gingerly, Ronnie attempted to pick himself up, whilst at the same time checking for any would-be injuries. There was no doubt he was visibly shaken by his ordeal, and a throbbing elbow added only misery to his misplaced demeanour.

By now, a small crowd had begun to form. Seemingly unaware of their presence, Ronnie stood, as if in a trance rubbing his arm. Realization had not yet set in, and his face gave no indication as to his present thoughts. Slowly but surely, the 'accident' came back to him with a jolt.

'How could I be that stupid?!' he cried out loud.

Just for once in his life, he'd been suckered, and made to

feel vulnerable. It was of his own making, a rash decision that could have proved fatal. That was bad enough, but what of Rossetti's involvement? His addled brain flipped from one consequence to another. One thing was certain: nothing he came up with was making any sense.

'Excuse me, guv, anything I can do for you?' The request came by way of an onlooker who'd witnessed the alleged accident. His plea fell on deaf ears, as the monotonous wailing emerging from an ambulance broke his chain of thought.

'Christ! The bloody gym!' he retorted.

'You sure you're okay, mate?' This time, the plaintiff request finally got through to him.

'Yeah, don't worry about it, but thanks all the same.' Reality had finally set in; nothing else seemed relevant anymore. From start to finish, the episode had taken only a few minutes. In that time, the traffic was still maintaining a steady crawl, although the fog at last was lifting somewhat. A welcome gap appeared in the traffic, and he seized the moment. On reaching the other side of the road, he paused briefly to collect himself. Breathing deeply, he regained his composure, and broke into his stride. Within minutes, a convenient side street beckoned; leaving the Kings Drive behind him, he readily swung in, and lost himself in the gloom of the night.

The door to the gym proved more than a welcome sight. Hurriedly, he grasped the handle, and in doing so his hand somehow slipped off.

'Damn!' he exclaimed loudly. Inwardly, he blamed himself for his mistiming. The second attempt wasn't a problem. On entering, he slowly closed the door behind him. The ever familiar smell of stale sweat and body oils filled his nostrils. Breathing a sigh of welcome relief, he removed the towel from around his neck, and wiped his face all over. Placing his hands on his hips, he glanced around, and began to take stock.

There was no disguising his feelings; the look on his face said it all, as he evoked a childish grin. His innermost thoughts said it all for him. *Home, bloody home!*

CHAPTER 2

A PUNCH IN THE RIGHT DIRECTION

The rhythmic staccato beat of a speedball filled the air in contrast to the swishing of busy ropes. This, in turn, complemented the irregular thud of leather on canvas. Above the din, voices issuing encouragement and mingled with orders were being expressed to heaving and grunting bodies from around the gym floor. As yet, Ronnie hadn't moved but continued to look on, as he relished every aspect of the round in progress. This was his own private domain, and he revelled in its being. A punch bag jerked spasmodically towards his direction. Nimbly sidestepping, he quickly made his way to the far end of the gym. As was the norm, Joe Public were allowed to spectate.

Tonight being no exception, a dozen or so 'disciples' could be seen lining the floor perimeter. Cries of 'Be first, jab, and move' echoed their singular enthusiasm. Turning round, Ronnie looked across in their direction. A wistful smile crossed his face, as he replied with a negative shake of his head. 'Bloody sideline trainers!' became the term he favoured above others. But their love for the business was never going to be an issue. Once clear, Ronnie turned his interest towards the ring. A sparring session, he noted, was in progress. The look on his face changed dramatically, as it went from pleasing to one of sheer disbelief.

'Cocky bastard, over the top, as usual!' he exclaimed out loud. The remark was aimed at the aggressor of the two men, who traded under the name of Dave Molloy. For a supposedly controlled situation, their sparring had now become a one-sided affair. Disgust on his part gave way to cringing, as Molloy forced his sparring partner back onto the ropes. Resistance became non-existent. Gloves held low, mouth agape, and nowhere to run formed the epitaph of a well-beaten man.

Molloy appeared unrepentant; full bloodied shots honed in from every conceivable angle, any form of defence was futile. Legs turned to jelly, as the weaker of the two slid down the ropes. Mercifully, the sanctity of the floor canvas halted any further onslaught. Ronnie had seen enough. Seething with anger, he leapt up onto the ring apron.

'What the fucking hell you trying to prove?' he shouted across to Molloy. His rant had little or no effect whatsoever. He was caught up in his own private war and the question seemed redundant. Turning on his heel, Molloy retreated to his corner. Reluctantly, for the time being, Ronnie decided to let the matter drop. It had happened before, and he knew it would happen again. But this time, there would be words. The 'old school' syndrome had become an integral part of Ronnie's portfolio. There was no reason to change the experiences he had fought for inside and outside of the ring. Square on, kill or be killed fighters had never impressed him. 'Never make war in the gym' – this was an unwritten law in his book, and he stood firm by it.

His credentials had served him well in the past. 'Ability plus a good head-piece,' as he would tell you, 'and you're halfway there. The art of the game is the skill to create openings.' Liberty-takers played no part in his warranted strategy.

'LAST TEN.'

Momentarily, his frustration was lost in the inference of the time keeper. The beat from the speedball gained momentum; around the gym, weary bodies forced aching limbs towards a punishing crescendo. The circuit was over; the prize, a one-minute rest.

With mixed feelings, Ronnie stepped down from the ring apron. He'd witnessed enough, and firmly convinced himself that a verbal one-to-one with Molloy could well be on the cards. Gazing around, he noted the usual crowd of faces was holding court over by the office. They consisted of a mixed bunch, ranging from bookies to builders, indeed from all walks of life. Between them, they all shared that one common bond for their love of the game. Although, some had more interest than their counterparts.

An exclusive camaraderie existed within the business. Managers, trainers, promoters, together they formed the backbone of this elite company of self-confessed connoisseurs. Conversation, it seemed, was running deep. A forthcoming title fight was giving way to heated opinions. One voice in particular, striving to make its mark, could be heard above the hubbub. 'Big' Tommy Russell, it seemed, could be heard ruling the roost. Any involvement coming from him was immediately ruled out. Other personal matters were on the cards. Moving swiftly, he made his way towards the locker room, closing the door behind him. Once inside, he discarded his soiled towel from around his neck. Opening his personal locker door revealed more neatly stacked towels. Like every other seasoned trainer, the attention to detail was paramount. With reverence, he removed one, and placed it over his shoulder. Clearly, this was no ordinary locker; to all intents and purposes it resembled a shrine. Aged photos of interest lined the interior like wallpaper. Past and present stopped right here. On the middle shelf he kept his 'corner bag', 'tools of the trade, mate,' as he would put it.

Just then, a figure emerged in the doorway. 'Give us a hand when you're ready, Ronnie.' The request came from a small dapper-built man, who went under the name of Wally Churchill. Employed as the chief 'whip', it was his task to 'glove up' the boxers, and ensure their wellbeing. The distinctive features of a well-worn gladiator etched his face. As an ex-pro, he held the distinction of going all the way. Unlike his namesake, he allowed his fists to do all the talking. Starting out as a featherweight ensured his apprenticeship within the business. Not long after, he moved a division to lightweight, thus creating his personal road to glory. It wasn't long before he became champion elect, reigning supremely for nearly a decade. His amazing prowess finally gave way to youth and a well-earned retirement. Like so many of his kind, further involvement within the trade was his way of giving something back. Plus it added a fresh new zest for life.

The business is like an incurable disease: once you're caught up in it, there's no known cure. Small and diminutive as he was, he still regained the posture of a true pro. His inborn, exaggerated walk became a giveaway – head forwards, shoulders rolling, and always on the move. Ronnie, on occasion, was often heard to sum him up: 'Bleedin' dinosaur if I ever saw one!' But right then, he was in need of a hand.

'Be right there, Wally,' came back Ronnie's reply. Grim-faced, corner bag under his arm, Ronnie strode out of the locker room. Heading directly towards the kit table wasn't doing his blood count any favours. Wally, meanwhile, could be seen removing Molloy's bandages. Completing the last snip, he centred his attention on Ronnie's approach. He was quick to note the look of an unhappy man, as his friend approached.

For a brief second or two, he felt uneasy. It wasn't the first time he'd seen that particular expression on his face. *Something is going down, I just know it.* His thoughts crossed his mind like telepathy. When you know somebody that well, it comes easy. Molloy made a motion to leave as Ronnie drew abreast of him. Confronting him was never going to be an issue. A problem was at stake, and he wasn't about to hold back. With eyes blazing deeply into Molloy's face, it had to be said.

'You took a right bloody liberty in there tonight!' His words were direct and meaningful. There was no response forthcoming, as Molloy chose to ignore the statement. Shrugging his shoulders, arms gesturing, he gave Ronnie a withering look, and sauntered off towards the shower room. Deep in thought, Ronnie watched him go. Nodding his head in discourse justified his decision that had been made some time back. Passing up an option to train him had proved his judgment to be valid. Wally couldn't wait to voice his own opinion.

'Bang in order, mate, fronting him like you did. The guy's an asshole. Who needs people like him?' The altercation died a death. As one they grinned; life was back to normality once again.

'It is common knowledge that boxer/trainer relationships aren't made in heaven. They are something special that you have to work at to achieve. Trust and teamwork are of the essence.' Without realizing it, he'd begun to talk out loud; it became obvious that Molloy had got to him in more ways than one. 'He wouldn't have reigned long, sooner or later—' was as far as he got.

'You say something, Ronnie?' Wally interrupted his chain of thought. 'You're bleedin' miles away.'

'Oh, sorry, cocker, just thinking out loud… what might have been, nothing important.' There was no way of knowing just how right he would have been. The Rossetti saga was still swirling around in his head, and Molloy's case hadn't helped his cause one bit. Taking in a deep breath seemed to put his frame on a new level. Any misgivings he may have held were quickly dispelled as he prepared his 'boy' for sparring. Gloved up and head guard secured, Eric Mercer was ushered by Ronnie towards the ring. The former was an up-and-coming welterweight out of Big Tommy Russell's stable – dedicated and easy to train. The two had formed a relationship once Mercer had joined the 'paid ranks'. As an amateur, he'd made quite a name for himself, and his skill hadn't gone unnoticed. The raw talent was there, and the advice he'd received from Ronnie hadn't been wasted. Obtaining a pro licence, needless to say, had been a formality.

Once the two were inside the ring, Ronnie headed towards the blue corner, and made his intentions known with a nod to Frankie Lyons, the opposing second. In his career, he'd generated more wins from that particular colour corner. That alone gave him a sense of achievement. The habit was purely personal, and bordering on superstition; all fighters are exclusive, making them a breed apart.

As a formality, Mercer's gloves and head guard were checked. From the back of his hand, Ronnie removed a generous helping of Vaseline, and proceeded to grease his man down. Instructions were short and basic, knowing that the opposition was an unknown quantity. 'Get up on your toes, be first, take the fight to him,' was enough for Mercer to know what Ronnie wanted of him. As the bell sounded, Mercer adjusted his gum shield, and immediately went after his opponent, working from behind his jab, as he did so. As a result, his sparring partner found himself forced to back pedal. Using the ring to his advantage, while showing no resistance, resulted in Mercer punching fresh air.

Ronnie couldn't help but notice the stranger's adept footwork. Any contact with leather was futile, and it was beginning to show in Mercer's utter frustration. Up to now, red corner hadn't thrown a punch, but more to the point hadn't taken one either. Purely out of character, all interest in the workout focused on the stranger, who, by now, seemed to dominate whatever Mercer threw at him. Upping his own brand of work rate, he appeared to be content to carry the fight. Briefly, Mercer cut him off and in doing so forced him into a corner. Ronnie hastily signalled to his man to open up.

'Let's see what the guy's made of,' he muttered under his breath.

He didn't have long to find out. Ducking and riding the combinations thrown at him, he cleverly pulled Mercer in, neatly sidestepping his man as he did so. Draped over the top rope with his back to the world wasn't the game plan. Frankie Lyons indicated to the sparring partner to back off; it wasn't necessary, as by now he'd taken command of the centre of the ring. With sheer frustration written all over his face, Mercer turned around, and looked towards his corner for advice. Momentarily, Ronnie's mind appeared to be elsewhere. Red corner's performance seemed to have had a numbing effect on him. In boxing terms, he hadn't put a foot wrong from the bell, and his added ring craft was something else.

'The kid's a bloody natural,' he concluded, and beckoned Mercer to come forwards. From the first bell it hadn't been his night. Chasing shadows, plus the indignation of feeling left out to dry, was affecting him personally. It had been a learning curve in every sense, and he needed to overcome it. Right now, Mercer needed something out of the session. There was still a minute of the round remaining. What then followed proved irrelevant to whatever he might have had in mind. Coming forwards from behind, his jab gave him some immediate success. For the first time they stood toe-to-toe trading combinations. His confidence began to ooze, as he honed in selective shots.

Without warning, red corner suddenly broke off, and took a pace backwards. Mercer had been caught flat-footed and defenceless. Even if he could have seen what was coming, there would have been no way out for him. The right-hand shot was full blooded, catching him square on the chin, as he desperately sought to right himself. His nervous system immediately shut down; at the same time his legs buckled and jellied. The ring canvas met his back, and he gazed upwards through sightless eyes. The speed of events left Ronnie shaking his head in utter disbelief. Finally, discipline got the better of him, as he leapt through the ropes. Turning Mercer on his side, he hastily removed his gum shield, while working a wet sponge to the back of his neck for the desired effect.

Ronnie breathed a huge sigh of relief, as Mercer's eyes tentatively began to flutter open. Shaking his head forcefully added to his sanity, and he declined the offer of water on demand. It became obvious that any pain he'd been subjected to was now overruled by embarrassment. Pride went hand-in-glove with feelings, and right now, his were at an all-time low. The steward's enquiry would come later; all he could think about now was the fact that he'd been decked in such a fashion. Ronnie, on the other hand, held a different view. Any thoughts of a sucker punch were quickly shoved to one side. Mercer was no mug – indeed, he'd become a rated boy – but the cold fact remained he'd been clinically taken apart on the night. Being the pro that he was enabled him to take the upset in his stride. In an effort to ease the situation, he grabbed at Ronnie's arm.

'Where the hell did yer find him? He's nobody's fool!' The best he got in return came from a sardonic smile. A few minutes had elapsed since the incident, in which time the sparring partner had exited the ring.

An interested Frankie Lyons walked across to air his views,

doing his best to console Mercer. 'You'll be alright, Eric, put it down to experience. We've all been there; you ain't alone, mate. Mind you, he was a bit of a mystery the geezer, here one minute and gone the next.'

Acknowledging his concern, Ronnie ushered Mercer from out of the ring. Worry was written all over his face; apart from Lyons and himself, the only real witness to the event had been Wally Churchill. Fortunately, the episode was over and done with inside of two minutes. Heaving a sigh of relief, Ronnie averted his gaze over towards the office. Luckily, Tommy Russell was caught up in his own verbal war.

For Mercer, his night was at an end. Ungloved and disillusioned, he made his way towards the shower room. An early bath night proved to be the best on offer, and he wasn't about to argue. Meanwhile, Wally couldn't contain himself, and was dying to express his own opinion.

'That was some right hand the kid threw in there tonight. Whose camp is he in?'

'You know as much SP about him as I do, Wally,' he assured him, and continued. 'By the way, did you see the going of him or, more to the point, get a name out of him?'

Wally shook his head and raised his shoulders, concluding, 'I couldn't get a whisper out of him. The minute I ungloved him, he was on his toes. I'm not sure, but I got the impression that he was under some sort of pressure, know what I mean?'

'Damn!' The sudden conclusion to the event was now finding its mark.

There was no doubt that the stranger had really got to him, in more ways than one. Once his brain began to churn, as he searched for some sort of an answer, letting the moment drop wasn't Ronnie's style. He did his best to reason with Wally.

'Do you reckon we'll see the guy again?' he asked searchingly.

'Your guess is as good as mine. One thing's for sure: that was no lucky punch he threw in there tonight.' Ronnie nodded his head in agreement, as Wally continued. 'I'd love an option on him, given the chance!'

Ronnie could only concur once again. Wally was no fool; he recognized a prospect when he saw one. Besides, he was endorsing only what he already knew himself. The rest of the evening session turned out to be nonplus. Any enthusiasm he might have held for the job in hand was taken over by questions that needed answers. Nothing, it seemed, made any sense. Too much had happened in such a short space of time. Deep in thought, head bowed, he stared long and hard at the floor. His fuddled brain flipped from one scenario to another. The Rossetti incident was still fresh on his mind; coupled with the Mercer saga, it had literally drained his resources.

From a positive attitude to one of speculation was a mode alien to him. It was a very relieved man who closed and locked the door to the gym that night. Once outside, he adjusted the towel around his neck. The night air seemed to penetrate his tracksuit top, and he gave a compulsive shudder. The sound of an approaching vehicle caught his attention, leaving his body to take over a new sense of relief.

'Please God, that's for me,' he said inwardly. His reference was made towards a taxi that had appeared from out of the gloom. Raising his arm, the cab swung over and came to a stop. Opening the passenger door, Ronnie almost fell into the seat.

Slumped sideways, Ronnie resembled a very subdued figure, as the car pulled away. Recognizing his fare, the driver attempted to draw him into conversation. 'You're looking a bit pissed off tonight, guv!' Ronnie locked in thought, the observation went clean over his head. Still the driver persevered. 'It ain't like you. Maybe a good night's kip will sort it out.'

Ronnie looked decidedly sheepish, and mumbled an apology. His thoughts, as usual, lay lost elsewhere. From the time he'd left home to go to the gym, the evening's events had come back to haunt him. Leaving Rossetti top of his list!

Accident... or just pure coincidence? And who was the stranger in the gym? Cupping his head between his hands, he wrestled with his brain for an answer. It just wasn't working, and it was late. Besides which, he was well past it anyway. Paying the cabbie off, he wearily entered his flat, and locked the door behind him.

Stepping out of the shower later, he towelled himself down, and made his way to the bedroom. After parking himself on the edge of the bed, he looked around the room. A nearby mirror on his sideboard reflected his drawn image. Peering intently at himself only added to his consternation. Staring long and hard, he began to meditate.

For a full second he truly felt his genuine age, as a wave of hopelessness swept over his body. Gritting his teeth, he playfully slapped his face. *Christ's sake, Callaghan, snap out of it!* His subconscious mind began working overtime with good effect. Without any warning, a surge of tiredness took full control of his body. It would seem that the cabbie's earlier remark had finally got through to him. Sleep, when it came, was a passport to happiness that he understood. After falling between the sheets, he slept like a baby!

CHAPTER 3

KID GLOVES

At 7.30 the following morning, he felt good. The drama from the previous night had become history. It was the beginning of a new week, and it was proving to be his saving grace. Pulling his curtain to one side in the lounge, he looked skywards, and noted the peculiarity of the cloud formation.

'Uhm, that's a mackerel sky if ever I saw one.' He grinned to himself. Sunday being Sunday entailed him driving to the gym, the intention being to arrive there earlier than he would have done normally. The time he gained was spent keeping the gym shipshape. Corner buckets would need slopping out, and corner water bottles needed to be recharged. Ronnie never looked on it as being a chore. 'A clean gym is a working gym', as he would say, and his reasoning was never in contention.

The ring itself was always the last to be checked over. After casting his eye over a loose top rope, he adjusted the shackle and tightened it, easing the problem.

'That'll keep 'em quiet for five minutes,' he mused. Jumping down off the ring apron, his face took on a serious look, as he surveyed the time that he'd spent. A satisfying grin followed. Methodical as he was, he really needn't have bothered. Averting his gaze, he checked his watch against the time keeper on the gym wall. 'Another ten minutes, and this gaff will be buzzing,' he reminded himself. Taking time out to digress, he went over his work routine, paramount being the kit cupboard. He was momentarily lost in his thoughts as the door to the gym slowly opened, leaving him unaware.

Engrossed as he was, an inner feeling that he wasn't alone crept over his body. A shadowy figure from out the corner of his eye then justified his awareness. Whipping sharply round, he confronted his suspicions. With one foot jammed in the doorway stood a young lad aged nine or ten, and scruffy in appearance. Despite his apparent youth, he portrayed an air of cockiness about himself. With eyes gawping, he digested every aspect within the gym, and what it had to offer. Aladdin's cave would have had the same effect on him if available, judging by the look of awe on his face.

For a brief second, Ronnie found himself wrong-footed. Obviously the kid was no threat in any way, which led him unsure as to his approach. Casually, he walked across, and confronted the youngster.

'Anything I can do for you, my son?' He added a body hint of authority.

Still caught up in his own little world, the kid continued to absorb the workings of the gym, and declined any offer of conversation. As much as he liked kids, rules were rules. Those who resided in the locale respected his wishes, and kept their viewing to the panelled windows at the far end of the gym. Content to continually glare all around, the kid once again chose to ignore the same question the second time around. By now, Ronnie was fast losing his patience, and the look on his face said it all. For a brief moment, an eye-to-eye confrontation set in. Removing his foot from the door, the kid took a step forwards; drawing himself up, he glaringly fronted Ronnie. A different approach now came into play. Placing his hands on his hips, Ronnie put on an enquiring attitude.

'Look, is it a message, son… or maybe something I need to know… what?'

A pregnant pause came into being, followed by a torrent of muffled verbal, which became lost in the process. Then it became standoff time, something Ronnie didn't have right now. Throwing the kid out on his ear wasn't an option. Besides which, he'd earned his minute of glory. Finally, humour seemed to be the only approach open to Ronnie. With a meaningful touch, he placed one hand on the kid's shoulder.

'So you want to be a champ... eh?'

Hanging on to his every word, the kid nodded vigorously. His positive reaction seemed to resurrect a dormant inner within Ronnie's subconscious. A feeling of déjà vu had quietly come home to roost.

How many times have I used that particular routine? he mused. *God only knows I could use a champ or two right now!* Faces from his past sprang to mind, long gone, protégés were singled out, men with that one burning desire wanting to go all the way! *They don't just happen along.* He continued to pursue his meandering on a relative level. *A dying man needs plasma... a trainer needs a champ...*

'Penny for yer thoughts, guv!' The kid had finally turned it all around. The spell was broken, and Ronnie found himself back in the world of the living. In a short space of time, the kid had now grown in confidence. Ronnie lowered his eyes, and patted the kid's head.

'By the way, what do we call you, son?'

The kid took a deep breath, and blurted out, 'Simmons, guv... Danny Simmons, and don't you forget it!'

'Saucy little git,' Ronnie concurred, but secretly admired his outward spirit. The kid was typical of his counterparts who frequented the neighbourhood: streetwise at an early age living solely on their wits. Their fight for constant survival came at a price; it was something even money couldn't buy.

'Are you Ronnie Callaghan?' It seemed that the kid wasn't finished just yet!

'Yes! I am, and that's mister to you. Now on yer bike, son, I'm opening up shortly.'

Pushing his luck to the limit, Danny stood his ground to the death. Finally, a playful raised fist was sufficient enough to convince him that Ronnie meant business. Raising two fingers into a proverbial 'V' sign, Danny turned on his heel, and flew through the door. For a minute, Ronnie stood there chuckling to himself. He found himself having to admit to a defeat of some kind, and had to agree that the kid had more front than he had at his age.

The fact that the gym was adjacent to a public house only added to its popularity. Eager to find room space, the nucleus of fight fans stood around in small groups. Ex-pros mingled with devotees, and they could well be excused for re-enacting past glories. Losses, as per usual, took a backseat. The all important factor being that they had all 'been there'. For them, their singular history had become a passport to the exclusive breed of men who had given their all in a controlled situation. Success was only secondary in the final analysis. Each man out to prove his prowess – collectively, they all shared that one common denominator: pain! Pound for pound, there was no exception; it was a human trait that went with the territory.

Unlike most evenings, the Sunday session was set aside for in-depth sparring and tactical ability. At the business end of the gym, mentors busied themselves, and prepared their men. Instructions were bantered around, as the warming-up programme kicked in. As was his standing, Big Tommy Russell's voice sounded prominent above the crowd. It also came as a reminder that the two needed to talk shop. It was no secret that Russell intended to give Eric Mercer an outing on a small hall bill locally. As things stood thus far, any ideas Ronnie might have held regarding any contract were best kept to himself. Mercer's fitness had never been an issue, but the events stemming from Friday's suspect sparring session warranted extreme consideration. As yet, there was a lot of work to be done on the man, both technically and mentally; more importantly he needed time. At the last moment, he changed direction, and made towards the locker room. Any involvement with Russell could well wind up with unnecessary grief. Up to now, Ronnie had been lucky; keeping his distance as he did suited them both.

'You get the boy ready, and I'll do the bookwork!' That was the deal. Sooner or later, Russell would be looking for a result; as from now Mercer's work rate warranted priority. The walls of the locker room seemed adverse to sound; even inside, the monotonous tone of the big fellow's voice resounded throughout. On the bright side, something inside gave him cause to smile; he'd heard it all before. 'Bread and butter verbal', as he would say. Anyway, he'd never met a manager yet who couldn't talk a good fight! Although Russell radiated an aura of power, his Achilles' heel stopped and ended at yours truly!

It all stemmed from their very first meeting. The well-worn fight adage 'Be first' had served Ronnie well indeed throughout his career; that particular day had been no exception. It was a case of David meet Goliath! For once in his life, Russell found himself forced to take a backseat. A simple nod of the head one way or the other was the best on offer. Cards on the table, he was forced to listen, as Ronnie stated his case regarding any form of partnership. It became clear that experience had conquered ignorance. The respect Russell had metered out to him, as a result, had never wavered over the years. As a firm, their track record had stood the test of time. Contenders and journeymen alike owed a great deal to their combined ingenuity.

On occasion, Ronnie would take time out to dwell on his

own selfish yearning. It would take the form of somebody – somebody special – who possessed that little bit of extra talent. To nurture such a prize would be payment in itself. The queue of realization was a long endearing one; right now he found himself at the back of the queue. Closing the locker door behind him, he glanced around the gym. For a second or two, a wave of hopelessness swept over his body. His mundane task of managing the gym momentarily seemed to have lost its appeal. Fighting to justify his apprehension wasn't what he was good at. A lifeline was needed. Briefly, Wally Churchill interrupted his chain of thought, and for some reason enabled him to review his pessimistic outlook. Looking across to where Wally was busy, up to his neck in gloves and bandages, doing what he was good at, there could be no denying the man's loyalty. Still unsure of his addled convictions, Ronnie approached to give him a hand.

'What the bleedin' hell are we doing here, mate?' he blurted out. Rapt in his own private bubble, the enquiry went clean over his head. The look of contentment on Wally's face shamed Ronnie into submission. Once again he sought an answer. 'Why do we do it, Wally?' This time he got lucky, as Wally was quick to reciprocate.

'Oh, that's easy, my son… it's the love of the game, but you knew that anyway!' In an instant, any seeds of doubt were blown away. Ronnie nodded his head in agreement, an assured grin now carpeting his face.

'Yeah, you're so right, mate. I just needed a little reminding, good game, innit?' After walking across to the back wall, he set the timer on the clock. Another session, it seemed, was now fully underway.

CHAPTER 4

FRIENDS

The punters in the municipal market were beginning to thin out. The majority of the traders had already begun to dismantle their individual stalls. As per usual, it had been a long and arduous day for most of them. Setting up entailed an early 6 am start, as wheeling and dealing continued right through to mid-afternoon. The pungent odour of fish and raw meat hung about in the air. Rotting vegetables littered the cobbles. Close to the main entrance, a couple of stray dogs were squabbling over the remains of a discarded bone. A well-directed kick from the ever-aware market inspector ('Granite') soon sent them packing.

'Spurs could have done with you Saturday,' shouted the owner of a nearby china stall. Acknowledging the spontaneous remark with a derisive smile, Granite sloped off to upset somebody else.

Three or four days a week, or when it suited him, Ronnie worked a stall here like his father before him. Ronnie's trading licence had come by way of inheritance, due to the demise of the latter, who was a local character in himself. The Irish blood that flowed through his veins ran true to form. The verbal wit of the man, you got for nothing; it only got better for the price of a pint! Not long after his death, Ronnie's mother also passed away, some said of a broken heart. They were testing times for him. Fortunately, the company of friends he could call on enabled him to pull through.

'Stick together, and look after yer own… it's family.' Wise words or not? But they were traits handed down through time, and they worked. On completing a sale, he made his way to the back of his stall to check his money pouch. The smug look on his weathered face summed up his demeanour. The day's trading had been better than most; in one sense he considered himself as being lucky. His infectious popularity, plus the know-how of buying in good stock, stood him in favour. Whatever, his regulars, should he be pushed, would always bale him out; holidaymakers alike were an added bonus.

His forte was, and always had been, flowers! 'They're a doddle,' he would readily tell you. 'They sell themselves, you don't even have to work at it.' Besides, he had only himself to worry about. Marriage, as far as he was concerned, was a no-no. Staying single suited his way of life, and he never looked back in anger. Moreover, money would never be an issue. The cut and thrust of his fellow traders went clean over his head. As far as accommodation was concerned, he'd previously paid up the mortgage on his flat some years ago. This, in turn, enabled him to enjoy a quality of life he relished. Coming and going, as he did, and a wedge besides, what more could he ask for?

'Looks like you've had a result, mate!' The enquiry came from the adjoining stall holder. The owner was quick to pick up on his smugness.

'Yeah, I managed to clear expenses, and a few quid on top. You don't miss a trick, do yer? I reckon you could sniff a tenner out from a bag of rotten apples.'

'So who's complaining already?' came back the reply. It became standoff time, as both men patted their money pouches, and burst into raucous laughter. The two men seemed to have a rapport born out of respect for one another. There was no questioning their apparent affinity, which was clearly in evidence. Together, the pair went back a long way, their origins stemming back as far as childhood. For his part, Siddie Levy was of Jewish descent, his family deriving from East End stock. Because of his ethnic background, he was constantly singled out by the so-called bully boys. Equality, in any form, had been a trait that Ronnie carried on his shoulders even as a kid. He'd fought for his beliefs in the past, including those of the underdog.

Siddie had been indebted to him on numerous occasions. From a problem shared, Ronnie was always on hand to pick up the pieces and stand his corner. From then on, the seeds of a lasting friendship were sown. Personality-wise, they were worlds apart. Siddie was a self-confessed pacifist in contrast to Ronnie's extremism. 'Minder' was a term easy to live with whenever their friendship became threatened. Siddie, on the other hand, played the 'headpiece', valued advice, a shoulder to cry on. It was his way of cementing their personal needs. To many, it appeared to be an odd coupling, but it had stood the test of time.

Ronnie's induction to the 'noble art' had been largely due to Siddie's superior business aptitude. From their early teens, Siddie had been quick to pick up on the respect meted out to Ronnie before and after pecking order was established. It didn't take long before he cajoled him into joining a local amateur boxing club. In time, his instincts were to prove beneficial. Having served his apprenticeship, it was time to move up the ranks, and his adopted career prospered, as a full-time pro.

Stifling a yawn, Ronnie decided that he'd had enough for one day. 'Time I wasn't here,' he exclaimed, not bothering to look around. In return, Siddie just nodded to acknowledge his decision; he was far too busy going for the kill. Money was changing hands; as befitted his creed, socialising gave way to business. The last of Ronnie's unsold stock had been loaded onto his handcart. Setting off, he made his way towards the main lockup at the far end of the market. Securing the key, he turned, and surveyed what was left of the current working day. The resident army of pigeons had now moved in. With extra space to work in, they darted between the cobbles looking for easy pickings.

On time as ever, their counterparts, the gulls, flying in numbers and homing in on any forsaken morsel. His interest started to grow, as he picked up on a group of punters that had gathered around Siddie's veg stall.

'He'll find a bloody clue,' he told himself, and laughed inwardly. Secretly, he admired his friend's salesmanship. 'Victims' fell for his brand of spiel and charisma that was peculiar to his creed. 'A nice Jewish boy doing what he's good at!' as Ronnie would say. Purely out of habit, he gave a token wave, and headed for the market café. It had become his habitual port of call, prior to making his way home.

His idea of 'coming down' would be, over a cup of coffee, to sit down and mull over the events of the day. Here, conversation was readily at hand if required. Indeed, for years now, the café had served as a bolthole for the many characters that worked in and around the vicinity of the market. Between them, they represented a broad spectrum. Distinction was non-existent; once inside, the environment took hold, and common ground became established.

Adjacent to the market ran Bailey Street. From end to end, Regency-style buildings formed a façade of yesteryear. The gentry had long gone; in their place, a labyrinth of commercial offices now existed. The predictable brass nameplates adorned every door. This represented the heartland of the local legal profession. Because of its significance, it had received a somewhat colourful reputation over the years. Hence the name Bailey was no longer used as a reference. To all and sundry, it became known as Justice Row. From messengers to lawyers, the café had become their exclusive watering hole. Often, deals were ironed out, conclusions reached, all on the strength of a coffee or tea. Here, felons brushed shoulders with the law. It was an acceptable situation that seemed to work for everyone concerned. In the past, 'a bunch of flowers for the good lady' in exchange for information received had served Ronnie well.

The unmistakeable tones of the proprietor greeted Ronnie as he made his way through the door. For the time of day, it was still quite busy, and he found himself forced to push his way through to the counter. It was well worth the effort. Par excellence became the order of the day. Toni de Angelo was his usual inquisitive self.

'You makka da monies today, Ronnie?' he enquired, the Latin overtones in his banter clearly evident to his Italian connection. Toni was a giant of a man; his dark swarthy features complemented his jet-black wavy hair. This, in turn, combined an overpowering air of old world charm.

'The guy's a bleedin' film star' was one way that Ronnie would label him. Wally Churchill on occasion settled for the second Primo Carnera.

'I managed to snatch a few quid today, Toni, please God it lasts,' he replied.

Nodding in agreement, Toni motioned towards the coffee machine; he knew his customers too well to ask. Placing his mug down on the bar top with acute reverence, Ronnie propped himself up on a vacated stool. Head bowed, spoon in hand, he gazed into the froth of his cappuccino. Slowly and deliberately, he began to stir. Deep in thought, he paused momentarily to look up. 'Must remember to re-order some fresh stock tomorrow.' As it was, his plea came out loud, as if in conversation; it was a habit of contentment, but then he was like that!

CHAPTER 5

THE MEET

The monotonous tones coming from his landline were beginning to get to him. Initially, Ronnie had chosen to ignore the unwelcome intrusion, in the hope that whoever it was would go away. Checking his watch did little to ease his frame of mind. Nine in the morning just wasn't his style, but still the would-be caller persisted. Monday onwards, he wouldn't have been at home anyway. Today just happened to be Sunday, and he didn't envisage any unwelcome grief. Besides which, his breakfast was far more important. The mocking tones continued to plague him; cursing the world at large, he made a half-hearted attempt to lower the gas ring on the cooker, and stormed out of the kitchen.

'This had better be bleedin' kosher,' he growled to himself, and lunged at the receiver. 'What!?' This was bluntness at its best, but then etiquette was never going to be his strongest point, at any time. Making the connection, the caller bided their time before replying. The alien voice came over as being strong and pushy, as the final connection was made. In spite of the fact that Ronnie was needled, he elected to see it through anyway.

'Am I speaking to Ronnie Callaghan?'

'Who the hell wants to know?' he replied brusquely. His attitude, it appeared, didn't cut any ice at the other end.

'If you're prepared to listen, it's purely regarding a business arrangement.'

34

'Arrangement… what sort of arrangement?' He was hedging. 'Do you realize its early Sunday bloody morning? Who the hell am I speaking to anyway?'

'You came recommended through—'

Ronnie cut him short; he was rapidly losing his patience. 'Get to the damn point!' His volatile persona had now struck a nerve, and the caller quickly responded.

'My name is Winters, Terry Winters, that is. I'm looking for a second opinion on a useful boy. They tell me that you're the man I need to approach.'

Ronnie swallowed hard. *Patronizing bastard*, he thought to himself. *Although, he talks as if he's in the business.* The name Winters wasn't ringing any bells, as he wracked his brains for some form of connection.

'Hello! Are you still there?'

Pulling himself together, Ronnie grunted something less audible, as the conversation continued.

'We obviously need to make a meet, that is if you're interested of course. I would like you to see the boy in action, know what I mean?' By now, the caller was beginning to show his own brand of impatience, by placing the emphasis on his tone. 'Look, I'll be at Slatteries Gym on Wednesday evening around eight o'clock.'

'I need to know—' was as far as their conversation went. The line went suddenly dead. The look hanging on Ronnie's face said it all, as sheer anger and frustration took over. 'What the fuck?' He slammed the receiver down. Trance-like, he lumbered back to the kitchen, and flopped down into the nearest chair. His eyes were blazing; whatever positivity remained in his mind began to churn over. The front of somebody, and a complete stranger at that, hanging up on him was bad enough in itself. Unanswered questions, and answers to them, were something else.

For a moment, he wrestled with his beleaguered brain. 'Winters... Winters!' The harder he attempted to focus, the worse it seemed to get. Nothing positive was coming out of it. Briefly, his chain of thought was broken by the distinctive smell of something burning. Turning his immediate attention towards the cooker, he made a vain effort to negotiate the control knob. He needn't have bothered himself; his futile attempt to resurrect his breakfast faded out of sight. Shortly after, over a belated sandwich, he'd decided to confide in Siddie regarding the Terry Winters scenario.

The session the following morning boded well, in contrast to his early morning spot of grief, allowing him an escape route. Eric Mercer became his saving grace. It appeared that the incident arising from the previous week had been a blessing in disguise. Ploughing their combined energies into technique pad work, he'd responded well enough to satisfy Ronnie that he was back on the case.

'You get caught out, son, you gotta learn by it,' he emphasized. It was a well-satisfied man who left the gym behind that morning.

The feel-good factor suited him well. Later, settling down in his armchair, eyes half closed, he placed his ice-filled glass of orange drink onto his forehead, and proceeded to roll it back and forth. The rest of the day belonged to him, a chance to relax. The soft drink never tasted better, as he eagerly quenched his thirst. The forthcoming week sprang to mind. Business-wise, the recent weather forecast created a bonus. Sunshine meant punters, and money over. After placing his drink to one side, he rubbed his hands together, at the same time allowing himself a miserly grin. With time on his hands, Monday seemed forever and a day away. Stifling a yawn, a sudden wave of tiredness swept over his body like a tsunami. Closing his eyes was too easy, as his brain slipped into meaningless thoughts.

Sleep finally took over, as two words hammered away at each other within his subconscious. 'Sunshine! Winters!' Again and again the words kept repeating. Deep down, something or somebody was trying to explain to him the relevance of it all. Mercifully, with little or no warning, his nightmare subsided. He now found himself wide awake, having gone full circle. He shook his head vigorously to offload the demons from within his distorted mind. It became obvious that the early morning phone call had temporarily locked itself away inside his mind. Only to manifest itself at its own convenience. 'Terry Winters!' he exclaimed out loud. 'Of course, it all makes blasted sense now. How could I be that stupid?'

His initial annoyance now appeared to be more than justified; intrigue had now entered the equation and, like it or not, wasn't about to go away that easily. Forcing himself from his chair, he paced up and down. His patience was now long exhausted, but this was Sunday, and answers to questions needed to be resolved. Tomorrow seemed light years away. The urge to talk it over remained paramount, and gave more credence to his earlier desire to get third-party involvement.

'Siddie! Must get Siddie on the case; he's bound to come up with some answers.' For the time being, he felt good inside, in knowing that a meeting with his mentor could well be on the cards. Without hesitation, he reached for his Blackberry. The text message he sent was brief and surgical. *Siddie, something has cropped up, we need to talk at yours!* That and goodbye concluded the extent of his call.

★

'Was that your mobile I heard, Siddie?'
Oblivious to his wife's demands, Siddie, for reasons of his own, chose to remain silent, as a discerning look shadowed his

face. Sensing a negative response, Rachael momentarily feared for the worst. In sympathy, the Jewish blood in her veins ran cold. Reaching out, she gripped Siddie's arm tightly.

'It's family business, isn't it?'

Slowly, he pocketed his mobile. Smiling reassuringly, he placed his arms around her shoulders.

'I should lie to you, of all people, yes, Bubula, it was Ronnie. He's got a problem we need to share. You know what he's like; it has to be when it suits him. I wouldn't be surprised, knowing that he's on his way over here now, already.'

'So I was right!' She emphasized her point with a characteristic shrug of her shoulders. In doing so, her face spontaneously lit up. 'Like I said before, it's become family business!'

For his part, Siddie was forced to concur. On reflection, he considered that Ronnie had appeared to be more than distant in his text content. The fact that Rachael, as well, had picked up on his response now confirmed his own misgivings. Having said that, the 'need to talk' had come as no great surprise. He'd read the script too many times before, but if anyone could mark his card, then he would!

Ronnie, it seemed, hadn't wasted any time. An hour after making contact, he'd showered, and was ready to face his mentor. The expression his face allowed gave nothing away. Siddie, now and in the past, had been a good listener. Right now he was digesting all the relevant facts. Having explained the turn of events, Ronnie appeared fidgety, finding it hard to control his emotions. His obvious impatience for conclusions was running deep. If he was affected by his attitude, then Siddie never showed it. Instead, his face remained impassive. In the past, an easy yes or no would have been sufficient; this latest episode, he considered, needed dwelling on.

At length, he glanced upwards. 'This Terry Winters schmuck, you say the name doesn't mean anything to you?'

Ronnie felt he wasn't in the mood to digress; his mind was going down one road only. 'Like I said—' was as far as he got. Siddie hastily intervened.

'Let's get this straight: you mentioned some sort of business deal... right?' befitted his creed, cynical as ever. Any would-be financial commitment threw more light on the situation. Selfish or otherwise, the crux of the matter became evident. Siddie knew that money was an aspect that Ronnie couldn't handle too well at the best of times. His renowned gullibility as being a soft touch was public knowledge. Aware of his pitfalls, he decided on the softly, softly approach. 'From what you have told me already, between us, we don't have a great deal to go on,' he remarked guardedly.

Ronnie took a deep breath, and exhaled almost immediately; his facial expression dropped to one of despair. Supposition began to creep in. His own reluctance to form conclusions of any kind doubled up as a reflection of Siddie's acute uncertainty.

'Christ's sake! Nothing's bleedin' easy, is it?' demanded Ronnie and gave vent to his feelings.

'I'm sorry, my friend, but this alleged deal, it doesn't ring kosher to me,' replied Siddie, and shrugged his shoulders.

Grim-faced, Ronnie walked across to the nearest window, and stared outwardly. Frustration had now run its course; he resigned himself to the fact that Siddie had every right to come across as being negative. Dealing with your own would never become a problem; the unknown was another league! Disparaged, Ronnie turned away from the window, and faced him.

'You're right of course, but I—'

'Don't say anymore, you're going to pursue it anyway.' The designer interruption was as predictable as it was implied.

Stubborn to the end, Ronnie made one last ditch to justify his case. 'I mean, what have I got to lose anyway, mate?'

Once again, Siddie raised his shoulders in his own indomitable way, adamant that he would have the final word on the matter. 'I can't stop you, Ronnie; all I suggest is that you watch your back!'

The following couple of days seemed like an eternity. Full of apprehension, Ronnie went about life aimlessly. His resolve to see the Terry Winters saga through had undoubtedly affected his wellbeing. On hand as ever, it fell to Siddie to take the brunt of his mood swings.

Slatteries Gym could be found at the Docklands end of the town, and set in a seedy locale. Over the years, it had become a breeding ground for notoriety, due to its choice of clientele. Lowlife took advantage of its non-existent credibility. Open house went hand-in-glove for the many desirables it seemed to draw in. Aside from the purpose it had been built for, they wheeled and dealt in a world synonymous to their type. Development over the years now included a snooker and pool room. This in turn reduced the gym as a front for the so-called patrons of the art!

The fact that Ronnie commanded respect on his own patch would do little to enhance his standing when dealing with the opposition. Leaving the main road, he swung into the car park, and reversed into a convenient bay. Filling his lungs, he turned, and approached the main building. At the last minute, misgivings began to cloud his judgment. Warning echoes from Siddie flashed through his mind. Steeling himself, he tentatively entered the gym. The sparse lighting that greeted him caused his eyes to narrow, and the distinctive aroma issuing from a cigar filled his nostrils.

Grimacing, he shook his head in an action of disgust. 'Fuck's sake! How the other half live,' he muttered under his breath. Peering through the haze, his eyes slowly began to adapt to the alien light. To his right, it became possible to make out a small crowd of figures, adjacent to what resembled a boxing ring. Voices were being raised; it became apparent that an argument was in progress. Stopping short, he glanced around to take in the rest of the interior. He needn't have bothered. It added only fodder to his initial thoughts.

Shit... utter shit! I wouldn't train a bleedin' dog in 'ere! became his immediate thoughts. Nearby, the door of what appeared to be an office of sorts opened, and an unrecognizable figure emerged.

'Oi! You looking for somebody?' The unexpected request was directed straight at Ronnie, and carried more than a hint of menace about it. In return, Ronnie elected to be awkward.

'That, sunshine, is my bloody business,' he replied flatly, and just stared ahead, fists tightly clenched. His inquisitor quickly decided that he wasn't going to win any medals, and called off what might have led to a possible confrontation. Needless to say, he still retained a parting shot.

'Please yer fucking self!' And he promptly disappeared back into the office, slamming the door behind him. The noise it made rose above the heated voices that were still in progression. The effect that it had on them suitably put paid to their indifferences. As one, they turned, and confronted him; an uneasy silence followed. For Ronnie, there was no turning back now. He'd come too far; to walk away now would prove nothing. But he was on his own, and any unwarranted grief was the last thing he needed right now.

Swallowing hard, the well-worn adage 'Be first' sprang to mind. It became the incentive that he was looking for. 'I'm looking for Terry Winters,' he enquired dryly. The name alone seemed to take an immediate effect. The resident atmosphere

THE FINGERLESS GLOVES

became less tense. At worst, Ronnie had broken the ice, which now put him in the driving seat. For the moment, his thoughts were put on hold.

'You must be Ronnie Callaghan... Glad you could make it.'

CHAPTER 6

DÉJÁ VU

The owner of the voice disengaged himself from the group, and made himself known. The alien cigar smoke that came with the face wafted into Ronnie's face, causing him to stifle a cough. The accent he afforded ranged from somewhere between Chertsey and south London, dependent on the company at the time. He was dapper in size, although the diamond cluster ring that took over his finger seemed to compensate for his standing. There was no doubting his dress sense. The cut of his suit suggested Savile Row, along with the monikered silk hanky he sported, hanging out of his jacket pocket.

Ronnie was far from impressed, but kept his comments to himself. *Bleedin' flash git*, became his initial thoughts, but he decided to stick with protocol. Accepting the podgy outstretched hand, limp as it was, he grasped it tightly, and squeezed it hard, for as long as it was permitted, and waited. Winters' face contorted into a sickly smile. Relaxing his grip, Ronnie quickly discounted any chance meeting that the two may have previously had in the past. Up to now, things were going along his way, but he still needed to be on the case. For his part, Winters wasn't given the benefit of continuing any pre-set conversation.

'You spoke about a second opinion on the phone,' explained Ronnie, in a casual approach. He figured that 'take it or leave it' attitude gave him an element of verbal control.

He quickly sensed that Winters looked unsettled, playing second fiddle, and appeared as being a new ballgame to contend with. 'Yes, yes, that's right,' he replied hesitantly. 'But I feel we need to discuss the details of the matter in my office.'

Once inside, Ronnie made himself comfortable, and awaited Winters' proposals.

'Drink?'

'No, thanks!'

'You don't mind if I—'

'Your liver, not mine,' interjected Ronnie, while allowing for sarcasm.

Pouring himself a large scotch, Winters mumbled under his breath, and sat down. Stabbing the remains of his cigar in the ashtray, he finally got around to making small talk.

'You're probably aware by now that I'm a stranger to the town, and that applies to the business as well.'

Ronnie held his silence, in spite of the alleged business disclosure.

Taking a large gulp from his glass, Winters continued to spiel, in an uneasy vein. 'I hope you don't mind, I took the liberty of talking around; favourably, your name kept cropping up.'

'Really, how did you manage to obtain my number?' The relevance of the enquiry took Winters completely by surprise.

Downing the remaining scotch, he nervously fiddled with some papers on his desk top. It was plain that he needed to buy some time before replying.

'Somebody who—' He didn't get any further. Without warning, the office door suddenly opened, just wide enough for a voice to be heard.

'The two boys are warming up, boss, ready when you are.' Any further thoughts centred around Winters came to a jarring halt. The hairs on the back of Ronnie's neck rose in protest. Immediate recognition took over his frame, as he spun round, hoping to catch a glimpse of the intruder. But he was long gone, leaving Ronnie with no illusions whatsoever. *I'd know that voice anywhere.* It was rubberstamped on his mind. *It had to be Paul Rossetti!*

Sensing a welcome lull in their meet, Winters smothered a sigh of relief. Briefly, he was off the hook. Moving quickly from his seat, he motioned Ronnie over to the door.

'We'd better not keep 'em waiting... you know what fighters are like!' His inappropriate remark went down like the *Titanic*. Taking it as a personal observation, Ronnie threw him a blinding sideways look. Laughing nervously, Winters endeavoured to redress the situation. 'Present company excepted of course!'

The guy was pissing Ronnie off from minute one, and he badly needed a change of scene.

'I don't think you'll be disappointed with what's on offer in the gym. Personally, I strongly believe that there's some genuine talent out there. But I need you to give me the full SP, that's why you're involved.' Opening the door, he ushered Ronnie towards the ring area. For the time being, any thoughts on Rossetti were put on hold. His current interest now rested with the two fighters waiting in the ring.

The poor lighting on offer only hindered his cause, so he decided to stand a few feet away from the apron, midway between the corners. Noting his keen awareness, Winters chose to hover in the background for the time being. With everything to lose, getting Ronnie had been a feat up till now. But he still needed to keep him sweet. Slowly, uncontrolled circumstances fell into line. The following ten or fifteen minutes figured highly in Ronnie's role within the charade. Any background knowledge or name linking with what was on offer hadn't been discussed as yet. Under normal circumstances, Ronnie would have been in full possession of certain facts prior to scrutiny. Inwardly, he blamed himself for allowing Winters the space to compromise his position. It was unprofessional, and somebody was going to pay to make it right!

Out of respect for the two boxers, he decided to linger awhile. Inside the ring, instructions were bandied around, and the bell signalled round one. The two men touched gloves, and squared up to each other. The first round did nothing to make Ronnie's decision to stay any easier. Both boys stood off each other, reluctant to mix it. Ronnie's face said it all; frustration was nibbling away at his motives to hang around. Into the second round, and both boys were beginning to open up, as they progressed, so Ronnie's interest grew.

It soon became clear to him that red corner was dominating the ring area to his own advantage. Basically a counter puncher, his style convinced him that he was always going to dictate the workout.

'I like the way he moves… could be interesting… reminds me of…' Fighters from his past suddenly came to mind. Struggling with comparisons forced Ronnie to conclude, 'They were all personalities.'

Meanwhile, red corner continued to keep on the move; even back-pedalling didn't stop him out-jabbing his opponent.

'He can't run forever,' mused Ronnie.

Now under pressure, a two-handed attack forced him onto the ropes. Claiming his man, he drew him inside, and tied him up. Pausing only to turn him, he rained in combination punches from all angles. Just then the bell went, signalling the end of the round. Anticipating a reaction, Winters sidled up to Ronnie's side. It wasn't hard to see a mark of contentment littering his face. Fortunately for him, the last three minutes of action had got him out of jail! It had given him the leeway he desperately sought.

SECONDS OUT

Unbeknownst to him, Ronnie had inadvertently done him a favour. His mind was already made up; he could have saved his breath. His singular interest in red corner had more than a touch of familiarity about it. For whatever reason and peace of mind, he was determined to see the session through.

'Give 'em another two,' Winters shouted to the corner man. The bell sounded, and another round got underway. Evading his opponent's lead by clever footwork, red corner continued to take the initiative. Bobbing and weaving in his exclusive way left his man punching fresh air. Totally frustrated, the underdog bulldozed him back to the ropes. Smothering everything that was thrown at him and neatly sidestepping at the same time left him floundering on the ropes. That last move seemed to have unlocked the key to Ronnie's uncertainty. Deep down, he felt there was an estranged affinity between them both.

More than ever, a face-to-face meeting was a priority as of now. Up to the final bell, the session had become a spectator's idea of fulfilment. 'Useful boy' was the only term Winters had got right all night! Ronnie's version would have sounded far more convincing had he read his thoughts. But the time for commitment was for his exclusive benefit only. Whatever the outcome, his evening had been turned around. In his own words, 'the kid's a classic act' belonged to him... full stop!

Breaking the spell, Winters loomed up on his shoulder. The body language Ronnie had given out over the last ten minutes or so now convinced him there could be a lot going down. A smirk of triumph filled his face; pinning Ronnie down for conclusions, or so he thought, would be a formality. Any judgment on offer would have to come out of professional attachment to the game.

'The kid's got a lot going for him, wouldn't you say?' Winters had decided to make the first move. Turning his head away, Ronnie attempted to hide his obvious enthusiasm;

47

biting his lip left him in limbo before replying. Turning to face him, Winters gave out an appealing posture. Any form of a breakthrough wasn't forthcoming; it now left him floundering in no-man's-land. Ronnie was holding all the trump cards, and he was making the most of it.

'I'd very much like to meet the guy in the red corner,' he remarked at length.

Eager to fall into line, Winters hastily nodded his approval. Making their way to the corner, Ronnie discounted any deals that might be offered and summed up Winters' unofficial motives. *The guy's an asshole, who needs him?* Meanwhile, the cause of his concern was having his head guard removed. The fact that his back was towards them both put any recognition on hold. Winters felt intent on getting things moving, and uttered the predictable lines.

'You're shaping up well, son. By the way, there's somebody I'd like you to meet. His name is Ronnie, Ronnie Callaghan.' In an instant, the boxer turned to confront them both. A smack in the mouth wouldn't have had the same effect. Stunned into silence, Ronnie found himself struggling for words. There was no doubt whatsoever in his mind that the two had met previously. He knew now that he was standing face to face with Mercer's antagonist! Words didn't come easily. Finally, it was left to the stranger to break the deadlock.

Grasping Ronnie's hand, he uttered a nervous, 'Pleased to meet you, the name's Mickey Gibbons.'

In reply, a grace-saving 'Likewise' was the best that Ronnie could come up with. Sensing the impact that he'd obviously provoked, Gibbons elected to smooth over the situation, and cast his mind back to the previous Sunday.

'I guess I owe you an apology, or at least an explanation. I'm sorry about the upset last week.'

'Don't be,' assured Ronnie. By now, he'd regained his full

faculties, and continued. 'You only do what yer good at, son, 'sides, nobody got hurt, so don't dwell on it.'

'To be honest, I feel bad about walking out of the gym like I did, it ain't me.'

Gibbons had made the point! If it was meant to come across as a confession, it had a ring of sincerity about it, which Ronnie quickly picked up on. There was no doubt in his mind having come this far that as it stood the outcome wouldn't become meaningless. Having said that, he was desperate for answers, stemming from a host of questions that was churning over in his mind. For Winters' part, their introduction had done him no favours whatsoever! From start to finish, he'd felt completely isolated.

The readymade conversation between the two had read like a script. Winters' face contorted with anger; every word that had been uttered felt like a knife in his gut, twisting and turning at leisure. Sweat appeared on his forehead, as his blood count rose and fell. Grasping the bottom rope of the ring, he made an effort to compose himself. Time was running out, and it was crucial that he was still part of the deal. Meanwhile, Gibbons had stepped down off the ring apron. Winters, his hand shaking, removed a silk hanky from his pocket, using his free hand to do so. Wiping his perspiring brow, he focused his full attention on Ronnie and made a brave attempt to make small talk.

'Strange, I can't believe that! If I didn't know any better, I'd have to say that you two have met before.' In the event, it remained futile and fell on deaf ears, as Ronnie completely blanked him. Not to be outdone, he targeted Gibbons. 'You kept that bloody quiet.'

'Meaning?'

'Callaghan's gym!'

'It's no big deal. Anyway, I'm my own man.'

Realizing he was on a hiding to nothing, Winters went for low key.

'You seem to forget—' Their conversation ended abruptly.

'Phone, guv,' a voice could be heard shouting from the direction of the office.

'Get 'em to phone back, I'm busy.' The reply had a sense of urgency about it.

'I reckon you'd better take it, it happens to be Charlie Cochrane.'

On hearing the name Cochrane, Ronnie's ears pricked up. As a manager/promoter, his name was well respected amongst the boxing fraternity. Based in London, it was common knowledge that he commanded a big slice of the action. The connection between him and Terry Winters gave credence to doubt any form of negotiation between them. Based on what he knew about Cochrane, the call had to be out of character, or was it? *Just don't ring right*, he told himself.

Momentarily, his chain of thought was interrupted by Gibbons. 'I need to get changed, Ronnie. You hanging about for a while?'

The latter relaxed his thoughts. 'Not for too long, mate, incidentally, can I give you a lift somewhere?'

'Yeah, I'd appreciate that! Shan't be long.' With that, he sauntered off into the gloom. Apart from the occasional raised voice, echoing from the nearby snooker room, Ronnie had been left to his own designs. Sitting on the ring apron, he gazed around the room. A strong feeling of nostalgia crept over his body, causing him to shudder slightly. *Some bloody good boys trained out of 'ere in the past*, he told himself. *Including Wally Churchill. Christ! If he was to walk in 'ere now, he'd never believe this karzy.* An overpowering feeling of anger caused him to choke; without realizing, his arms appeared waist high, fists clenched. A look of menace crossed his face. Full of intention, he made his way to the nearest punch bag. Drawing his arm back, he allowed a full bloodied right-hand shot to follow through. The bag rocked, and shook on impact.

'That's for nothing,' he grunted between gritted teeth.

'I wouldn't have liked to have been on the end of that!' The patronizing sound of Winters' voice jammed his frustration, as he continued. 'Sorry about that! The phone call, you know how it is.' It was the first positive thing to have come out of his mouth all night. Expecting some form of confirmation regarding Gibbons' performance, he gave Ronnie a pleading look, and held his breath. Whatever hopes he had of getting a verbal result disintegrated! It wasn't coming tonight, or any other night.

'Blimey, is that the time?' Ronnie gestured towards his watch, his ill-timed move leaving Winters feeling totally deflated. Conversation was going nowhere; he'd been hung out and left to dry.

'Ready when you are.' Gibbons had signalled his intention to leave. Not that a get-out clause was warranted, but Gibbons' timing proved to be perfect.

Ronnie grunted a half-hearted, 'See yah,' turned on his heel, and headed for the exit, leaving Winters to choke on what might have been.

As he approached the door, a furtive-looking figure emerged from the darkness of an adjacent corridor. Contempt blanketed his face, as he watched the two disappear into the night. Hate-filled eyes narrowed, as he cursed under his breath. 'This ain't over yet. You've got it all to come, Callaghan!' It was stated with great intent, but that's all; Rossetti excelled at... talking.

With time to contemplate what might have been, Winters was slowly coming to terms with the past events. Given the facts, Ronnie had hijacked any hidden motives he may have held with Gibbons in mind. Putting it mildly, he'd lost control of the situation. The last hour had run like a nightmare, and left him hurting. As of now, any long-term plans were frozen by proxy.

'It needs to be sorted, and someone is going to have to pay for it!'

Glancing across to Rossetti, he beckoned him over. He made a meagre attempt to remove a cigar from within his suit pocket, his hands still shaking uncontrollably with temper. After forcing it into his mouth, he finally got a light to it, and proceeded to pace up and down. Inhaling deeply, he spoke through gritted teeth.

'Callaghan!'

Every syllable became highlighted, as he spat it out, his rage now in full control. Anticipating a hiding to nothing altercation, Rossetti's yellow streak came out of hiding, in turn, forcing him to take a step back, colliding with the office door, as he did so. Backed into a corner on demand, there was nowhere for him to run. Slowly, Winters closed in on him; his facial expression read like a script. Using his lighted cigar as a pointer, he repeatedly thrust the lighted end within stubbing distance of Rossetti's face. With slow verbal deliberation, he spelt it out.

'Listen up, you nonce. Here's the deal, I need to know what's going down between those two. I need connections, addresses, the full SP. Callaghan took the piss out of me tonight. I intend to put that right! You understand?' With his free hand, he slapped Rossetti's cheek a couple of times, and imparted an insidious smile. 'You won't let me down, will you!' Turning on his heel, he made his way across to the snooker room, leaving a pathetic-looking Rossetti wondering what had hit him.

★

The night had indeed belonged to Ronnie. Once outside of Slatteries, Ronnie paused to raise his head skywards. The freshness of the still night air filled his lungs, as he gulped inwardly. 'Bloody nectar, I needed that!'

Gibbons readily concurred, as they made their way across to where Ronnie was parked. As they approached, his attention, for some unknown reason, was now drawn to a large saloon car, parked nearby. It caused him to falter in his stride, allowing him a secondary glance. A quizzical look appeared on his face, and just as quickly vanished.

It was quite clear that his eyes hadn't deceived him; the vehicle in contention just happened to be a red Mercedes! By now, Mickey had picked up on his curiosity.

'Blimey, you don't get many of them to the pound, especially in this area!'

Ronnie was forced to nod in agreement, although his private thoughts remained indifferent. The colour alone seemed to be telling him something. Slowly, it began to dawn on him that his reasoning wasn't so nonsensical after all. The recent altercation with Rossetti had involved such a car model. Plus the voice that he'd heard in Winters' office earlier in the evening, that alone had touched a raw nerve. He'd been emphatic that it belonged to Rossetti. Coincidence or not? Whatever, there was plenty to think about.

Driving back to Gibbons' place, in comparison, turned out to be a quiet affair. As he still persisted to wrestle with his brain on what had gone down, foremost in the frame came via the Mercedes car. To his way of thinking, the latter held the key to a host of nagging unanswered questions. The plain fact that the Mercedes could be seen parked outside Slatteries certainly gave credence to a possible link between Rossetti and Winters. In summing up, he concluded, *That alone is one fact I'm assured of.*

By the time the pair arrived at Gibbons' place, he'd diplomatically decided to drop the present scenario; delving only created involvement, besides he didn't need the grief.

The evening, for his liking, had entailed a double whammy of sorts. On the one hand, meeting Mickey Gibbons was a right result. Winters, on the other hand, could now be seen as a perpetual enemy. Given the choice, Gibbons counted for all the satisfaction he needed at this stage.

'Anywhere here will do fine, Ronnie, thanks.' Bidding goodnight, they jointly arranged a meet at the gym for the following Sunday.

Glancing at the dashboard, Ronnie noted it was now fast approaching ten o'clock. Any 'I told you as much' was put on hold until tomorrow's market. Eager as he was to contact Siddie, it folded there and then.

Tiredness got the better of anxiety as he drove home. Once indoors, his bed became his saving grace. Slumber, it seemed, would never become a problem!

CHAPTER 7

WIN SOME - LOSE SOME

Early the following morning, Ronnie drove into Bailey Street, parked up, and crossed over to the market. The time was just after 6 am. One could sense there was an air of wellbeing about him. Toni de Angelo was out and about as usual, busy carrying crates of milk into his café.

'Morning, Toni, weather looks promising for today, be lucky.'

Shifting his attention, Toni looked across towards Ronnie and placed his load down. A picture of concern, followed by one of astonishment, forced him into scratching his head. On any given day, the best that life could offer would have been a token grunt in pidgin English! There could be no denying Ronnie's mood change. The recent prospect of having witnessed Mickey Gibbons at work in the gym had left him with something to relish.

Being at ease with the world at large had assured him that the stable had a future. Siddie Levy was engrossed in setting up his pitch; the melodious grinding noise made from the wheels of the handcart interrupted his habitual mundane routine. It took him a double take before realization set in.

'Blimey, mate! You're early, you must be on a bet.'

Ronnie grinned back, and returned the enquiry. 'Don't knock it, pal, it could well become a bleedin' habit.'

Uttering a desperate 'Please God!', Siddie offered his hands up in reverence, on the assumption his pattern behaviour might have a bearing on the previous night. Anticipation then came into play, as work ceased, with baited breath, Siddie waited for a possible explanation. It was clear that Ronnie was on a high. Just for the craic, Ronnie promptly decided to get him at the waiting game.

'Oh, meant to ask yer, did you manage to get the forecast for today, mate?' To smother mirth meant turning away after he spoke. The fact that his friend was on a loser didn't affect him one bit.

After picking up a cauliflower, Siddie made a half-hearted attempt to aim it at him. 'You schmuck, Callaghan!' and swore at him in Yiddish.

Unable to hold his feelings any longer, Ronnie held his hands up in mock defence. 'Sorry, pal, I should have known better.' Together, they burst out laughing.

If, for a moment, he thought he felt good, then Siddie had the edge on him. Fully aware of the facts at last, he expressed his relief knowing that his mate had come out of the Winters saga with a result. Later, sitting in the café, they digressed over coffee.

'I'm pleased with you, already, the meet could have turned out nasty. This Mickey Gibbons you spoke about, seriously, has he got what it takes?'

A direct question deserves a positive answer and Siddie was at the heart of the matter. Any doubts that were possibly borne were just as quickly allayed. Without pausing, Ronnie's rapid response summed it all up.

'Take it from me, Siddie. You heard it 'ere first, the kid could go all the way, as far as I'm concerned.'

Pleased as he was at Ronnie's success still left Siddie to play the Devil's advocate. In his opinion, there would be 'I's to be dotted and 'T's to be crossed. In his book of reasoning, it was all too easy. He strongly felt that Winters' role in the build-up shouldn't be dismissed that easily. The latter's personal interest in Gibbons, bent or otherwise, wouldn't run to any third-party involvement. That being the case, then any newfound pact Ronnie may have established would warrant serious consideration. Feeling obliged to emphasize his point left little or no impact.

'That asshole Winters can go to hell!'

Leaving Ronnie adamant in reply. 'It's not as if the kid's under any sort of contract anyway,' he added.

Technically, Siddie was forced to agree, under the circumstances. Although deep down, he could sense some form of aggravation on the horizon. As they left the café, the heavens opened up, and they were forced to run to the safety of the lockup.

'You and your kosher forecasts,' Siddie echoed.

The rest of the week could have been better. Continuous bad weather had now affected trading all around. Ronnie appeared to have taken it all in his stride. His new lease on life seemed to override any loss on profit. In contrast, Siddie took the world on his shoulders.

'There's no money about. Is it something I've said already?'

And he put it all down to a personal vendetta. Although there was a humorous side to his reasoning, Ronnie did at least sympathize with his cause.

'You need to look at it from a fighter's point of view, Siddie. Some you win… some you lose!'

'Yeah, try telling Rachael that!' came back the response.

Saturday soon came round, and with it a smile on their faces. The weather was set fair, bringing the punters back in force. Ronnie had just settled with a punter. Glancing around, he looked across in Siddie's direction. Shaking his head, he stifled a laugh, as Siddie proceeded to check his wedge.

'You'll be on a winner tonight, mate, second honeymoon, I reckon.' A simple gesture off the hand put it all in perspective. 'Thank gawd he's back to normal at last,' and carried on rearranging his flower show.

The door to the gym opened, and Wally Churchill appeared. He sighted Ronnie, broom in hand, giving the floor the once over. His face evoked a cheeky grin. 'You'd make somebody a half-decent housewife if you're not careful.'

Bachelor as he was, domestic innuendos didn't rub off on Ronnie. Momentarily, a reply was hard to come by. Muttering something like, 'I'm too bleedin' ugly, it would never work anyway!' he promptly discarded the broom. By now, bodies began to filter into the gym, creating a welcome atmosphere.

'You got the keys to the glove cupboard, Ronnie?' enquired Wally.

'There yer go, sunshine,' replied Ronnie in anticipation, and handed them over. 'Oh, meant to tell you, I paid Slatteries a visit in the week.'

'Yeah! And I knocked out Don Tyson,' Wally fired back ruefully, as he emptied the shelf. A mute silence ensued, as Wally busied himself arranging the gloves on the kit table. Sensing a verbal sequel, he looked up. Ronnie's face carried an all too familiar look. 'You're flaming serious, ain't yer, son? What the hell were you doing in that karzy?'

'Well, it wasn't out of choice, but—'

'It's a bit off the manor, mate,' Wally interjected. 'Besides, it ain't the sort of place you need to get involved in!' A distant look crossed his face, leaving him to momentarily digress. 'I can remember when the gaff was rated. Where did it all go wrong?'

Ronnie had sensed his intentions into making an issue out of it. There was no denying he'd earned the right to the memories he passionately held. Thinking swiftly, Ronnie placed his arms around his shoulders.

'You're an old sentimental sod, but you're right of course.' His actions quickly dispelled any other alien thoughts that Wally may have been harbouring. Briefly, he explained his reasons for going. The fact that Ronnie had confided in him had given him an added sense of importance. Familiar voices now filled the air, as more bodies began to make themselves known. It was back to business, as usual.

'Good morning, Ronnie, Wally.' The commanding voice of Big Tommy Russell inadvertently broke them apart. 'A word in your ear, mate.'

Leaving Wally to his own designs, he sauntered across to confront Russell. Truth to say that he felt uneasy.

'Problem, Tommy?' His investigative enquiry, unconvincing as it was, became brushed aside.

'You ought to know me better than that!?' replied Russell decisively. His face then took on a discerning look, as he pulled his frame up to full height. The conversation that followed was predictable in every sense. 'One word... Mercer!'

Forced into a corner, Ronnie issued a weak smile. For reasons best kept to himself, he'd played down Mercer's upset, should it become public knowledge. His thoughts began to cloud as concern became a factor. A verbal 'Be first' attitude kicked in.

'Look, if it's anything to do—'

Russell cut him short. 'You can rest easy, I know exactly what happened. The kid explained everything. I told him, it's no big deal. Let's hope he's learnt by it! Now then... business!' Rubbing his huge hands together, he emphasized his point. 'I've managed to get Mercer an eight-rounder on a supporting card, up in town. It's a small hall venue, and the outing will do him good. Timing is of the essence, as you know. You've only got a couple of weeks to get him prepared. Is there anything else I should be aware of, at this stage?' he concluded.

Inwardly, Ronnie breathed a sigh of welcome relief. Any outstanding tension had eradicated itself. Now he could feel relaxed. 'I can't fault his fitness, that's for sure,' he declared. 'So I guess, sparring and plenty of it is on the cards.'

'Fine, makes sense to me. Right, I'll leave it in your capable hands. Incidentally, Ronnie, I'll bell yer tomorrow regarding weights and the SP on his opponent.'

Quietly contented, Russell went on his way, and left Ronnie to it. Around the floor space, bodies were warming up in readiness. Ronnie cast an anxious eye on his watch, and gave a disparaging glance towards the main door. As yet, there was no sign of Mickey Gibbons. Seeds of doubt began to cloud his thinking. *Maybe he's in the locker room*, he mused out of desperation.

'You working the time clock, mate, or shall I?' Wally conveniently brought him down to earth with a bump.

'Oh, sorry, cocker, you carry on, as if I ain't 'ere. I'll be in the locker room for a minute or two.'

What's eating him, I wonder? thought Wally. Looking slightly bemused, he threw the switch to operate the timer.

Wishful thinking on his part only added to Ronnie's disappointment. The locker room, as he suspected, was empty.

'Damn!' His feelings were running high. Caught up in his own selfishness, benefits of doubt were now cast aside. He'd felt so sure that Gibbons would make an appearance. Being a stickler for time only exasperated his anxiety, leaving worry to come back and haunt him. Totally dejected, he stood there looking vacant, lost in thought. Secondary thoughts began to emerge. *I shouldn't have taken so much for granted*, he rebuked himself. *I don't get it. It's just that the kid seemed so genuine at the time.* Finally, he conceded through experience what he already knew to be true. 'Fighters are more temperamental than most women are. They'll wind up breaking your bleedin' heart!'

as he would say. It all but left him with a ray of hope. 'If it happens, it'll happen when he's ready.'

Looking somewhat sober, Ronnie shrugged his shoulders, and left the room. Any hang-ups were soon lost in the atmosphere that the gym created. *This is where it's all at*, he convinced himself while crossing the floor. Raising his voice above the sound of the speedball, he hollered out instructions to the corner man.

'One more on the light bag, and then get Mercer gloved up.'

Adjacent to the ring, Molloy was working out on the big fellow. Annalistic as usual, he caught Ronnie's eye. Watching intently for a minute or so, the bell went for the last ten. Rocking and lurching, the bag rose and fell as Molloy applied full-bloodied shots from every angle.

Full of admiration, Ronnie felt obliged to confide in himself for a moment. *Whatever his shortcomings are in the ring, he can certainly bang a bit. There's certainly hope for him yet!* he concluded. With that, the final bell went, signalling the end of the round. Wally Churchill approached to attend to Mercer. Any lesser man would have failed to pick up on Ronnie's observation. Glancing across gave him the opportunity to endorse his own point of view.

'Bloody good job the bag don't hit back,' he remarked, with a glint in his eye.

'I know exactly where you're coming from, cocker, get them gloves sorted' – which basically said it all, as he tried to stifle a laugh. Mercer appeared to be brimming with confidence. Three rounds of technique work on the pads under his belt had paid dividends. The corner man removed his mouthpiece and head guard. Overworked sweat pores caused his singlet to stick to him like cling film. Head bowed, he grasped the top rope, enabling his body to support aching limbs. Between rasping breaths, he attempted to voice his performance, as Ronnie sponged him down.

'Bloody nectar… but—'

Ronnie cut in before he could continue. Critical as he was, compliments were, in his case, quick to surface. 'That little chat we had last week seems to be rubbing off. You're beginning to use the ring more to your own advantage; make sure you keep it that way.' He emphasized his point with a playful slap on his cheek, and went on. 'Basically, you're a good counter puncher, so let the other guy do all the running.'

Mercer listened intently, hanging on to his every word. 'I felt good in there tonight, and yeah, back-pedalling gives me time to think.'

'Name of the game,' Ronnie concurred. 'You certainly impressed me.'

Mercer climbed out the ring. That last remark from Ronnie had worked wonders to enhance his ego.

Removing his gloves, Wally chipped in. 'Yer looking pleased with yerself; I hope it's catching. By the way, I couldn't help noticing you looked the business in there tonight. Keep it up, my son.'

Being on a high, Mercer endeavoured to drag him into fight politics. It hadn't gone unnoticed.

'Don't stand there catching a bleedin' cold, you've got yer ground work to do yet.' Ronnie was exercising his authority.

For a couple of seconds, Mercer felt slightly deflated. 'What a bloody task master,' he muttered, but managed a grin.

Wally took him to one side. 'He's only thinking of you, son. Remember, winning comes easy, losing comes ruddy hard!'

Mercer was forced to succumb to experience, as his work rate began to take its toll. Pain became etched on his face, as he strained his body to the limits, and beyond.

'Don't overdo those reps, just keep 'em routine,' Wally advised. 'Remember, quality input beats quantity!'

Meanwhile, Ronnie hadn't missed out on Mercer's show of force either. Turning to Wally, he gave him a quizzical look. 'What did you say to him?' he questioned.

Wally winked, and smiled. 'You don't really want to know, mate,' was all he said on the matter. The session came and went. Apart from Tommy Russell working in the office, it only left Ronnie, busy clearing up. The gym was empty. Methodical as ever, the last of the remaining equipment was now stored away. As per usual, he made a strong point of checking to see if he might have missed anything.

Pausing merely for thought, Ronnie turned to reflect on the current morning's input. Mercer's contribution had been inspiring. Even Molloy came in for praise. All in all, he figured, the stable was showing positive. Without warning, a voice from the background jolted his mood.

'Still 'ere, Ronnie? I thought you'd have been long gone by now.' The voice belonged to Russell, who had just emerged from the office, looking drawn.

'Same as that!' exclaimed Ronnie. 'It's not like you to hang about.'

'Yeah, to be honest, it's been one of them mornings. The bloody phone's taken a right hiding; I can well do without it.'

Ronnie gestured a sympathetic nod of agreement. 'Never off the case, eh? Who'd be a bleedin' fight manager?' There was no doubting that Russell was looking uptight. It was plain he needed to chill out. 'Verbal battles,' as he would say, 'were far worse than physical ones.' Deliberately changing tack, his mind converged onto the public house that adjoined the gym. Respecting Ronnie's attitude towards the 'demon drink', he decided to push his luck.

'God! I could murder a bloody pint. I don't suppose...

what I mean is, I could use the company.' Short of pleading, the expression on his face spoke volumes.

Meanwhile, Ronnie maintained a cold silence. *I must be bloody crazy to even consider the idea*, he told himself. But then again, Russell did have this exclusive aura. At length, he caved in. 'You're a bleedin' liberty taker, go on, you've talked me into it,' and ceded, 'Fight manager! Huh, ruddy actor more like.'

The two departed the gym, like a couple of kids on an outing. Once inside the busy pub, size had priority over manners, as Russell carved his way through a sea of people to get to the bar. It was left to Ronnie to make the apologies on his behalf. *I really don't need this shit*, he told himself. His obvious disinterest in the pub, as a whole, had now started to show through.

Finally, they made the bar. Ronnie ordered a soft drink, and managed to find refuge in a nearby corner. Once settled in, Russell made the first verbal move, by deciding to talk shop, airing his views on Mercer's forthcoming outing and finishing by emphasizing the importance of a result. It was 'old ground fodder', and Ronnie's patience began to falter. He also sensed that Russell was holding back on something.

'Are you in a position to name the opposition at this stage or do I wait for the next phone call you get? Only, I've got this distinctive feeling that yer holding out on me.' It was sarcasm at its best, but needed to be said.

A pregnant pause followed, allowing Russell to toy with his glass. A look of apprehension appeared on his face. It became blatantly obvious that he was hedging.

'As I said before, if he comes through this one—'

'A name, Tommy... gimme a name,' demanded Ronnie. He'd had better replies in the past, and judging by the look on

Russell's face left him in no doubt whatsoever. 'Why Harrison, of all people?' Ronnie was needled.

Calling on diplomacy, Russell chose to take it out on his beer, rather than pursue the topic. Taking the top of his beer at worst gave him a few seconds of respite. The answer to Ronnie's nagging question needed tact. There was no disputing the fact that he now felt uncomfortable with the present situation, especially knowing Ronnie as he did. It was going to take a lot to win him round to his way of thinking, when it came down to justifying his choice of selecting Mercer's opponent. The open fact that Harrison was a rated fighter could not be ignored. On a par, his track record justified his ratings in the division. Russell, in the past, had never been one to push his boys. Selective opponents were always readily available, until such times the fighter proved his standing, his reason being that it served as a stepping stone to any future success. 'You don't win any medals bumping fighters off' became an adage he genuinely believed in. Personalities apart, Russell felt convinced that Mercer was ripe for the occasion. Downing the last of his beer, he placed the defunct glass down to one side, and turned to face Ronnie.

Their conversation had been a complete mismatch, doomed from the start. Conversation was going nowhere. If that wasn't bad enough, the illicit smoke wafting in from a nearby open window was invading Ronnie's space. Cursing under his breath, he signalled his intention to leave. As far as he was concerned, any duel decisions in the making were put on hold. For his part, Russell's mind had already been made up. With or without Ronnie's blessing, the Harrison–Mercer match would go ahead. With the pub now a distant memory, the two exchanged goodbyes, and parted company. Shoulders slouched, Ronnie sauntered off in the direction of his car;

mixed feelings consumed his body. Outwardly, he looked as if he had the world on his shoulders.

'Oh well, tomorrow's another day!' he concluded. It became the only positive statement that seemed to be appropriate at the time!

CHAPTER 8

TRIALS & TRIBULATIONS

If for a minute Ronnie thought that his problems were all self-imposed, then he wasn't alone! Competition appeared rife. Circumstances were out in force creating Rossetti with a similar outcome. Living like he did in a fantasy existence had more than its share of pitfalls. His day-by-day vision of survival entailed finding more clues than a crossword puzzle. Lady Luck also had a large part to play. Whatever money that he'd managed to hustle that particular morning, playing pool, was classed as lent. To his mode of thinking, money was made round to go around!

Leaving Slatteries that morning saw him heading for the nearest bookies. One by one, defunct betting slips littered the floor space around him. His so-called alleged inside information had been well and truly left behind in the weighing room. As of now, his credit rating had lost its charm as a result.

The trouble was the winners' queue was a long one and he just happened to be on the end of it. Checking the last of his wedge made him grimace. Running his digit down the list of runners on his card forced him into making a decision involving a four-horse race. Blinded by the odds on offer, his selection rested with the favourite, his thinking being classed as 'getting out stakes'. If his horse won, then he would be only thieving his own ante back. But then that was Rossetti!

He glanced up at the board to get a show of the betting odds. The bookie was laying 4/6 on, bar the field. The overhead Tannoy made his mind up for him. 'Under orders Kempton Park.' Hurriedly, he thrust his betting slip through the grille to be processed. His idea of a racing certainty was on a par with an underwater coloured candle! Three minutes later, he vacated the office, the SP echoing from the Tannoy ringing in his ears. 'Result Kempton Park... winner number four... 8/1... second the favourite even money.' Like the rest of his cop-outs, his latest betting slip joined the rest on the floor. Turning on his heel, he slunk out of the office.

Like a man on a mission, he'd swiftly decided that a return to Slatteries could be his last remaining trump card. As per usual, he still needed to find that all elusive clue! It wasn't going to happen today, or indeed, any other day.

The endearing term 'loser' had become a virus. In his ignorance, he could have turned to reverse psychology and made a winning book on it. But that was Rossetti. A glimmer of hope interrupted his thoughts. He suddenly realized that Terry Winters still owed him a few quid, on the strength of an illegal errand. *That ought to bale me out for a while*, he considered. Ducking and diving came as second nature to him. His unearthly existence suited the bent society that he ran with. Like it or not, Winters, he envisaged, would become his next passport. For his role, Terry Winters had to enforce his control over the unlawful regime he'd set to establish. In a short time, it had matured into a world set apart from the norm. The extreme power generated from protection rackets to money laundering endorsed his standing in the local underworld as being the ruler. What he couldn't do with muscle went hand-in-glove with ill-gotten gains. Over time, he'd now managed to create a major foothold within the world of crime.

Rossetti craved a percentage of the local action, and his

conniving way of life hadn't gone unnoticed. Winters suitably put him on the payroll, while using him for his own ends. From day one, he'd become bracketed; what little brain he had ran only to number one whipping boy. Running messages, and the occasional use of a red Mercedes saloon car, didn't figure too highly in his book. Right now, his twisted mind was flowing with optional ideas. His intention to use Winters, in the short term, lay claim to a stepping stone aimed at wishful thinking. More than ever, it was paramount to gain Winters' confidence in him. Sucking up to the man seemed the favourable option.

In one respect, Rossetti did have one asset going for him. Winters, by definition, was classed as a new face on the manor. Whereas, he was on familiar territory. Along the way, he'd managed to gain access to certain profitable information. In maintaining his standing, with that in mind, Winters would have been prepared to pay dearly for such knowledge. Especially in knowing that they were linked to a local protection racket. Obtaining full control on the manor could only boost his rating within the seedy underworld he'd ruthlessly created.

For Rossetti, the SP he retained counted as money in the bank!

At any time, and if the timing was right, it could become his pension! Keyed up, he entered Slatteries; the office beckoned. Shortening his stride, he stopped short prior to entering. For the time being, any monetary thoughts were put on hold. From within, the sound of raised voices was in progress. Staying put gave him a ringside seat, as the argument got decidedly heated. It was plainly evident that Winters and a third party were involved in a dispute of some kind. Straining his senses for loose information caused the hairs on the back of his neck to rise. Above the hubbub, the name Callaghan became clearly audible. 'For fuck's sake!' he thought out loud, and retreated into the shadow of a nearby corridor.

His blood began to pump on overtime, as he continued to grasp the extent of the altercation. The reference to Callaghan on its own created a personal fear factor. His mind was racing; various combinations rapidly filled his head. *What if Callaghan recognized me last Wednesday night, when I interrupted the meeting? And what about the car accident?* ... No, that was a different scenario. Grief was the last thing he needed right now. Without prior warning, his fantasy ambitions were beginning to look dented. *Just supposing, what if Callaghan had put two and two together?* Cold sweat broke through on his forehead, and his breathing became erratic. For a second, his exclusive nightmare was left in limbo, as the office door suddenly flew open.

Retreating further into the shadows, he managed to wedge his body behind a cupboard out of sight. Winters appeared first, followed by a figure he immediately recognized as belonging to Mickey Gibbons, still sticky with sweat, as he was. Relief swept over his pathetic body; for the time being, he decided to stay put.

His face fully contorted with rage, Winters squared up to Gibbons. 'You pulled a right stroke on me the other night... so don't expect me to forget it!' Their rant continued.

'I don't owe you anything,' retorted Gibbons. 'You and me are over, mister... I don't owe you a thing... end of story... got it?!' Turning his back on Winters, he sauntered off towards the exit.

Rossetti's mind appeared to be on overtime. He recalled the word 'contract' had been mentioned during their argument. Had Gibbons reneged on a deal of some kind? Or was it something even more sinister?

Meanwhile, with arms flailing, Winters continued to rant. 'You can't do this to me... you bastard... you fucking owe me! Don't think this is the end of it, you'll get yours...

you'll see.' He pointed a trembling fist in Gibbons' direction. Totally exasperated, he fought for the right words to say. 'Just watch yer bloody back in future, and that goes for your pal Callaghan, as well.'

Gibbons never looked back. He appeared to be oblivious of what was going down, and exited the building. Emerging from out of the shadows, Rossetti hesitantly approached Winters.

'You, in my office now!'

It just hadn't been his day. Lady Luck, it seemed, had decided to take the day off. Any money he thought had been owed counted for nothing; it didn't appear on Winters' agenda. Cursing the world at large, Rossetti followed him back into the office.

★

That night, Ronnie had two phone calls. The first one had been previously arranged. With time on his hands, his flagging patience began to take its toll. Moody and irritable, he continued to clock watch in anticipation. Phone or no phone, it wouldn't have eased his current temperament. The changeable weather from the previous week had resulted in a few soakings. Suspecting a chest infection might be on the cards, he'd been advised to lie low for a couple of days. A bear with a sore head would have made better company. Mooching from one room to another wasn't his style. Right now, he craved some sort of company, verbal or otherwise. He was just about to doze off, when the first of the calls came through.

It made a welcome respite; any form of contact thus far would be tolerated. Heaving a sigh of relief, he lunged for the receiver. With so much time on his hands, his main concern rested with the gym. Fortunately, Wally had paid him a fleeting visit in the morning, on a pretext that something was going down. He'd called in at the market for a waffle, and happened to notice Ronnie's empty pitch. Acting on Siddie's advice, he left clutching a large bag of grapes. On arrival, Ronnie soon put his anxious mind to rest. His cold hadn't affected his awareness. Having said his goodbyes, Wally got halfway through the door when Ronnie checked him.

'Who were the grapes for?' he enquired, half-knowingly.

'Blimey, mate, I almost forgot,' replied Wally sheepishly. 'Siddie asked me to pass 'em on to you.' Chuckling to himself, he made his way out.

Shortly after his departure, the phone rang again. Feeling wide awake, the handset was lodged in his hand in no time.

'Hello… that you, Tommy?'

'Speaking!'

'What's occurring, mate?' He made out as if it wasn't important. In the background, he could hear Russell clearing his throat.

'Sorry to hear you're iffy. I would never have known if it hadn't have been for Wally. But I did say I'd get back to you.'

Recalling their last negative conversation, Ronnie prayed that a compromise could be on the cards. Russell then picked up where he'd left off.

'Now, it's imperative that we discuss a working business plan. Firstly, I respect your judgment regarding Mercer. Having said that, and I've given this a lot of thought, by going up market with the kid, he's got nothing to lose. Okay, so it's a gamble, but I firmly believe it's one that we need to take. Harrison is a good fighter, but if Mercer delivers the goods on the night, it can only do his rankings a power of good. In my book it definitely makes sense… what do you think?'

'Maybe I overreacted the other morning,' suggested

Ronnie. 'Sunday morning, in a boozer, wrong time, wrong place, know what I mean?'

Sensing a climb-down of sorts, Russell levelled their differences, and continued to spout. 'The thing is, mate, I've got the contract in my hand, as we speak. The only foreseeable problem, as I see it, will be levelling the weight situation.'

'I hear what you say, Tommy. I'm prepared to go along with the contract; besides, the kid's worked hard, he deserves a crack at the big time. Making the weight could be awkward on the day. Just make sure you arrange an early weigh-in; hopefully, he'll come in fully blown on the day. Knowing Harrison as I do, he's gonna struggle to make it, so it should by default give Mercer the edge... okay?'

Russell heaved a sigh of relief at the other end. 'Glad we got that sorted,' he exclaimed thankfully. 'I'll be in touch.' With that, he hung up.

Ronnie was left to reflect. The deed had been done. Mercer was now the priority, and the sooner he could get the kid back into a working rhythm, then so much the better for everyone. It was a very relieved Ronnie who replaced the handset! His armchair beckoned; plonking himself down, he made a futile attempt to reach out for a newspaper. It became short lived, as the phone burst into life once again.

'I don't believe this is happening,' he exclaimed, although deep down, he did have a hidden suspicion. Tentatively, he raised the receiver to his ear, and spoke. 'Ronnie Callaghan speaking.'

For reasons of their own, the caller bided his time before replying. 'Hello!'

Once again, Ronnie forced the issue. This time he got lucky, as the caller responded.

'Erm, I'm sorry, I wasn't sure if I had the right number or not. I did try to get through a while back.'

Listening intently, as he spoke, Ronnie thought that the tone of voice somehow seemed familiar to him.

'It's me, Mickey Gibbons. I'm phoning about last Sunday.' For a minute, nothing seemed to register. 'Sorry I never showed, nothing personal, you understand. Bad timing... circumstances, you understand. Saying that, I needed to keep in touch.'

Then it dawned on him. 'Mickey, yeah, how could I be that dumb? Please God, don't hang up.' His concern proved to be invalid; Gibbons had other ideas.

'Trouble is, things got a bit heavy since we last met. As a result, I was forced to give Sunday a miss, know what I mean?'

Mickey's emphasis on the word 'heavy' made an instant impact on Ronnie's line of thinking. Maybe the kid was being leaned on, and then, of course, there was Slatteries to consider. In retrospect, it was the only real connection that the two shared. Question was, what was Gibbons doing in a dump like that anyway? What little he knew about him didn't count for much, although his genuine side had left its mark.

'Winters!' His subconscious cut in; the name was reaching out, trying to tell him something. For once, his reasoning was slowly beginning to make sense at last. He recalled Winters' reaction to Gibbons' confession saying Ronnie and he had met previously.

'Problem? Look, there ain't no problem. As far as I'm concerned, things happen, that's part of life, mate. Is there anything I can do for yer?'

'As it happens, I'm in need of a favour.'

'So try me!'

'I'd rather not discuss it over the phone. Any reason why we can't make a meet?'

'Look, save messing around, why don't I come round yours? I know where to find yer now. By the way, are you working at all?'

'No, not as yet. Tell you what, if we said 10.30 am tomorrow morning, or thereabouts, I'd be well happy.' Ronnie wasn't about to hold a steward's enquiry on that and was quick to respond.

'You got it, mate, see yer then.' What had transpired with the last hour left Ronnie feeling outwardly calm, all things considered. Although, underneath, his mind was on a par with a cat on a hot tin roof, with one sequel overlapping the other. 'First things first,' he was quick to remind himself, and commenced pouring himself a soft drink. Semi-relaxed, he took the top of his orange juice, and once again eased his frame back into the armchair. He dismissed Gibbons' call to one side; Tommy Russell appeared to have invaded his thoughts.

Previously knowing that he'd given his allegiance to Russell gave him cause to focus his attention on the decision he'd made to sanction the Mercer fight. Whatever the outcome, Harrison, he considered, would have known that he'd been in a scrap. The fact that his camp had more to lose was a plus, as well. Besides which, a trip up to the smoke wasn't such a bad idea. A chance to see a few old faces in the business, yeah, why not! There and then, he closed the door on any likely outcome. Instead, he channelled his remaining thoughts on the Gibbons' scenario once again; at least it brought about a smile of satisfaction on his face.

In all honesty, his unexpected call had taken him completely by surprise. At worst, it meant that Gibbons was now back on the scene. That in itself boded well. Given the chance, he thought, and working on an assumption, the idea of signing Gibbons up via Russell could not be ignored. 'People like him don't just fall out of trees. The kid's a gilt-edged asset,' he convinced himself.

What with the calls, and the time spent fact finding, the evening had slipped by. The wall clock caught his eye. 'God! Is that the time?' he exclaimed. Downing the remaining orange juice, he caught sight of the grapes that Siddie had sent over. 'Must remember to thank him when I get the chance,' he concluded. Ten minutes later, the evening, as such, became history. Pulling the duvet back, he climbed into bed, and turned out the light. *I don't suppose I'll get much sleep tonight*, reigned foremost in his mind. He was right... he didn't. Whatever sleep went begging that night appeared to be lent in lieu of anticipation.

The following morning, with a full English inside of him, found Ronnie on his way over to see Mickey Gibbons. It didn't take long for the early rush hour traffic to swallow him up. Thankfully, some twenty minutes or so later, the road leading to Gibbons' came into view. In the light of day, it appeared to be hardly recognizable from his previous late night visit. Although having been familiar with the locale, the years, and alleged progress, had now taken their toll of the once elegant Regency dwellings. Scrupulous landlords could be found on a par with the unfortunate tenants they financially squeezed. Peering through the windscreen, Ronnie shook his head and grimaced.

'I must be getting bloody old,' he mused. 'It ain't the manor I used to know!' Finding a space to park was testing his patience. Luckily, a bay became vacant within walking distance of Gibbons' place.

After parking up, he headed back up the road in the opposite direction. It didn't take him long to find the house in question, although the number of doorbells representing the flats began to wind him up. Scanning the name plates led to a clue at last. Expressing relief, his digit hit the button. A few minutes went by with no response from within. Uncertainty began to cloud Ronnie's mind. The right road... the number? No, he was right the first time. The next time around, he literally hung on the doorbell. Slowly, the door opened. The unmistakeable face of Mickey Gibbons tentatively appeared. Relief washed over Ronnie's face, and he decided to let Mickey do the talking.

'God! Am I pleased to see you. Glad you could make it.' Without hesitation, Mickey hurriedly ushered him through into a large hallway. Before closing the front door, Mickey proceeded to make a distinctive point of looking up and down the road. Straight away, Ronnie picked up on his behaviour, but, just as quickly, decided not to pursue his logic. At first glance, the spacious hallway appeared to be rundown. The token dated newspapers and junk mail littered the floor, almost serving as a carpet.

'Shit! How the other half live,' he thought out loud.

'In here, Ronnie.' After pushing a discarded armchair to one side, Mickey opened a door, and swiftly motioned Ronnie inside. Once inside, he hurriedly shut the door behind him, leaving Ronnie to take stock of the surroundings. Initially, he found himself taken aback by the size of the room, until he realized that it included a bed in one corner and a sink in the other. A mobile clothes horse standing against one wall seemed to double up as a wardrobe of sorts. The outline coming from a one-time cooker complemented what wallpaper there was hanging off the walls.

Just then, Mickey interrupted his space. Thrusting a dilapidated chair in front of him, he said, 'Here, park yourself down for a minute… I won't be a moment.' With that, he disappeared through a side door.

Left to his own designs, Ronnie glanced around. He could just make out what looked like a blanket spread over a piece of furniture or other. His interest got the better of him; grasping the cover, he pulled it to one side, fully exposing a bow-fronted cabinet, as he did so. It took a double take before he realized what it contained inside. Both shelves were littered with silverware, ranging across trophies, cups, and medal shields, all of which depicted various aspects alluding to the noble art. A look of admiration caused his face to light up.

'Blimey! That's the nearest I'm ever going to get to see Aladdin's bleedin' cave.' Just then, Mickey re-entered the room. Looking up, Ronnie raised both arms high. 'Sorry, mate, just being plain bloody nosey!'

'Don't worry about it, I'm not.'

'Been busy, ain't yer?'

'Oh, those! Something I picked up from my amateur days.'

'Think yourself damn lucky, mate. All I ever got as a kid was a glass of lemonade and a poxy currant bun voucher.' Whatever strained tension had pre-existed vanished without trace as they laughed heartily. Grabbing another chair, Mickey sat down, and made himself comfortable. A questionable look took over his face.

'Uhm, where to start?'

'From the beginning sounds good to me, son. I'm a good listener.'

'I don't want to bore you with any verbal crap,' he insisted.

'I'll be the best judge of that!' Ronnie hit back.

It was enough to put Mickey at ease. He went on to say that he'd been fostered out as a kid living in London, never having met either one of his parents. Shunted from one situation to another finally brought things to a head. Any form of security in his torrid life proved non-existent. He'd had a gutful of being institutionalized. So at the age of seventeen he made the decision, wrongly or rightly, to go solo. Checking him momentarily, Ronnie pointed towards the cabinet. Mickey shrugged his shoulders before replying.

'They're just mementos I picked up along the way. They gave me an outlet to offload my aggression, know what I mean?'

'At least it was controlled aggression, son, and that's the difference. I reckon you got it right.'

Nodding his head, Mickey concurred, and went on. 'I badly needed a change of scene. Eventually, I found myself here in Stonewater. I was desperate to get me head sorted, so much shit in my head, you understand?'

'Probably more than you realize, Mickey... go on.'

'Well, I managed to get a start, labouring on a construction site; then I happened to meet this guy in a bar one night. We got talking...' He hesitated slightly.

'Go on, my son, let it all out. Don't stop now, yer on a roll.' Desperate for conclusions, Ronnie made the point. 'This guy, name... gimme a name!'

Mickey averted his gaze; he appeared reluctant to continue.

'What's in a name, Mickey? It can't be that important, surely?'

'Guess you're right. The guy called himself Rossetti... Paul Rossetti!'

A stunned silence kicked in. Ronnie's face could now be found on the floor, leaving his blood count to rise in sympathy. This latest revelation from Mickey had left him feeling slaughtered, struggling as he did, trying to make some sense as to what was going down. Name and situations were pounding away inside his subconscious.

Slatteries! ...The red Mercedes car. Slowly, it all began to make sense at last. Especially the car scenario, it all fitted into place. It was the last piece in the jigsaw, confirming what he'd suspected all along. Proving that Rossetti had been at Slatteries the evening of the meet. Winters might have been calling the shots, but together they were both part of a hidden conspiracy bent on using Mickey as a monetary asset. The sudden change in Ronnie's demeanour hadn't gone unnoticed. Even at best, he was white with temper.

'Was it something I said?' enquired Mickey.

Doing his utmost to play it down, Ronnie endeavoured to sum up his thoughts. 'I'll tell you all about it one day, son. So, I presume, Rossetti introduced you to Winters… right?'

It was now Mickey's turn to take a step back. 'How could you have known that?! I'm confused.'

'I'll explain later. So where did it lead to from there? After you meeting Winters, I mean.'

'Previously, I'd already told Rossetti I was looking to get a living as a pro. That's when he got me involved with Winters. The idea suited me, a chance to make something of myself. I was grateful. He said I could use the gym whenever, but I wasn't impressed with his set-up and the pressure he was putting on me. I put up with the grief for a while, and then I told him I wanted out.'

'You summed that up about right,' Ronnie chimed in. 'What happened next?'

'He didn't want to let me walk, so he arranged for me to obtain a licence, providing he could manage me. Like a fool, I went along with it. Getting the licence was the easy part; the hard part came when dealing with him. Winters, to be honest, didn't have a clue when it came to management – unless any dealings were bent, then he was in his element. All I got out of the guy was promises. I knew I wasn't going anywhere. Not only that, his involvement with unlicensed halls isn't exactly a reference… is it? To keep me sweet, he said that he would get me a trainer to do the business for me.'

'And that's when I came on the scene. What a conniving asshole! Bloody good job you gave him the elbow, knowing what you know now.'

'Yeah, right! Trouble is, he didn't take it too well, and that's when he put the frighteners on me, and on you as well for that matter.'

'I can see now why you made such a fuss about opening your front door. My gut was telling me that something iffy was going down.'

'One thing's for sure: Winters means business. The sort of faces he runs around with tells you something. His threats need to be taken seriously. I'm not in this dump out of choice, you know, Ronnie. I was forced to leave my last flat in a hurry. I was informed that two faces were asking after me, so I didn't stop to meet them. Hence the reason I'm here now. Thing is, it's easy saying don't let him get to you; it doesn't work like that!'

Ronnie held up his hand, intending to cut him short. He was desperate to express his own views on the situation. 'I've said it before, and I'll say it again. Winters is a down and out asshole, and as for that devious bastard Rossetti, he'd better get off my back if he wants to stay healthy.'

Knowing that he was in good company, a much relieved Gibbons asked the all-important question. 'So where do we go from here, then, Ronnie?'

It was clear he was seeking assurance of some type. Ronnie quickly endeavoured to put his mind at rest. 'For the time being, lie low, don't put yourself about needlessly. Obviously stay in touch, as well. One thing's for sure: you can't stay 'ere. Leave it with me, I'll get something sorted, trust me... right?'

Leaving Mickey with plenty to think about, Ronnie said his goodbyes, and departed. For the time being, self-control was paramount. A personal threat couldn't be taken too lightly. On his own, Rossetti was a non-runner, although a double act was different again. But he didn't envisage losing sleep over the situation; after all, he was a Callaghan!

Once out of sight, he checked for the time of day: it was nearing 11.45. With time to play with, he headed out of bedsit land, and headed directly towards the market. Fifteen minutes later found him on home turf, parking up in Bailey Street. Grim-faced, he made his way towards the entrance. Like it or not, Siddie Levy in the past had been a shoulder to cry on; today would be no exception to the rule. As of now, he badly needed a shoulder to cry on; his timing as usual remained irrelevant as sweetener, but that's the way he was. Should he ever need an excuse, then Siddie's benevolent bag of grapes would get him out of jail! Siddie, by chance, had already spotted him, as he entered the market. Leaving his stall in the hands of a minder, he hurriedly made his way over to meet him. He figured that Ronnie's sudden appearance could mean only one thing... trouble! Knowing he was a non-gambler, he still would have put his stall on it.

'Don't worry about it, I needed a break already,' Siddie assured him. Seated in the café together, Ronnie was making a bad job of explaining his lousy timing. Brushing it aside, Siddie jested, 'So I'll bill yer for the grapes! Now get to the point.'

Taking in a deep breath, Ronnie went into grief mode. 'It's all come on top, mate... bleedin' long story, know what I mean?' he blurted out. He then sat back, and waited for a response. Any underlying doubts that the reason he appeared to be holding back on, in relation to Terry Winters, now confirmed his suspicions that Winters happened to be the root of the problem. It would have been far too easy to have said, 'I told you so,' and promptly left it at that! But this was Siddie Levy talking.

'Before you go any further, I'm telling you now, this guy Winters is a schmuck! And you've let him get to yer already. If you feel yer need a waffle, then let's do it. For what it's worth, I knew the strength of him from day one!'

Expressing his forthright opinion had somehow left Ronnie feeling totally inadequate. God! He envied him, and his uncanny gift of hindsight. Glancing an anxious eye towards his stall cut short any further discussion on the matter.

'Tell yer what,' he suggested. 'Why not come round mine tonight? Rachael's doing matzoh ball soup with bagels for supper.'

That was an offer he couldn't refuse. 'Nice one, Siddie. I look forward to it, say around eight o'clock?' And he went on. 'I ain't got nothing in anyway.'

Siddie was forced to grin as he castigated him. 'Callaghan... you're a shnorrer, but don't be late.'

★

Fed and watered, Ronnie sat back from the table and sighed. Easing his waist belt, he patted his stomach.

'Rachael, that happened to be the absolute business. They broke the mould when they made you.'

Rachael playfully threw her arms up in the air. 'Schmaltz! All I ever get from you is schmaltz!' she replied, and winked at Siddie. 'I'm sure youse two have plenty to catch up on. I'll clear the dishes, and catch up on some paperwork.' She then left them to their own designs.

Ronnie looked directly across at Siddie. 'You are one bleedin' lucky guy, mate, she's a bloody diamond!'

Nodding vigorously, Siddie fired back at him. 'So I know that already. More importantly, what's occurring?' Getting impatient for a story, he urged Ronnie to open up. It wouldn't have been hard to relate the facts, but Ronnie being Ronnie somehow seemed to lose the plot. 'You just don't get it, do yer?! Okay, so you get Mickey Gibbons. But at what price? The threat from Winters isn't going to go away overnight.' Siddie, as usual, was saying it as it was, which meant including the flipside to the coin. He continued. 'You have to see it from his side; no wonder the asshole is taking it personally. Mickey would have the wedge in his pocket; suddenly, you come on the scene and break the chain. So now that's all he's got to think about, which makes him one dangerous putz. And, from knowing Rossetti, we really don't know who else he's firmed up with. Except to say that whatever plans he's got for your health, you need to give them some serious thought.'

Forced to listen, Ronnie leaned forwards, resting his elbows on the table. Hands clasped tightly, he inhaled deeply. His eyes narrowed as the truth of the matter came home to roost. There was no disguising the impact that Siddie had laid on him. Right now, he bore the hallmark of a much worried man. Realization had now set in. At length, he spoke up. 'It ain't a game anymore, is it?' It was the best he could come up with at the time, short on words, and gave no indication as to his true inner feelings. For his part 'tomorrow is another day' seemed grief enough. Two more coffees, and a hell of a lot wiser, he said his goodbyes, and departed.

An early night, or what was left of it, seemed appropriate. He intended working his stall the next morning. As he drove home, his thoughts returned to focus on Mickey Gibbons. For somebody who he hardly knew, there was no doubting, in his mind, the form of affinity he had towards him. Pushing his own problems to one side made him realize just how vulnerable the kid was; out on his own and living the way he did didn't add up to much. Through no fault of his own, his card had been marked. It wasn't going to take Rossetti long to find out his whereabouts. Ronnie needed to act fast. His priority would entail getting Mickey away from bedsit land, even if it meant him staying at Ronnie's flat. Without the use of a contact number, he decided to take a chance by calling on him the following evening. The need to respect Winters' open threat had finally sunk in. Looking into his car mirror reflected the serious look emblazoned on his face. 'As from now, I need to keep in front of the game,' he stated purposefully.

CHAPTER 9

WISHFUL THINKING

Elsewhere in town, Rossetti had an evil look about him, but then he didn't have to work at it! Slamming the door to Winters' office, his face contorted from one of evil into one of blinding hatred. For a start, his recent clumsy attempts to locate Mickey Gibbons had fallen flat, and for somebody who allegedly thrived on know-how, the week had cost him dearly. The fact that he'd dropped a monkey at the bookies ran only secondary to the pride that was eating away inside. Then there was Winters of course giving it large at the top end! Reasoning didn't appear in the latter's makeup, so any excuses that Rossetti came over with were consequently shot down.

Slouching out of Slatteries, he could still make out Winters' parting shot ringing in his ears. 'Useless bastard!' That became the knife in his back. Cursing him with every stride, he hailed a nearby cab, and directed the driver to the nearest off-licence. After telling him to wait, he returned minutes later, clutching a bag full of spirits.

'Where to nah, guv?' enquired the driver.

'Martin Street, this side of the basin, and don't hang about.'

The cabbie duly obliged, and proceeded to boot the pedal. Canal Street formed the heartbeat of Docklands. Its reputation over the years had grown as large as the community it imbibed. Nationalities from every quarter became drawn to its illicit atmosphere that it had generated over the years. Pocket ghettos now existed. Creeds and cultures became segregated as a means of trading within their own locales. Catering provided the major blood flow of Docklands; because of its intensity survival incurred competition. It ran deep throughout each regime, creating a volatile undercurrent. The respect metered out by their counterparts was as high or as low as the takings they produced.

In turn, the reigning underworld media had been quick to capitalize on the situation. Thus, the protection racket established itself like a leech, sucking away on survival blood, by preying on disillusioned restaurant owners. Collectively, they imposed a wave of misery synonymous to their kind. On a felon scale, they were a breed apart. Working in teams on a grand scale, despair gave way to muscle.

'Pay up to survive' became a way of life, ruled entirely by fear and violence. For the short time that Terry Winters' firm had been operating on the manor, he'd managed to gain a substantial slice of the business. His standing in the underworld was now on the way up, made beneficial by the ungracious henchmen he employed. Because of their fear factor, they were well respected by counter villains alike. From the clubs and pubs that he frequented, like a magnet, Rossetti became drawn to their evil circle. The fact that he was out of his league meant he was always going to be on the outside looking in. Although in his ignorance, and blinded by egotism, he felt that he was part of the action. Blinded by false illusion, his company was tolerated only by the amount of money he could put about at any one time.

His misguided art of perception gave him a lifeline when it suited him. Over a period of time, gilt-edged inside information he'd managed to accumulate had cause to fester on his reasoning. Time and places, pickups, and drop off zones could be readily called upon. In reality, it meant that a small firm using the right man to front it could turn out to be a nice little earner! In the past, his total lack of bottle had always held him back. But pushed into a corner, with no way out, who knew what his twisted mind could cope with?

After paying the cabbie off, he entered his flat, and took no time pouring himself a copious amount of scotch. Throwing it back in one go forced him to shudder as the raw alcohol bit the back of his scrawny throat. Three more shots later, relaxation took over his useless body. His inner thoughts were centred around the last Winters altercation, which also included money, in that order. The nectar he was knocking back began to flow by now, and in doing so helped to create a false sense of being. Scheming came to the fore, inducing an uncontrollable leering mask of Dutch confidence to consume his pitiful frame.

For a moment, the end of his self-made tunnel didn't appear to be as dark as before. Pouring another drink, submerged in thought, he sipped away at it in a mechanical fashion, totally rapt in his delirium. His day would come, he promised himself; with the aid of a further drink, an idea began to manifest itself in his mind.

The little sensibility that remained was lodged in his brain the following morning, as he finally made contact with the real world. The heavy sound of traffic tentatively aroused him from his stupor. His bloodshot eyes, still full of sleep, laboriously flickered open. With difficulty, he made a vain attempt to take in the surroundings. Recognition slowly oozed through his negative mind, as he quickly realized that one wing of the armchair doubled up as a prop between himself and the floor. A pall of smoke hung eerily between himself and the ceiling. The stale odour it resonated filled his nostrils, causing him to involuntarily heave. Beside the half-filled bottle, which lay at his feet, the dregs coming from another added their own contribution to his induced misery. Instinctively, he rubbed his eyes to adjust to the sparse existing light. It became wasted on the pain that honed in, as he made a meagre attempt to focus.

'Fuck's sake!' Cursing himself only caused him to grimace, as he leaned forwards in the armchair. The supposed blood flow to his head momentarily stopped him going any further. Somewhere, a pneumatic drill was thumping away; in seconds, he realized it came from the inside of his head. A few feet away, the clock on the wall seemed to mock his sanity; bloodless eyes narrowed at his attempt to locate the time of day. He needn't have bothered; the clock was a million miles away. Finally, forcing himself out of the armchair, he stumbled his way through to the bathroom. Filling the basin with cold water seemed to have the desired effect. Dunking his head for the third time slowly brought him back into the world as he knew it. Glancing in the shaving mirror, he hastily grabbed a towel, and feverishly wiped his face down to rid it of its zombie-like appearance.

A form of sanity now began to fill his resident twisted mind, allowing him to curse the world at large. But more important were the decisions he'd previously made via the scotch, which were now stencilled inside his brain. To turn back now seemed almost inconceivable. For the time being, retribution needed to be placed on ice. Terry Winters, he quickly reminded himself, was still his meal ticket. At all cost, it was essential that he kept him sweet. In the end, it all comes down to opportunity, even for Rossetti. Feeling good, he afforded himself an insidious smile of self-belief.

He felt resigned to the fact that the top rung of the ladder of success was now achievable. For the first time in his paltry life, he knew he was destined for better things. The plans to make his dream come to fruition were looking rosier by the minute. Loaded with black coffee and a change of clothes brought him back to reality. Foremost on his mind: keeping Winters sweet. Five minutes and a cab later saw him en route to Slatteries.

CHAPTER 10

RELOCATE

Getting the use of a transit van at such notice proved to be a win. On his way over to Mickey Gibbons' place that evening, Ronnie could only hope that he'd find him in. No contact number at hand forced him into making an eleventh-hour decision to go ahead. For whatever reason, business in the market had been unusually quiet in the morning. This in turn had given him time to dwell on the Winters' threat scenario. Naturally, he once again confided in Siddie, who managed to come up trumps, by obtaining the wheels. Approaching bedsit land, apprehension was running high, as his adrenalin flow pumped away. Without realizing it, his state of mind began to wander. Fragments from his proactive career began to filter through.

'Hell,' he told himself. 'I haven't felt this way since my last fight!'

His overworked brain desperately sought for a name to add to a conclusion. Digging deep, he cast his mind back some twenty-five years. A satisfying smile blanketed his face.

'Got it, just come to me. No, it couldn't have been him. Shit! Who was that guy?' he exclaimed. With one hand on the wheel, he used the other free hand to scratch his head in frustration. Just then, Grafton Street loomed up, cutting short any further quandary. 'I probably lost the fight anyway,' he concluded, and turned into bedsit land. Two minutes or so later, he pulled up outside of Mickey's place. Grim-faced, he stepped out of the van, and looked around in both directions. Two resident call girls, he noticed, were touting for business. 'Each to his own,' he muttered. After securing the van, he made his way to Mickey's front door. Assuming it was a possibility, then Ronnie's gaff would serve as a convenient safe house in the immediate future. Dependent, of course, on the strength of Winters' idle threat.

Ringing the doorbell, he looked skyward, and muttered, 'Please God,' and hung on the bell. What followed became music to his ears, as the sound of footsteps became apparent. Seconds later, the door flew open and Mickey appeared, clutching a baseball bat in his hand. Relief swept over his face, and he lowered his insurance. In no time, he vented his feelings.

'Shit! Man, am I pleased to see you, Ronnie.'

'Likewise!' Ronnie countered.

'Come in. I presume you're stopping for a while.'

'Only for as long as we have to!'

For a minute, Mickey appeared mystified. 'We? You said we, I don't understand, mate.'

Ronnie made his case clear to him, in no uncertain terms. 'You're going to have to trust me on this one, Mickey. I'll explain my reasons later. In a nutshell, I want you out of 'ere as soon as. If you don't go, then sooner or later you'll be playing into Winters' hands. Well, it ain't gonna happen; from now on, like it or not, you're my responsibility.'

Mickey wasn't about to hold a steward's enquiry over his decision. 'Go? When do—'

Ronnie cut him out in full flight. 'You start packing, as of now! It's as quick as that.'

It was plain that Mickey was struggling to take it all in. His current situation had accelerated. 'You're the last person

I expected to see, I also hear what you say, and yeah, it's time to move on again… seems to be the story of my life, wouldn't you say, mate? Saying that, I've got no damn regrets about leaving this karzy behind me.' Mickey swiftly adjusted to the situation in hand. 'One thing's for sure: packing won't take a lot of time up; I've always travelled light.' Stopping short, he threw an appealing look at Ronnie and gestured towards his silverware.

Bowing to nostalgia, Ronnie quickly assured him. 'It ain't a problem, wherever they go, you go, right? The wheels are outside ready and waiting. Let's do it.'

Gibbons didn't give it a second thought; between them they got things sorted. In less than an hour, they pulled up outside of Ronnie's place. After ushering Mickey inside, he soon put him at ease.

'Help yourself to whatever you need, mate; what you can't see, then just ask. You'll soon get the hang of the gaff.'

The mood was electric, seated around the kitchen table ten minutes later, having a cup of tea. Ronnie endeavoured to make him feel at home. Tapping the side of his misshapen nose, he winked. 'It's not what you know that counts, Mickey, it's who you know. From now on, mate, you're family.'

Secretly, Ronnie welcomed the sudden, but necessary intrusion into his exclusive way of life. *Reckon it was meant to be*, he mused. As for Mickey, he'd been on his own for far too long. From being a mere kid, he'd become mature beyond his years. Forced into uncalled-for situations throughout his short life meant he had to grow up fast. Independence and survival came unexpectedly to him from an early age. He was also quick to show his gratitude.

'I just want you to know, I appreciate your concern…'

'But nothing!' Ronnie questioned. 'You can stay for as long as it takes. From where I'm sitting, like it or not, it's obvious we're in this together. It goes without saying, the gym, as of now, is at your own disposal too; there's a few people I want you to meet.'

'I won't let you down, Ronnie, and I mean that.'

'I feel sure you won't, mate,' he responded quickly, and continued. 'In fact, I know that better than I know myself.' Spontaneously, they shook hands in a surge of friendship. In time, their pact would be put to the test. For the time being, though, the future boded well.

Acting on a whim, Ronnie decided to drive to the gym that night. The fact that Gibbons was now going to be around for a while had influenced his decision. The fact that his own lifestyle had come under scrutiny meant changes needed to come into place. In spite of earlier warnings on behalf of Siddie, his eagerness to get to the gym hadn't gone unnoticed, having reflected on his erratic driving. This prompted Mickey to remind him, 'Steady, you almost ran that red light, what's the hurry up for?'

'Shit! That bad, eh? Yeah, yer right, I should know bleedin' better.' He was still dwelling on his stupidity when the gym loomed up. Once inside, the atmosphere took over. Mickey's presence seemed to rub off on everybody, especially Eric Mercer, the latter being well aware that, with two weeks to go before his forthcoming outing, density sparring would be at the top of the agenda. Introducing him officially to Mickey created an immediate rapport. Belated apologies fell onto deaf ears, as they recalled their previous encounter. Mercer, the pro that he was, welcomed Mickey's services as a sparring partner. Feeding off each other's variant styles could only prove to be valuable on the night, and also took some needy pressure away from Ronnie. The only hurdle left, if there ever was one, would be down to Tommy Russell. Granted, he hadn't witnessed Mickey in action, but after watching him work out with Mercer, he wasn't about to mince his words. Turning to Ronnie, he looked him square in the face.

'I kid you not, apart from the fact that I wished we'd met earlier, I can't fault the kid. For a twenty year old, he's a natural, and more importantly, he's got a good headpiece to go with it. That is a rarity. Handled right, he's got the potential to go all the way.'

Putting aside Mickey's future involvement now left Ronnie with a lot to think about. As a result, the rest of the session flew by. Driving home, an anti-climax kicked in. Deep in thought, he appeared reluctant to utter a word, instead, concentrating on his driving.

'You're quiet, Ronnie,' Mickey quipped, and continued in the same vein. 'You're allowed to do thirty miles an hour, you know.' His over cautious remark seemed to break the tension, as they both laughed heartily.

CHAPTER 11

DECISIONS

Elsewhere, Rossetti found himself under orders, having shelved an inevitable showdown for another day. In return, Winters had texted him, telling him to make himself available. Pent up and standing outside the office door, he took a deep breath, forcing himself to keep calm. He reminded himself once again that lip service was the priority for the time being. Any confrontation at this juncture would virtually wipe out any God-given chance of retribution that lay in the offing. His eyes narrowed to combat the alien lighting.

'Poxy place, but it won't be for fucking ever,' he told himself. It almost seemed that even Slatteries had gone beyond its sell-by date, according to his reckoning. But then this was the self-elected heir to the throne talking. As far as he was now concerned, life for him was going only one way, and that was up!

The Paul Rossetti of yesteryear had required a fresh persona; as from today, he'd become his own man, or so he imagined. As per usual, his timing proved to be way off. Pushing the door open, he gave a nervous cough and walked in. Winters, predictable as ever, was in a foul mood.

'So nothing changes,' he observed, while fiddling with some paperwork on his desk. He took his time before finally looking up. 'Nice of yer to fucking turn up.' He snorted.

His level of sarcasm felt like a smack in the mouth where Rossetti was concerned. *It's only words*, he told himself, and sensibly allowed the remark to go clean over his head. 'You left a message to—'

Winters cut him short before he could finish. 'You got a problem with your poxy memory, Rossetti? I pay you for information, and it's not happening! Callaghan! Gibbons! Nothing, you tell me nothing!' he raved, then stopping off abruptly. In a split second, his attitude traversed from a to z. The warning he issued was loud and clear, and spoken in a delicate tone of voice. 'You have the benefit of a week; I suggest that you use it wisely. My reputation, as you're aware, depends on results. Unfinished business is bad business; in the end, somebody has to pay. I'm sure that we understand each other?'

Rossetti shuddered as he felt his blood run cold. In sympathy with his blood count, his nerve began to waver. Threats were only threats, but the message behind them was non-negotiable. Winters had spelt it out for him. *The man's a fucking psycho*, he convinced himself. Pushing his luck, he fired back, 'My man tells me that Gibbons has been spotted in bedsit land recently. So it's only a matter of time before he surfaces; nobody can keep their nut down for that long.'

It was never going to be the best offer he could come up with; at least it gave him some breathing space, and he was a desperate man.

'In that case, I'll leave the situation in your capable hands, Rossetti. Like I said, you've got a week!'

The atmosphere in the office mellowed briefly, and Rossetti once again took advantage of the fact. 'Right, so now I'm 'ere, what's going down?'

Winters got up from out of his chair. 'I've got an errand I want you to run for me. I need you to make a drop at the bank. The sooner you offload it, the better I like it.'

'Okay, no big deal, nothing I can't handle, but I'll need some wheels.'

'You'd better take the Merc. Oh, one other thing: just watch yer back, you'll be on yer own... right?' The passing remark took a couple of seconds to sink in, giving Rossetti something to think about.

Can't believe this is happening. On my own? Any other time I'd need a minder with me. Like he was worried! The look on his face suggested he'd just won the lottery. For once in his abysmal life, he felt he was on a roll, and decided to push his luck. 'Ain't Rogers about, then?' His newfound confidence started to ooze, as he pursued the whereabouts of the firm's driver. In the event it backfired on him; without warning, Winters brought his clenched fists hard down on the desk top.

'I'm surrounded by fucking losers,' he screamed. 'Rogers thought it clever to mouth off at the old bill while they were carrying out a spot check last night. Not content with that, he decked a sergeant, so now he's fucking banged up. So it's all down to you. Just get the poxy job done, will yer?' Winters was almost pleading for a form of sanity. 'Make me happy, do the business, for Christ's sake.' Shaking his head in frustration, hands shaking, he removed a large cigar from out of a gold-plated container. Slowly and methodically, he placed the cigar in his mouth, and gave Rossetti a look of expectancy. He didn't waste any time; he was still part of the charade, and the starring role belonged to him. Moving quickly, he grabbed a nearby cigarette lighter from off the desk, and offered it up to the extended cigar. Momentarily toying with the flame, Winters pulled long and deep, until finally exhaling, at the same time ensuring that Rossetti received the full impact of the offensive smoke directly in his face.

You passive bastard! he told himself, and was forced to grit his teeth. *It won't be long, and yeah, I'll do the fucking business alright, but on my terms in my own way.*

Sweeping the offending smoke to one side, Winters

attempted to clear his throat before continuing. He allowed a sardonic smile to crease his face. 'Good! Good, now we agree on something, here's what I want you to do.' After strolling over to the wall behind him, he pulled a self-portrait picture to one side to expose a designer wall safe. Fully aware that Rossetti was standing behind him, he carefully dialled the combination to open it. After reaching inside, he removed a bulky package, which he threw on the desk top. 'There's £15,000's worth of wedge for deposit, all in used notes. Nothing complicated... you go to the bank... you pay it in... you come back, end of story. Now get out of my fucking sight. Oh, yeah, you'll need these, as well.' Throwing the car keys belonging to the Merc at his feet, he erupted into a contemptuous laugh. 'Now fucking pick 'em up.'

Rossetti sank to the floor like a dying man, hands beyond trembling with temper as he grasped the keys, and regained his feet. After picking up the package, he stuffed it inside his overcoat pocket. The value of the package ran a close second to his existing blood level, which by now had reached boiling point. The keys contained in his clenched fist threatened to tear his skin from the tension he was giving out. Winters' final putdown had fortunately pushed him through the pain barrier, although the resident thoughts harboured inside his brain had involuntarily moved up a league. *Wrong time, wrong place,* hammered away like an out of control drill inside his deflated shell-like body. Judgment day, as far as Winters was concerned, would be placed on hold. Slowly, he released the pressure on his clenched fist. The keys almost fell out of his useless grasp. Almost immediately, a surge of blood returned, to pound mercilessly away at his hand. Gritting his teeth, he threw Winters a murderous look and slunk out of the office. Standing outside of Slatteries, the sight of the Mercedes drew him in. It appeared to be the lift that he needed. Opening the driver's door was proving difficult, due to his hand throbbing. Picking the keys up for the second time out of the gravel, he eventually manoeuvred the lock and got in. Grasping the wheel with both hands instilled a fleeting sense of power inside his puny frame. Taking his time, he eased himself back onto the plush leather seating. Turning the key in the ignition came with a positive smile, as the sound of the engine burst into life.

For a short time, as if in a trance, his erratic frame of mind went into overdrive. *It all starts 'ere. No more shit, this is the new Rossetti and nobody is going to say different! As from now, the rest of the poxy world can go to hell. I've arrived, and I'm on the fucking case.* Strong words indeed from somebody of his calibre, when trying to convince himself that he could handle his newfound motives. Especially without an audience to fire back at him. As was the case, his prattling had about as much potential as a chocolate fire grate… useless!

Or could this be the genuine ranting emerging from a newborn Rossetti? He wasn't that stupid to realize that it was going to take more than money and brain power to achieve his future. Patting the bulge in his overcoat, the wedge felt good; in fact… too good. For the time being, he would have to settle for feel good. Not only that, things were moving fast, plus the potential could well be in hand. Time, at least, was on his side. A continuous smirk etched his face, as the accelerator dipped and purred contentedly. Silently, the Merc picked up speed and slid out of the car park.

For the time of the day, the traffic appeared heavy. Bumper to bumper fast became a recipe for grief. Progress and the lack of it brought him down to earth. Using the traditional route into the town centre had seemed to be a good idea at the time. Right now, he began to curse his judgment. Ten minutes later, and his patience was beyond its sell-by date. Other solutions appeared in the frame.

As if on demand, a junction ahead came into view, giving him an option as a cop-out. Hanging a left, a feeling of relief swept over him as he entered the side street. For reasons of his own design, he swung into a bay, and parked up. The thought of chilling out for five minutes wouldn't go amiss; besides, his head was still spinning from the earlier grief.

'I don't need this shit!' he echoed. 'Not only that, the poxy bank can wait.' Setting off once again, following a ten-minute break, he sped off into a maze of back doubles in a complete change of direction from the town centre. Totally ignoring Winters' orders, he headed for his flat down at the harbour basin. He couldn't wait to get inside. He threw himself into the nearest armchair, and began to cradle his head. 'Fuck's sake!' he exclaimed. 'I need a drink, can't think straight.'

After rising from the armchair, he made a beeline for the drinks cabinet. He couldn't help but notice the sweat on his palms. Opening the cabinet didn't work for him. 'Damn!' In complete contrast, he turned on his heel, and opted for a black coffee instead. 'Just as well,' he confided in himself, and helped himself to a couple of painkillers, which he proceeded to swallow. 'Can't have the old bill giving me a tug.' At least the pills worked for him; ten minutes later his head began to clear. For some reason, his attention was drawn to the wedge in his pocket.

For no apparent reason, he removed the package, and placed it down in front of him on the kitchen table. Like a magnet, it seemed to draw him in. The longer he stared at it, the more his eyes became transfixed. He felt that it was trying to tell him something. In contrast, a nagging voice from somewhere deep inside of his brain had other ideas. 'Don't let it get to you,' it repeated over and over again. Giving out a maniacal laugh, Rossetti suddenly lunged at the package, and proceeded to swing it from side to side, just like a ragdoll.

As if in a trance, his deluded mind rose to fever pitch, as he increased the rhythm.

What happened next was inconceivable. With no warning available to him, the package ripped apart under the pressure he was exerting. Notes of all denominations spilled out in all directions, showering the air around him. His ramblings came to an abrupt halt, as a mask of sheer and utter disbelief etched his face. And then it was over. For a few seconds, he looked shell-shocked, his addled brain struggling to comprehend his stupidity. Lowering his arms, he made a futile effort to gather in what notes lay scattered on the table. Despair took over from frustration, causing his blood to chill. This latest intervention was turning into a nightmare for him. The alleged £15,000 would have to be checked, no question, and time wasn't on his side. Checking his watch only mocked his misery. An hour had almost passed since he'd left Slatteries. He now found himself stuck in no-man's-land, along with a pile of money that didn't belong to him, and as much grief besides. He couldn't give it away. The more he looked, the bigger the pile seemed to grow, as he took stock of the situation. His body involuntarily shivered at the thought of counting it all. There was no turning back now; clearing his head, he rubbed his hands together to inject some warmth. To get the count correct the first time around would be a result to savour.

Whatever his failings were, Rossetti was always good where money was concerned. He could handle it well; trouble was, it always seemed to be other people's. But when it came down to his own, he could hold his breath longer than he could hold on to a fiver. The pile of notes slowly diminished, as he feverishly worked his way through them, stopping only to place a selected wad to one side in formation. Up until now, his method had gone smoothly. He quickly realized that he required only a grand to end his ordeal. Briefly, a pensive look crossed his face, as he hurriedly scanned the notes that were now left. 'Uhm, must be all fives and tens,' he considered, and continued counting.

Two long minutes and a grand later saw him placing the last wad alongside the other fourteen he'd made up. And therein lay the problem, or in this case Rossetti's. Slumping forwards onto the table, he buried his head in his hands. It was a lousy attempt to conceal the fact that there were still notes unaccounted for! Self-doubt began to creep in, as he focused his full attention on the alleged £15,000 he'd meticulously checked. At least he hadn't lost his confidence.

'There's no poxy way I've got it wrong, I know my count will hold up.' His thoughts then took another stance. 'Supposing, just supposing, Winters has got this all wrong? … Or maybe it's just a bloody plant?' The time to dwell on conclusions had now run out. Forced into a hasty decision, he quickly decided to pocket the difference, and funk that Winters had lost the plot. On second thoughts, it was a feasible explanation, knowing the grief Callaghan and Gibbons had given him of late. Checking the residue of the alleged wedge twice over, the result came back the same: it came to £600. 'Not a bad morning's work, if it don't all come on top,' he concluded, and promptly slipped it into his back pocket. A few minutes later, and slightly richer, he left his flat and headed for the town. Driving back to Docklands, Rossetti felt relaxed and well within himself. The drop had proved successful, leaving him on top of the situation. To his mode of thinking, Winters had done money in cold blood. Also, in the event it all went belly up, he'd figured out a delay excuse should it arise.

On arriving back at Slatteries, he parked up and headed for Winters' office. In spite of his earlier win, his newly found zest for Lady Luck filled him with apprehension as he gave the door a thump. Surprisingly, there was no answer.

'Strange, maybe he's in the pool room,' he muttered, with a ring of hope.

'Hi, Rossi.' A nearby sounding voice momentarily broke his chain of thought. Spinning around, he immediately recognized the owner. 'If yer looking for him, he ain't 'ere. The last thing he said to me was to tell you to wash the Merc and call in tomorrow.'

Rossetti didn't stop for a steward's enquiry. Wearing an evil grin, he turned and made for the exit.

'Don't get any better than this!' he reminded himself.

CHAPTER 12

OPTIONS

Unlike the vast majority of streets and cuttings that formed the harbour basin, Wharf Street had somehow managed to escape the ravages of new development, consistent to the locale. Seemingly locked in a time warp, high-rise blocks of flats overshadowed its existence from every possible angle. Any sunlight that did manage to make its way through became obsolete, as the concrete jungle surroundings soon swallowed it up. At best, it remained dark and dingy at any given part of the day. Somebody was once heard to say, 'This is the street that time forgot.' Well over half the houses had been vacated over the years, due to the re-housing programme. Windows and thresholds alike were unceremoniously boarded up, as a stark reminder to inevitable progress.

Its only claim to the outside world lay in a public house, situated at the water's edge, at the bottom end of the terraced street. The sign that hung above the main entrance served only as a contradiction in terms. Depicting a voluptuous mermaid riding a dolphin saddle was obvious by name to anybody setting eyes on it. Over the years, its far-reaching reputation for low-life punters gave credence to a change in name. To all and sundry, it was renamed the Rat and Trap. Sociability became non-existent. Basically, the pub became a meet. You had a drink… you did your business, and you left. In Rossetti's case, it was as close to a local as one could get.

He'd used the place for years, purely on the strength of what it stood for.

On a personal level, he would liken it to his office. Nobody questioned his motives, and nobody cared anyway. His long-time distorted personality had long distanced him from his own. The fact that he lived only a five-minute walk away more than added to its charm. Getting the Merc washed was never going to be a chore. Within an hour, it was back in the car park. After getting a cab, he made his way back to his flat. The time was just after 1.30 pm. He felt restless, on account of the wedge concealed in his pocket. There and then, he quickly decided that, following a crucial phone call, a belated liquid lunch was on the cards. Minutes later he left, heading for the basin and his 'office'. The resident bookies caught his eye, causing him to momentarily falter in his stride. Patting his back pocket assured him that for the time being his wedge was safe. At least, he was quietly confident in knowing it was destined for better things that lay in the offing. He was well aware that laying out his money as an inducement would fetch a far better return, depending on the strength of his crucial call. Although, he was under no false illusions, should the deal he had in mind go pear-shaped. His main problem lay with the two faces he needed to complete his game plan, consisting of three men. The fact that they were on Winters' payroll could literally make or break him. The only trump card he held would be contesting their loyalty to Winters. Although, it was public knowledge that their outright opinion of him ran to a bullet short of a shooter!

Grim-faced, he entered the Rat and Trap. After ordering a scotch, he manfully downed it in one.

'You look as if you needed that?' the barman enquired. 'I take it you want a refill?'

Slowly, Rossetti eased the glass away from his mouth,

taking in every last drop. It caused him to shudder slightly, from the effect of the liquid kicking the back of his throat.

'Tell yer what, make it a large one this time with a lemonade top, and put yerself in.'

'Don't mind if I do,' replied the barman. 'I'll have half a lager with you, cheers.'

Rossetti's facial expression remained passive, as he laboured to gather his thoughts.

'How's the gee-gees treating you, then, Rossi?' the barman enquired, eager to small talk. Rossetti chose to remain oblivious; his mind could be found a million miles away, trapped on a tightrope of self-ambition. And he just happened to be smack bang in the middle of it. *What the hell do I do?* Somewhere inside of his pickled brain, a voice attempted to reason with his dilemma. *You have three chances: you either go back… go forwards… or you simply fall off!*

'Penny for your thoughts, Rossi.' The barman inadvertently broke his bubble of convenience. 'You look like a worried man. Can't be all bad, can it?'

'No, no!' responded Rossetti. 'I might have been, worried, that is, but I ain't anymore. I need to use yer phone.'

'No problem, it's down the other end of the bar, help yourself.'

Without hesitation, Rossetti made his way across to the phone. Calmly, he dialled a contact number for the pool room at Slatteries, sat back, and waited for a connection to be made. He wasn't about to be disappointed.

'Jack? Yeah, it's Rossi. Listen, I need to talk to Ricky Peters a bit lively, is he about?'

'Hang about, Rossi, I'll give him a volley.'

He could hear him yelling at the other end, which stopped as Peters got through. 'What's occurring, Rossi? I'm in the middle of a frame, and it owes me! Know what I mean?'

'Something kosher is going down... we need to talk because—'

Peters swiftly interjected. 'You ain't listening, Rossi. Like I said, my pocket's taking a bloody hiding, so what's with yer problem that you need to phone me about?'

Rossetti could feel his deal slipping away from underneath him; impressing a man like Peters wasn't going to be easy.

'Just hear me out, Ricky, forget yer bleedin' snooker or whatever. What I've got in mind will more than compensate yer, trust me! If yer interested, do yerself a right favour, and meet me down at the office. I'm gonna be there for a couple of hours yet. Oh, and bring the travelling man with yer, not that you need insurance. What d'ye say, you in or out?'

The line went silent; it became obvious Peters was playing him at the waiting game. Rossetti's blood count began to rise, causing him to fidget. He couldn't hold back any longer.

'Hello, you still there, Ricky?'

'Yeah, yeah, but listen, this deal or whatever, it had better be viable. I hope for your sake it ain't a poxy wind-up. You know what the Traveller is like if he gets upset.'

'Like I say, Ricky, I'd have to be crazy to fuck with the guy. Take it from me, the deal I've got is kosher.' A further pause followed, as Peters deliberated.

'Rossi, give us an hour, I'll be there.'

'Nice one, Ricky, you ain't gonna regret it, see yer then.' Sighing with obvious relief, he replaced the receiver. A wan smile took over his face. 'There's no turning back now,' he stated with conviction. Any further misgivings coming his way were lost in the amount of scotch he put away. This in turn gave the barman a chance to catch up.

'None of my business, you understand, Rossi, you celebrating something, or what?'

Choosing to ignore the intrusion, Rossi was content just

to let his mind wander. Insistent as ever, the barman continued to ply him.

'I know, don't tell me, your mother-in-law just died!'

At least he made an impact. Rossetti's face screwed up, causing his eyes to narrow. Shaking his head, he glared at him. 'Yer bleedin' sick, d'ye know that? But, yeah, yer right about one thing: it's gonna be a long session.'

The added pressure from the alien hand mounted on his shoulder caused him to whip sharply round. A total look of relief blanketed his face, as two figures confronted him, both of which were instantly recognizable. The smaller of the two spoke up first.

'Bit jumpy, ain't yer, Rossi? Who'd yer think it was, the old bill?' Standing midway between five and six foot gave him cause to look up to Rossi, as he continued. Whatever he might have lost in height, he seemed to gain in stature. For a small dapper being, he evoked a strong aura of presence, which kicked in the moment he opened his mouth. On a par, his exclusive outward appearance gave no indication as to his persona.

From his feet upwards, highly polished black brogues complemented a dark blue chalk-line, three-piece tailored suit. The silk, immaculate white shirt he wore formed a backdrop to the crimson polka-dot tie he sported. The mother of pearl cluster pin, containing the tie, represented the jewel in the crown, in anybody's language. His swarthy complexion, with coal black, heavily greased hair swept back off his forehead, appeared to give him an edge of hidden importance. His pushy attitude remained undeniable, and he was well noted for starting and ending any form of conversation that looked like developing!

As far as he was concerned, black was white, and stripes were circles. Somebody once remarked, 'If he'd have gone straight, there's no question to my mind, at worst, he would have made a prime minister.'

'You do what yer good at, so flaunt it!' became his by-line. 'Me!? I negotiate in a big way!' For a small being he made you believe that. So there we have Ricky Peters. Villain and career criminal in one. In direct contrast, his sidekick dwarfed the two of them. Well over six foot, and the physique to carry it off, enabled him to virtually dominate the scene irrespective. From out of powerful shoulders, a bull-like neck ably supported a large, close-shaven head. Evidence of old scar tissue was plainly visible all over, a past reminder of the bleeding business! Poking out from granite-like facial features, distinctive small piggy eyes constantly flicked open and shut from behind a semi-glazed mask, resembling a face. Scar-lined eyebrows, void of hair, drooped down at each end, supported by pot-line flesh, and what looked like a mouth! Somewhere in the middle of all this mess could be found the remains of what was once a nose, only becoming visible in daylight!

From the waist upwards, his years of bouncing and unlicensed bills had finally taken their toll. His half-addled brain now struggled to control his long-gone prowess. The first stage from being punch drunk had long set in, although he was still capable of starting World War Three! He was born and, up until the age of eighteen, raised in the Balkans... somewhere! If asked for confirmation, his usual reply would be, 'I am a Bungarian gypsy!' The grunts that followed you filled in yourself, and any sane man never questioned his validity. It's been said that he made his way across into England, via a state circus. When it suited him, he did a runner, and lost himself in society. For years, he survived on his wits, or the lack of them, and too many times... his fists. The law constantly breathing down his neck meant he would always be on the move.

Meeting up with Peters became his biggest break. From

the moment they both met, they seemed to gel. The two formed a formidable team, working for the highest bidder. Eventually, their reputation in the business grew. As a result, they were dubbed the Muscle and the Mouth! Owing to the big fellow's track record, Peters subsequently nicknamed him the travelling man! And nobody ever questioned as to why!

Rossetti nervously laughed at Peters' jibe 'old bill'. 'Who me!? I ain't involved with noncing anymore.' The question was aimed at Rossetti's dubious past, as a habitual felon, and he continued. 'You know me better than that, Ricky. I'm squeaky clean these days; the only grief I'm getting at the moment is from that bastard Terry bloody Winters.'

Peters seemed impatient to delve, and it showed in his manner. 'I ain't 'ere on a bleedin' mercy mission, Rossi. So what's going down?'

Casting his eye around the bar, Rossetti pointed towards an empty corner table. 'Park yerself down over there, Ricky. I'll be over in a minute with some drinks; then we'll talk.'

The Traveller looked at Peters for some sort of approval. After he nodded, the pair made their way across, and waited. Minutes later, full of apprehension, and armed with a tray of booze, Rossetti joined them, eager to make conversation.

'Well, I remember your poison, Ricky, but I had to guess the Traveller's, know what I mean?'

Peters sneered, and gestured. 'That ain't a problem, Rossi, he drinks what I tell him!'

Smiling like a Cheshire cat, his partner nodded vigorously, as Peters pointed at a tin of coke. His own preference lay in a glass of brandy. Head lowered, he methodically rolled the glass backwards and forwards, between the palms of his manicured hands. Finally, he looked up from his glass, before levelling his eyes directly at Rossetti. Through narrowed eyes, he made his point.

'Why do I get the feeling that fucking Winters is in the frame somehow?'

'I'd be a liar if I said he wasn't, Ricky,' he fired back, at the same time detecting a swing of allegiance in Peters' reasoning. 'I ain't a bad judge, am I, Rossi? Mind you, thinking about it, he's given you some shit lately, from what I know.'

The Traveller heaved his massive shoulders, and grunted something inaudible to endorse Peters' reply.

'That noticeable, eh, Ricky?' Rossetti concurred with a shrug, and continued his verbal assassination. 'One way or another, the bastard's gonna fucking pay! This is what this is all about, the meet, I mean. But I need yer help to make it happen. On my own, I ain't got a chance in hell, but the three of us mob-handed can make a noise.'

Peters appeared unrepentant. 'Unless you've got something gilt-edged for me, yer in over your head, sunshine.' Adamant as ever, Peters pressed home his point. 'Money! The guy's corrupted with it; he can buy and sell people, all day and every poxy day. He's got full control over at Docklands, and that's why he can walk all over yer. And don't even think physical; there are a few mean bastards on his books.'

Rossetti nodded in agreement, saying, 'Don't worry, I've given it a lot of thought; as far as I'm concerned, his heavies don't come into the equation. There's only one way to hurt an asshole like Winters, and that's through his pocket!' Throwing Peters a pleading look, he continued to rant. 'Believe me, I know it can work, but like I say, we need to be firm-handed to make it possible.'

Peters was beginning to show signs of doubt. Getting involved with another man's vendetta wasn't what he had envisaged.

Rossetti had his back to the wall at this point. He needed more from their meet. 'Look, I ain't talking about just one specific heist, that ain't enough for me. I want to squeeze him dry long term.'

This last chosen remark seemed to have touched a nerve in Peters' mind. 'You've obviously thought about this, ain't yer?' he suggested.

'More than you'll ever know, Ricky, so what d'ye think?'

'Seeing as yer ask, I'll go along with your pocket scenario. I agree, it's worse than a knife in the back, although carrying it out would be something else. Think about the planning alone. I'll be frank with yer: you've got more chance of swimming the poxy Channel with a rope around yer neck than getting Winters' money.' The Traveller then threw in a few grunts of his own, as he hung on to Peters' every word.

Draining his glass, Rossetti fixed Peters with a withering look of desperation. 'It's got to work, for fuck's sake, it has to work.' He was beginning to lose it, and it showed in his manner.

As for Peters, he hadn't been taken in right from the word go. His time and patience were at an all-time ebb. 'Rossi, listen to me, up to now, you haven't told me anything that I don't already know, so unless you can come up with some way of putting one over on Winters, then I'm out of 'ere.' Drowning his remaining brandy, he half rose from his seat, only to be checked by Rossetti's outstretched arm.

'There is a way out, but it'll take a lot of front to pull it off,' he blurted out. This was his last remaining ray of hope, and he knew that the odds were stacked up against him. The Traveller wasn't impressed by his show of arrogance either. His pig-like eyes bored into Rossetti's face; at the same time he raised one clenched fist that said everything! For a second or two, a cold silence reigned, leaving Rossetti to break the impasse. 'Winters' protection rackets!'

Peters calmed the Traveller down, and levelled with Rossetti. 'What about them?'

'Can't you see? This is what I've been trying to tell you about.'

'Could have fooled me, but go on, I'm listening.'

'It's simple, you and the Traveller are doing two or three hits a night, right? The worse way, a dozen a week.'

'Keep talking, but keep yer bleedin' voice down, will yer?'

For the first time since the three had sat down together, he could actually feel that the tide at last was beginning to turn in his favour. Clearly, he was on a roll; getting Peters to exploit a possible loophole had been paramount to his game plan. Inwardly, he now felt certain that he'd done enough to convince him. Pulling his chair up closer to them, he leaned forwards, and spoke in a lower tone.

'This is the way I see it. And I reckon it's foolproof, assuming we're firmed up. Every time we carry out a hit, we up the ante and cream off the difference. Divvy it up three ways, and everyone's a fucking winner! Except Winters of course, but then his cut is there anyway. He's still getting his wedge, so he shouldn't worry. I realize there could be a problem with his clients at first, but...' He threw the Traveller a look of confidence. 'Would you want to argue with him? Like I say, we could bottle our way through to the front, and leave the muscle to the big guy. Can't be that hard, money for old rope!'

Peters leaned back in his chair, all the while staring intently at Rossetti, his face giving nothing away as to what he was thinking. For someone who wouldn't even register on a brain scale of one to ten, he had to admit the scam held a viable proposition. There was no love lost between himself and Winters. In the end, everyone's got a price, and the longer he pondered on the deal, the more viable it seemed to get. There was, of course, another angle he needed to sort out.

'Before I give you an answer, Rossi, there's something

we need to get out of the way.' A question of loyalty was at stake. Peters' voice took on a chilling attitude as he reminded Rossetti, in no uncertain terms, 'How the hell do I know you ain't setting me up?'

A much relieved Rossetti called on his past. 'You know me better than that, Ricky. If yer looking for assurance, I've got a monkey 'ere as a down payment.'

Surprised, Peters wanted confirmation. 'Where'd ye get that sort of wedge from?' he demanded.

Rossetti couldn't wait to fire back at him. 'Would you believe, courtesy of fucking Winters, and d'ye know what? The stupid bastard will never ever know!' Reverently, he removed the money from his pocket, and placed it on the open table. 'Does this convince yer? Go on... take it, this is only a start.'

For a split second, Peters ogled the money; then swiftly snatching it up, he feverishly stuffed it inside his suit pocket. 'That does it for me, Rossi, you've got yerself a deal. Obviously we need to discuss a game plan, but I can't see us having a problem with that. As for the Traveller, he's in anyway, because I say so... right?' Shoving a nifty in the gorilla's hand, Peters pointed him in the direction of the bar. 'Make sure they are doubles, and watch yer change.'

Grunting, he ambled off to do the business, tray in hand. For his part, Peters was eager to get things organized. As for Rossetti, he was wearing the look of a man who'd just won the state lottery!

CHAPTER 13

BUSINESS AS USUAL

'There yer go, guv, one bunch of dahlias and there's change as well. Get those home in one piece and you'll be on a promise, guaranteed!' Completing a sale, Ronnie glanced across towards Siddie Levy. 'I dunno about you, mate, but I think I'll knock it on the head; it ain't been a bad morning's work, what d'ye think?'

Siddie didn't hesitate to answer. 'I like it already, but are you going to tell Rachael? She ain't expecting me home for at least a couple of hours. Truth is, I need to shift two boxes of Victorias before they turn.'

'Guess yer right, but at least have a coffee and a waffle before I go. Charlie will mind yer pitch.'

Siddie nodded, and signalled his intentions across to the holder of an adjacent china stall. Looking at ease with the world, they both made their way over to the market café. As per usual, Toni de Angelo was in form.

'Hi, waddya know, two of my best customers, you luvva my coffee, huh? For that, I only charge you for the milka.'

'Schmaltz!' remarked Siddie. 'The guy is full of schmaltz already. By the way, Ronnie, it's your call.'

'You do it to me every time!' said Ronnie laughing, and handed Toni a fiver. Making themselves comfortable, Siddie raised his shoulders in his own exclusive fashion. At the same time, a characteristic look crossed his face. 'Well, is there anything I should know about?' he enquired.

116

Ronnie looked up from stirring his coffee. 'Well, if you mean Terry Winters and that nonce Rossetti, then no, but I still make a point of looking over my shoulder, though. Know what I mean?'

'What about the boy? Mickey Gibbons, is he settling in?'

'As it happens, I don't even know that he's there half the time. It seems he's got a young lady in tow. The only other time, of course, is back in the gym. Still, he's his own man; I just wish he wasn't so bleedin' independent. Oh, and before I forget, I won't be around next Friday, I'm going up to town.'

Lowering his cup, Siddie felt inclined to frown. 'Yeah, business or pleasure?'

'Bit of both really, mate.' Ronnie was quick to discount any underlying fears he may have generated before continuing. 'Ain't like you to forget, we only spoke about a week ago.'

'So give me the full SP, then?' pleaded Siddie.

'York Hall, Bethnal Green, ring a bell?' replied Ronnie casually.

Siddie sat bolt upright and smacked his forehead, as realization set in. 'Meshuggeneh! How could I forget? Yeah, it's all coming back already. Mercer's big night. Forgive me, my friend.' He gestured his arms in an act of apology.

'That's gonna cost you another coffee, in case—'

He didn't get any further. Siddie waylaid him before he could finish. 'Promise me you'll phone me a result through, and give him mazel tov from me. The guy really needs this one; not only that, a good result won't do the stable any harm either.'

'If I didn't know you any better, Siddie Levy, I'd say you were stalling on the coffees.' Just then, he caught Toni's attention. 'Two more, mate, and put 'em down to Siddie, he's loaded.'

Toni shook his head and smiled with a ring of conspiracy. 'No monies, huh? You have the coffees on me.'

Ronnie turned to Siddie; a look of utter disbelief etched his face. 'You've bleedin' well done it again, what is it with you?'

'My father always said I was full of chutzpah!' Together they both fell about laughing.

★

That evening, while on their way to the gym, Mickey Gibbons happened to notice that Ronnie appeared to be looking a bit vacant. 'Penny for 'em, mate, you're bloody miles away.'

Giving an exaggerated blink, he shook his head. 'Blimey! That noticeable, eh? For a minute I was somewhere else.'

'Yeah, just concentrate on the traffic, will yer?'

'Sorted, won't be long now.' Five minutes later, they pulled up outside the gym. On entering, Ronnie threw the switches on the light grid. In a split second the gym erupted into life. Placing his kit bag on the floor, Ronnie stared intently towards the ring. For a brief moment, his private thoughts became lost in another time. At length, he spoke. 'Would be good to be able to turn the clock back, knowing what I now know,' he muttered under his breath. His aloofness hadn't gone unnoticed.

'You're in a strange mood tonight, mate. I get the impression you've got a lot on yer mind.'

Ronnie pursed his lips. Tentatively shaking his head, he replied, 'Nothing you need to worry yer head about, son, but...'

'Yeah, go on.'

'I'd give anything to be in Mercer's shoes on Friday night.'

'You sentimental old sod, I just knew that something was bugging you on the way over. You never will hang 'em up, will yer?'

'Can't help it, Mickey, it's in the blood. C'mon, we'd better get you changed; the rest of the gang will be 'ere shortly.'

The evening had been pencilled in as being Mercer's last session prior to his big night. Temporarily, the gym was available only for evaluation purposes. Criticism would be high on the agenda. The build-up over the last three weeks' grind stopped here! Any last-minute judgments needed to be ironed out alongside fitness input. Apart from Ronnie and Mickey Gibbons, the likes of Wally Churchill and Tommy Russell, their roles would remain as mere spectators. In a way, it was a coming together of the stable. The time spent in preparation had been intense. The combined sweat and toil under Ronnie's jurisdiction would now come under the hammer. Any praise coming Mercer's way had been more than justified.

With Gibbons on hand as a bonus, the two had formed an all-important collusion where sparring had been involved. The stable had now come full circle, and any likely outcome rested squarely on Mercer's shoulders. Wally busied himself in his own indomitable manner, while Russell took up a prominent viewing position at ringside.

'Get yerself warmed up, Eric, and we'll go through ten minutes on the pads, get rid of the cobwebs.'

Dishing out instructions to get the night underway, Ronnie held no qualms as to how the session would go; as a result, he was quick to mark Mercer's card.

'Just remember, there's no pressure at this point, you've done the graft, so tonight enjoy yerself. Any hang-ups you might have, save 'em for Harrison on the night, okay?' His singular policies within the fight game had always been his greatest ally. Having reassured Mercer as to his commitment, there was nothing left to prove at this point. In the past, overtraining had resulted in the downfall of many a seasoned fighter over the years. 'Leaving it all behind in the gym' had become a well-worn adage, leaving many a frustrated manager to tear their hair out. In Mercer's case, Ronnie had ensured that was never going to happen. As a result, Tommy Russell wasn't about to lose any sleep either. It was a proven concept. Two or three days off prior to an important fight strongly influenced a fighter's wellbeing. Hanging loose with no physical attachment became the order of the day.

Their pad work had gone according to plan and Ronnie called for a welcome respite. 'Presume yer using the fifteen-ounce for sparring, Ronnie,' enquired Wally. A positive nod answered his question, leaving him to prepare two sets of gloves. Equipped with head gear and gloved up, Gibbons and Mercer climbed up into the ring. Looking on, Russell fidgeted in anticipation.

'Give us ten to finish with two-minute rounds, Wally, unless Tommy says different, yeah?'

Wally concurred and set the clock in motion. Last-minute orders were voiced, and the sounding of the bell got the session underway. Wasting no time, Mercer responded immediately. Working off the back foot, he continually punished Gibbons with three-punch combinations, as he endeavoured to draw his man in. His work behind his jab became a pleasure to watch. Overall, six rounds of sparring had shown a wealth of quality on show, readily picked up on by Russell. His face evoked a smug look of satisfaction, and he lost no time in expressing his views.

'Got to tell you, Ronnie, you've done a great job on the kid. I'm more than impressed.'

'Not just me, Tommy, remember.'

'Well, that apart, if he can reproduce that sort of form on the night, a man couldn't ask for anything more!'

'Forget it, mate, we've all worked together on this one.'

Wally was in the throes of removing Mercer's gloves as Tommy approached. 'Well done, my son, you did the business tonight. Ronnie's done his part, the rest is down to you now. Personally, I don't have a problem with Friday night; I just feel that you're going to do a good job. In the meantime, enjoy your time off. I'll be in touch regarding travelling arrangements.'

'Thanks, boss, I'm really up for it, trust me,' Mercer replied. By now his confidence had begun to ooze. 'Whatever way the fight goes, Harrison will know he's been in a fight.'

Russell nodded approvingly, and loosened his head guard. 'You'd better do your groundwork before you catch a cold, then grab a shower; we'll talk later on the phone.' Turning on his heel, he made as if to go, then checked himself. 'Be in touch, mate,' he shouted, and gave Ronnie the thumbs up before departing.

Driving home later on that evening, Ronnie felt contented. Gibbons looked across at him eager to speak. 'Well, Tommy Russell looked happy enough when he left tonight. I reckon that's half the battle over. Is the guy a hard man to please, Ronnie?' he enquired, forcing Ronnie to take on a stern attitude.

'You find me a manager who ain't, and when you do, send him up to Sotheby's, he'll make you a bleedin' fortune!'

'Shit. What have I let myself in for?' A worried look crossed Mickey's face.

'Only kidding yer,' Ronnie assured him. 'The geezer's a diamond at heart. If he can't do yer a good turn, he won't do yer a bad one either. He's been in the business a long time, gained a lot of respect. Remember, if he's earning, so are we all! You could do a hell of a lot worse.'

Mickey heaved a sigh of relief. 'Trouble with me is that I've been on my own for far too long now. It ain't easy having to understand people, know what I mean?'

Ronnie was forced to agree, although remained adamant. 'You've got to put the past behind yer now. Your life started the minute you walked through the door of the gym. Call me sentimental, but things are meant to be; you've got a lot going for yer right now. From where I'm standing, you can only go one way, and that's up. Yer a natural born talent, so use it well.'

'Yeah, right! I need to chill out, I'm more settled now than at any time of my life.'

*

Across the other side of town, Canal Street was about to change the course of another individual hell bent on monetary ambition; the similarity between the two ended right there! Rossetti could be found embarking on a self-elected crusade, alluding to extreme fear and violence, although not necessarily in that order. The two individualistic pretenders seemed to have been cursed with an air of affinity. Their paths had previously crossed before, resulting in unfinished business. This time around, they were fated to meet up once again, this time in violent circumstances. As of now, both men were on the bottom rung of their chosen paths, but they both shared a palate for ensuring their own singular success. Time and fate alone would now rear their heads in more ways than one to act as judge and jury in their case!

CHAPTER 14

INDUCTION

For the third time in as many minutes, Rossetti checked his watch and downed another scotch. He was feeling uptight and it was showing. Glass in hand, he paced up and down in his lounge like a restless bear. Approaching the window, he forcefully yanked a curtain to one side. Peering intently through the opening resolved the answer to his problem, although it didn't ease his blood count. He observed a car pulling up on the opposite side of the road; within seconds, recognition set in.

'Ain't before bloody time,' he muttered under his breath. Without warning, a sudden surge of expectation washed over his body. He felt sticky and uncomfortable; at the same time, his stomach decided to go on a sponsored walkabout.

After removing a hanky from his pocket, he wiped his sweaty brow.

'It's time to go,' he reminded himself. The simple task of turning a key in a lock was fast becoming a problem for him. The Rossetti syndrome had begun to manifest itself inside of him.

Easing the key into position, he momentarily felt rooted to the spot, followed by another wave of nausea. His legs buckled, forcing him to grasp the door handle. Up to now, his pathetic actions had gone unnoticed by Ricky Peters, who was halfway out the car by now.

Leaning on the car door, he glanced across to where the lone figure of Rossetti appeared to be. 'What's the sodding hold-up all about, Rossi?' he shouted. 'We ain't got all fucking night, yer know.'

Wincing at the thought that Peters had witnessed his weakness, he made a ploy out of tying his shoelace. 'Gimme a minute, why don't yer!' he hollered out. By now his stomach was doing cartwheels, but the idea of turning back wasn't an option. You didn't do dress rehearsals in the world he'd carved out for himself; this was premier-league reality. Steeling himself, he stood up and walked to the waiting car. Peters, meanwhile, was getting into the front passenger seat. The door still remained half open at this stage; oblivious of the fact, Rossetti's shinbone collided with the sharp edge of the door, forcing him to grimace with the pain.

'You poxy blind, or what, Rossi? You'd better get yer head sorted.' Agitation wasn't Peters' strong point. 'This aint a poxy Sunday school outing, so wise up. Remember, if I ain't happy, then the Traveller becomes a very sad person.'

Rossetti eased his unsettled frame behind the wheel. From the back of the car, a succession of ominous verbal erupted. The thought of twenty-stone-plus gorilla breathing down the back of his neck had the desired effect. It became put up or shut up time.

'Yeah, I get the message, Ricky, but it's been one of those poxy days, know what I mean? Winters was giving it large this morning over that asshole Callaghan guy poaching his pension – a boxer called Gibbons – and me! I'm stuck in the fucking middle.'

Peters wasn't impressed; sympathy didn't wash in his vocabulary. 'Yer gotta be yer own man, Rossi. Don't take it so personal. I've told yer before, take the fucking money and run! Tonight, it'll be different, you get a bonus. Winters has given me two hits to carry out, so watch, learn and listen to what's going down. You'll soon get the SP, but remember, once we get established, yer gonna become a known face on the manor, which means you keep a low profile. Throwing money about and mouthing off ain't in the script. Just keep shtum, that way you get to keep yer health. Just call it insurance. Personally, I pay a high premium for mine!' Swivelling round, he pointed at the Traveller. 'I got a lot of dough invested in you, ain't I, mate?'

The torrent of verbal that followed was unintelligible, but Rossetti got the message loud and clear. The Traveller's features loomed up in his mind, forcing him to cringe. The sheer volume of the man registered fear. He even looked dangerous when he smiled, and yet Peters had this incredible Svengali control over him. The last ten minutes had brought home the meaning of the term 'another league'! Suddenly, it was reality, a new image was required to boost Rossetti's egotism.

God! How he envied Peters' way with words. If he had said, 'I climbed Everest this morning,' you'd have to believe the guy. Gritting his teeth, he managed to pull himself together. Turning the key in the ignition, it roared into life, leaving his subconscious to lay the ghost of the 'old' Rossetti. From now on, the top rung of the ladder beckoned, but at least there was a purpose behind the mayhem that lay ahead!

'So, where we headed?' Rossetti's request had more than a ring of confidence about it, suggesting that Rossetti was back on track.

A pregnant pause followed, before Peters finally replied. 'Papulous... Theo Papulous, does the name do anything for yer?'

'Heard of him of course, but I know his brother a whole lot better. The slimy bubble owes me a nice few quid from a card game, going way back.'

'Yeah, is that so? Then you must know the family run a business off Canal Street, a steak house by all accounts. It's called the El Greco.'

'Course I know it, can't say I've ever used it, though.'

'That's just as well, then; they're top of my hit list tonight. So let's do it.'

Five minutes later, they turned into the bottom end of Canal Street.

'What time you got, Rossi?' enquired Peters as Rossetti manoeuvred the car into a nearby bay.

'It's on the dashboard!'

'Nah, poxy thing don't work.'

'In that case, I make it just after 12.30.' Turning the engine off, he surveyed what he could see of the street. *Bloody busy for a weekday*, he thought to himself.

'Good!' Peters replied with a glint in his eye. 'If they're out there, then they're bleedin' well spending... right?'

After getting out of the car, they crossed the road to where the restaurant was situated, and entered unchallenged. Apart from two waiters who were drinking coffee at a table at the far end, the place appeared to be deserted. Peters halted after taking a couple of steps, and slowly absorbed every aspect of the eating area. He noted that every table was void of cutlery, and that the table cloths hadn't been changed.

'They've taken some good money in 'ere tonight, Rossi.'

'How d'ye know—'

'Bloody obvious to me,' he interrupted, and they carried on walking further in, except for the Traveller, who remained vigilant at the door. At this point, due to the subdued lighting, the two waiters were unaware of their presence. 'Hey, youse two!' Peters attempted to draw their attention. Startled, they both looked round and left the table. One of them approached, Peters gesturing as he did so.

'I'm sorry, gentlemen, we have finished serving tonight... no more meals... we are closing, yes.'

Peters switched into business mode. 'You got that fucking right, sunshine. Okay, Traveller, do the business,' he shouted.

Reversing the entry sign on the door, the gorilla waited diligently for his next command.

'You must be new 'ere?' demanded Peters of the waiter. 'I ain't 'ere to bloody well eat, where's the guvnor?' And he took a step forwards as he spoke.

The other waiter turned and vanished through the service door en route to the kitchen. Rossetti glanced across to Peters for a clue. Nodding, he started to count out loud. 'One, two, three...' He was never allowed to finish. The service door suddenly flew open, and the irate figure of the proprietor appeared, closely followed by the waiter. Arms flailing, he pointed towards the exit door, protesting in pidgin English.

'What the hell you do? I no want you here!'

'Theo, Theo. That's no way to treat yer insurance.' The mocking tones from Peters' sarcastic introduction halted the owner in his tracks. His arms dropped to his side in a forlorn gesture of defeat, a look of hopelessness embedded in his face. After grabbing a serviette from a nearby table, he hastily mopped his sweaty brow. Again he raised his arms upwards, but this time in a pleading manner.

'Mr Peters, I did not know, my staff are new here, they no tell me. I have the big problems, my staff have one week... they go. Last Saturday, my main window, it get broke... so please, no more grief for me... huh?'

'But that's what you pay me for, Theo. What happened last week will get sorted, but...' He hesitated. 'We're talking time and money 'ere, as you know. Mr Winters is a reasonable man and, like yerself, has overheads, which he has to offload of course. So I ain't leaving 'ere with nothing less than a grand... right!'

'You bloody mad people... my business, it get ruined. How can I afford to pay so much? It now go up £400 from last time. I phone Mr Winters and say £600 we agree from start.'

In spite of the Traveller's presence, Rossetti squirmed at the mention of his name. Peters was unrepentant. 'I'm beginning to lose what poxy patience I've got, Theo, which makes me feel unhappy, which in turn isn't good for him!' Slowly and deliberately, he pointed straight at the gorilla. 'I'll spell it out for yer: he hasn't had any exercise for a week. I'd hate him to get upset, so be fucking sensible and fetch the money. And oh, before I forget, that brother of yours, I happen to know where he's living, so I'd forget the phone call if I was you, and I'll forget to pay him a visit, know what I mean?' They say that 'blood is thicker than water' and Peters was about to prove the point.

The proprietor was now beside himself. 'I pay... I pay, please, not to hurt my family, Mr Peters.'

'Now that wasn't hard, was it, Theo? So run along to the office and fetch the rent!' He turned towards Rossetti. 'Better go along with him, Rossi, and make sure you check it.' The proprietor was still protesting as Peters gestured to him to leave, closely followed by Rossetti. Meanwhile, the two waiters remained cowering in one corner, not knowing what to expect next. Peters decided it was time for a laugh. He motioned the Traveller forwards. Words were not necessary. Stopping, he faced the two square on. Raising his arms, he gave out a chilling bellow, lunging at them with hands like shovels. The sheer terror latched on their faces never left them as they fled out of the restaurant into the night.

Peters broke into a laugh, and called the Traveller back. 'Easy now, mate, we don't need the bloody publicity right now. I reckon they got the point. As for him...' He left off, to point at the owner's portrait on the wall. 'I only hope for his poxy sake Papulous does the right thing.'

The gorilla concurred by smashing one huge fist into the palm of his opposing hand. A few minutes later, Rossetti appeared with a smirk on his face. In his right hand, he held aloft a money pouch.

'I'll take that, Rossi, if yer don't mind. I presume it's all there?'

'Don't even ask!' he retorted.

'Good! That's a result. Now, nip out and get the wheels sorted; I need to get the bubble straightened out on a few facts. Know what I mean? I'll be with yer in a couple of minutes.'

Rossetti slid behind the wheel of the car. He inhaled deeply as his head dropped back against the headrest. A smug look creased his face, and his obvious body language oozed cockiness. For the first time that evening, he felt completely relaxed by allowing the moment to grab him.

'That wasn't so bad after all,' he assured himself; just for once in his useless life he was probably right. His induction to the business had in his words. The added thought that a slice of the wedge would be coming his way was something else. *Surely it can't be as easy as that every time?* he told himself. Just then, Peters and the Traveller interrupted his meandering, by joining him in the car. For the time being, any further questions and answers remained in the foreseeable future. Booting the pedal, they drove off heading down Canal Street. In no time, Rossetti's newly found arrogance got the better of him. 'I can't believe we just did that! Although something is bothering me.'

'What's yer problem, Rossi?'

'Well, when you put the frighteners on Papulous, you made it plain that you knew where his brother lived.'

'Yeah, so?' Peters wasn't in the mood for a steward's enquiry. Although, Rossetti had other ideas.

'It's just that I happen to know that you've never met the guy, let alone know where the asshole lives.'

'You gotta lot to learn, Rossi. I couldn't give a shit if he lives in fucking Greece! The thing is I made him think I knew, and that's the difference between you and me. As for the Traveller, he's got an excuse: he's a bleedin' Bungarian!'

Rossetti stifled a laugh, as a set of lights loomed up, forcing him to stop.

'Hang a left 'ere, and first right,' ordered Peters. 'It's about time we invested in a Chinese takeaway.'

Rossetti gave Peters a strange look, as if questioning his motives. He had no idea Peters intended to wind him up.

'Yeah, apparently this particular Chinese joint has a happy hour once a week. They reckon you can just walk in, and order as much wedge as yer fucking want for nothing!' There was a short silence, followed by a snigger. The Traveller finally made the connection, and laughed in his own imbecilic way.

'Stuff you, Ricky, I should have known better. So what's this gaff called?'

'The Mandarin Palace, d'ye know it?'

'Yeah, reckon I do, mind you they all sound the bloody same to me.' In no time at all, Oriental Street appeared.

'Slow down, Rossi, there's a cul-de-sac at the bottom of the street, and drive down to the bottom and come back up again. Just make sure you go beyond the gaff when you park up... right?'

'Any particular reason why, Ricky?'

'Yeah, two reasons. I don't want to broadcast the fact that we're about. And secondly, if it all goes fucking pear-shaped and you've got half of bleedin' China chasing yer, the car needs to be facing in the right direction... got it?!'

'Yeah, I do now.'

'Not only that, the Chinks seem to stick together more than the bubbles do. For what it's worth, a bit more insurance might be a good bet. There's a baseball bat in the boot; you'd better fetch it out, Rossi.'

Rossetti swallowed hard at the possibility of violence creeping into the equation. If that was the case, then he needed to adapt his persona to suit. Having parked up, the three made their way back to the restaurant. The neon lighting sign hanging above the doorway threw out intermittent coloured beams of light, creating a strobe effect. At the last minute, Peters pulled up; together they slunk back into the sanctuary of a welcome alleyway. The sound from raised voices carried on the night air. He placed a warning finger of silence to his lips, as the sound from the voices increased.

'What time yer got, Rossi?' Peters whispered.

'Twenty past one,' came back the reply.

'That's handy, looks like we just got lucky. That must be the bulk of the staff knocking off.'

'Please God, Ricky, that'll cut the odds down. D'ye recognize any of 'em?'

'You're having a bleedin' laugh, ain't yer? You should know the Chinks as well as I do, once you've seen one, you've see the bloody lot!'

His remark caused the Traveller to utter an emphatic grunt.

'Keep the bloody noise down, can't yer?' Peters then kept a vigil, until he was satisfied the majority of the staff had left. With sweaty palms, Rossetti maintained his grip on the bat, waiting for a sign from Peters. They'd been holed up for only five minutes, but already he was feeling restless. As usual, Peters was quick to pick up his body language. 'Five more minutes, Rossi, and not before. Then, we do it. Just relax, the wedge ain't going anywhere except in our pockets.'

'Yeah, right, Ricky. I need to get me head sorted.'

'Look, let's just go over this one more time. Unless we get

any unforeseen grief, remember the same rules apply as before or unless I say different. Should things start to get heavy, the Traveller will sort it. Failing that, yer on yer own. The Chinks won't bottle it; they're resilient little fuckers, and when it's off, they come out of the woodwork fighting. Putting the ante up isn't going to help us one bit. I might even have to do a deal with 'em, we'll see.'

The restaurant owner exerted all his power, in a vain attempt to keep the door shut. Purely by luck, he'd spotted them coming, but by then it was too late. The gorilla had acted swiftly, and had managed to jam his foot over the threshold. 'Go for it, Traveller,' demanded Peters. He duly obliged. Twenty stone of muscle in tow with a glass-panelled door proved to be a complete mismatch. Like a knife slicing through butter, the door buckled inwards with a rush. The unfortunate owner found himself shunted backwards and collapsed in a heap on the floor inside the restaurant. Sheer terror filled his eyes, as he looked upwards, completely powerless. After raising one foot, the gorilla proceeded to place it on the diminutive owner's chest, almost treading him underfoot.

Peters, meanwhile, lost no time in getting organized. Ignoring the crumpled form on the floor, he shouted to Rossi. 'Get the bleedin' door shut somehow, and then check out the kitchen. There's no way this geezer's on his own.'

Bat in hand, Rossetti made his way towards the service door. In the background, the Traveller had removed his foot, and hauled the owner up on his feet. Waving the Traveller to one side, he turned his attention to the distraught proprietor, who attempted to make conversation.

'Mr Peters!' He was desperate to appease his tormentor. 'If I had only known, you could have been anybody who—'

Peters cut him short. 'That is crap, Johnny Loy, and you know it. I have to say I'm disappointed, we have an arrangement that suits us both. You have a domestic, and you look to me for protection… right?'

The owner nodded his head vigorously, in a vain attempt to gain favour once again. Peters was far from impressed, and spelt it out.

'For the service I provide, you pay me on a weekly basis. What I don't need is the fucking aggravation like that!' He pointed at the door.

Giving a token glance at the door, Johnny Loy wrung his hands in despair. Unlike his forefathers, he wasn't blessed with the spirit of survival. He hadn't got the stomach to deal with the likes of Peters. Being third generation, as he was, meant he was British born and bred, well educated and spoke better English than Peters. But, then, so did everybody else. For the time being, the inquisition was put on hold, as three small figures suddenly emerged from a door adjacent to the pay desk. At first glance, they appeared to be brandishing weapons of some description. Johnny Loy took the initiative as they came into view. He screamed out at them in Cantonese; momentarily it held them back in check. Only then did they decide to advance forwards.

Peters shot a warning glance at the Traveller and indicated at the three. Nevertheless, Peters was feeling slightly edgy himself. The fact that one of them was supporting a meat cleaver justified his cause. He needed to balance the books, before things got out of control. The only trump card going for him came by way of the owner, held in a grip by the Traveller. A sudden movement from behind the three figures caught Peters' eye. Slowly, the service door opened; he could just make out the figure of Rossetti creeping up behind the unsuspecting trio. Once again, they attempted to remonstrate. Immediately, Peters was on the case.

'Tell 'em to back off, Johnny, or you're going straight through the fucking shop window… your choice!'

It was a ploy, hoping to gain time for Rossetti, who by now was breathing down their backs. Raising the bat above his head, he endeavoured to create as much impetus as he could. *Don't fuck up now, Rossi*, Peters told himself. *Unless yer looking for a blood bath.* At the last second, a nearby mirror almost gave him away. But by now, the bat was already set on an arc of destruction, as the figure carrying the cleaver got the message. The bat struck the victim above the temple with sickening force, before he could confront Rossetti. Synonymous with an action replay, his legs buckled and collapsed like a wanton pack of cards, in sympathy with his numbing brain. He made an instinctive effort to stop himself falling, by grabbing his partner, but succeeded only in dragging him down with him, minus the cleaver. Rossetti had left his mark, but wasn't finished just yet. Using the butt end of the bat as a ram, he promptly struck the third victim full in the face. As he stood there, bewildered by the sudden chain of events, his face exploded as the weapon met flesh. Blood sprayed out everywhere. Finally, he sank to the floor whimpering like a dog, as Rossetti stood over him in a state of retaliation.

The whole unrehearsed episode had taken only a few minutes from start to finish. From a life-threatening situation, the scenario had been transformed in their favour. With no fight left in him, the senseless figure on the floor was propped against the wall by his terrorized companion, as Rossetti backed away. For the first time in his torrid life Peters found himself short on words. Playing the spectator didn't appear in his CV. Deep down, he found himself having to admire Rossetti for his show of tenacity. Up to now Rossetti had won all the points; he badly needed to level the score.

Turning his attention towards Johnny Loy could be one way of venting any loss of face. 'You just don't fucking learn, Johnny… do yer?!' he yelled. 'You have to do it the bloody hard way, which means me having to up the ante for the aggravation. As from tonight, I'll be calling in every week instead of fortnightly. At the moment, you're into me for £600, so I'll settle for £800. Ignoring Loy's pleas, he waved Rossetti over. 'Nice one, Rossi, yer using yer nut at last. That could have been a bit nasty if you hadn't have come up trumps.'

'It felt sorta good, if yer know what I mean?' His blind egotism began to surface.

'What?'

'Being in control, yer know, when I whacked the geezer, it gave me a hell of a buzz.'

'Really,' Peters concluded, and threw him a withering look. *I always fancied he'd turn out to be a right nutter one day*, he told himself, and returned to Johnny Loy. 'Don't keep me waiting for the dough I want out of 'ere, so move it. Rossi, you go with him, and make sure you check it.'

With a nice fat wedge on his hip, Peters and the other two departed the restaurant, leaving behind them a trail of untold grief and fear at the owner's feet.

Locking the door behind them, Johnny Loy watched them as they vanished into the night. Cradling his head in his hands, he attempted to shut out the torment and frustration before it reached boiling point. Any conclusions found wanting were now on a downward spiral, heading for a bottomless abyss.

Thankfully, the injured waiter had returned to the land of the living. The loss of the alleged protection money somehow didn't seem to be important anymore. The rules of the game had taken on a new slant. Pay up and look good, he was prepared to suffer; uncontrolled violence was something else. The fact that his shop front window remained intact he could class as a bonus.

Any other night, he would have dealt with a double act; now there were three! The insidious face of Rossetti haunted

135

his subconscious. A picture of pure evil wielding a bat. He almost retched, as he recalled the incident, leaving him drained of emotion. His life, he considered, would never be the same again. He felt that he'd taken his last order. It was time to sell up, move on. His prize for realization firmly planted in his mind, Rossetti! In another month's time, it could well be some other mug's problem. Corruption, it seemed, has patience; the availability it allows will always reign supreme.

For the winners, the night was yet young. Travelling along Canal Street, Peters began to lord over the past events. 'Results! That's the name of the game, and tonight we proved a point. Wotcha think, Rossi, give it another go?'

'Absolutely! Gotta be done, besides, I've got the flavour now. There's nothing to hold us back. Poxy Winters has got his wack, and we've got ours… sorted!'

A torrent of malignant verbal erupted from the back of the car. Even Peters evoked a laugh of sorts.

'Looks like you got yerself a friend there, Rossi. The Traveller obviously likes yer style. Saying that, the way you performed tonight helped to solve a few problems. I gotta say, I was impressed.'

'Tell me something, Ricky. If I hadn't of done the business with the bat, would you have let the Traveller throw Johnny Loy through the glass window?'

'Nah, there wouldn't be any point. I called his bluff. I happen to know it's made of toughened glass; I've still got the bleedin' billhead somewhere.'

A sinister smile appeared on Rossetti's face. 'And you reckon I've got style? So when do we get to do it again?'

'We don't! We give it a rest, chill out for a couple of days, let the dust settle down. Yer forgetting Winters' part in all of this. There'll be fucking murders if it ever came out, you know the SP by now. We need to keep him sweet and then hit him again when it suits us. In the meantime, the Traveller and me carry on the business as usual. What I will do, though, is carry out a roll call, pick out the soft targets; we don't want a repeat of the last hit. Another thing, socially, we don't mix; the least we see of each other, the better. The slightest hint that we're firming up on Winters, it's over... got it? And like I've said before, you don't mouth off, especially in the Rat and Trap!'

Dropping Rossetti off at his flat, Peters opened up.

'You did well tonight, Rossi; money-wise we made a profit. Your share's £300.'

'Thanks, Ricky, not bad for a couple of hours' graft.'

'Yeah, this is only the start of it, though. From now on, I'll make sure we don't have the grief. It'll be gilt-edged, trust me.'

'You can count on it. What about the Traveller's cut?'

'Easy, mate, I'll give him £100, and tell him the difference is in a Bungarian bank; he'll believe me.'

'Yer a hard bastard, Ricky.'

'Yeah, I know, and that's why it bloody works. Anyway, I'll text yer tomorrow night, see yer.'

With that, he drove off, leaving Rossi with plenty to think about.

CHAPTER 15

CONTROLLED WAR

Friday arrived in no time. They left Stonewater behind them, and the motorway beckoned as Ronnie alongside Mercer continued their journey up to town. Included in the stable were Wally Churchill and Mickey Gibbons, as additional support. At the last moment, Tommy Russell decided to make his own way up there. The weigh-in for the evening entertainment was scheduled for 1 o'clock, so Ronnie allowed himself a good two hours for travel and convenience time. In no time, they'd left the city behind them, in exchange for the grind of the Whitechapel Road.

'Poxy traffic,' Mercer commented.

'Won't be long, and we'll be out of it,' Ronnie assured him.

Mercer concurred with a guilty look on his face. 'Sorry, I didn't mean to sound off like that!'

'Forget it. At least yer fired up, so save it for tonight; that's where it's all at— shit! I've missed the bleedin' turn-off.'

'Who's stressed now, then?' Mercer replied jokingly. The four men erupted into laughter. Five minutes after doubling back, they manipulated the Hackney and Bethnal Green road without difficulty. Finally parking up within spitting distance of their venue, York Hall, Ronnie couldn't disguise his obvious relief, knowing that the pressure from their trip was now history. Alighting from the car, Ronnie lost no time in issuing out orders.

'You three go ahead, I'll catch up with yer inside; I need to sort the kit out.'

On entering the hall, Mercer stopped short, and nudged Wally.

'I can't believe this place. I know Ronnie mentioned it as being a small hall, but seeing is believing.'

'That's as may be, son,' agreed Wally. 'But it's big in atmosphere. There'll be bodies from floor to ceiling in 'ere tonight, and I should know. This place holds a lot of memories for me and Ronnie. Venues like this one are a shrine within the business. It seems to bring out the best in fighters, know what I mean?'

'In that case, I hope it rubs off on me, then!' Mercer quipped.

'Amen to that, Eric! Right, let's find the dressing room. You can put yer feet up and chill out while we're waiting for Tommy to make an appearance.' With that in mind, they sauntered off down to the end of the hall. Some ten minutes later, Ronnie caught up with them.

'Right! Let's get this show on the road. Time yer changed, Eric. Everything is 'ere in the kitbag. I'll leave it with yer, Wally. Mickey and myself will be at the weigh-in; in the meantime, I need to get hold of Tommy as—'

The unmistakeable tones of the big man's voice echoed down the corridor and into the dressing room.

'Better late than never, Tommy,' chided Ronnie.

'Sorry, mate, bloody traffic, you know how it is.'

'Yeah, we had our fair share. I presume you've verified the contract with the inspector?'

'No problem, it's all sorted. No amendments, pretty straightforward.'

'Fine.' Together, they made their way to the main hall. It wasn't long before Mickey and Wally appeared, closely followed by Harrison and his entourage. Almost immediately, the hubbub coming from the press boys and the ever present media increased.

'Gentlemen, please!' The steward made a plea for silence. 'Good afternoon, everybody. Let's keep the noise down.' As far as the paparazzi were concerned, it fell on deaf ears. Their chief interest lay in the top of the bill fighters. The underdogs didn't figure in their press. 'Harrison to the scales, please.' The steward began pressing for action. Mercer's opponent duly stripped off and obliged. Deliberating for a few minutes, the steward declared his findings. 'Gentlemen! Harrison, scales ten stone and four pounds.'

For whatever reason, Harrison looked directly across at his manager, while shrugging his shoulders; a look of consternation crossed his face. It was clearly obvious that something was bothering him. The woeful glance was a giveaway.

Ronnie was quick to pick up on the incident. His initial instincts were beginning to make sense. The camp had problems; in the past, Harrison had always struggled to make the required weight.

'Gentlemen, if you don't mind! Mercer, to the scales, please.'

Removing his gown, Ronnie ushered him forwards. A minute later a conclusion was reached.

'Gentlemen, Mercer weighed in at ten stone and seven pounds.'

'Yes!' Ronnie exclaimed through gritted teeth. He was now aware that the blood and sweat from the last three weeks had paid dividends. Levelling the stipulated weight gave Mercer a three-pound advantage to exploit, including a psychological bearing as a backup. With that in mind, he lost no time reminding Tommy Russell when returning to the dressing room.

'We mustn't get too carried away 'ere. Let's not forget that Harrison is a class act, so Eric's got it all to do. Saying that, the kid's oozing with confidence. I'm sure he'll be there at the death.'

The rest of the afternoon belonged to them. Ronnie's idea of a belated steak lunch seemed to fit the bill. Even after the meal, there was still ample time to put their feet up and relax.

'Put up or shut up' time came around quickly. With all the preliminaries out of the way, Mercer loosened up in his corner, awaiting the bell signalling round one. Ronnie's last-minute instructions were ringing in his ears; his eyes were completely focused on Harrison, as he drew in what fresh air remained available. A sudden adrenalin surge emphasized his fight plan, as he banged his gloves together. Framed in his mind, Ronnie was spelling it out for him once again.

'The guy's gonna hustle yer from the bell. Avoid mixing it with him, get up on yer toes and move. Use the ring, back pedal and jab him off. If you spot an opening, utilize it; you have the reach, height and weight advantage, so use it!'

'Seconds out! Round one.'

The time keeper brought him down to earth with a jolt. Ronnie's assumption had proved to be right. Harrison shot across the ring before Mercer had left his mark. It was a split second act of aggression on his part, leaving Mercer somewhat vulnerable, and with nowhere to go. From somewhere behind him, a voice could be heard screaming at him to get motivated. Instinctively, he moved to Harrison's right and threw a token jab, which met only fresh air. The inevitable reply came from under his own lead. Crouching low as he slipped the jab gave Harrison the opening to exploit his busy style. Hooking from every angle, he once again crowded Mercer back onto the ropes. A selected body shot left him clawing for air, as he attempted to fight back. With nowhere to go, he was beginning to own the ropes! In desperation, he glanced down at Ronnie for advice. It became his undoing; a well-timed short right-hand caught him flush on the chin. Instantly, the numbing sensation in his brain began to forge a link with his sight. Eyes semi-glazed, he could just make out Ronnie screaming at him to move. The increased roar of the crowd didn't help his cause, by obliterating any advice on offer. The numbing now doubled up, as yet again he got caught by a further blow to the head. His mouth gaped open on impact, spewing out his gum shield, which flew across the canvas. The referee swiftly kicked it to one side.

Through a haze of mist and dancing lights, the will to survive still lay in his corner, as he fought to rid the paralysis eating away at his nerve ends. The ropes supporting him finally gave up the ghost, as his legs parted from his useless co-ordination. Leather and flesh met canvas, as he hit the deck, subsequently rolling over onto his back. Through sightless eyes, Mercer constantly blinked at the overhead ring lights. In the background, the hall was in an uproar, the fans were getting their money's worth.

Meanwhile, in spite of the racket, Ronnie still had a job to do. Wally appeared to be less confident. 'It looks like an early bath night for Eric.'

Ronnie was quick to respond. 'You reckon? Well, it ain't over yet, mate! If he survives this round, he'll come back a different man. I know Harrison; Eric just took the best shot he could offer. The guy can't dig and he knows it; Eric got suckered in, don't write him off.'

That apart, Mercer hadn't thrown the towel in just yet. Having got to one knee resting on the canvas, he averted what brain cells he had left, striving to clear his head. Glaring upwards, the ref took up the count. Using his fingers, he repeatedly thrust them into Mercer's face, as he accentuated the count. The density of his actions seemed to stimulate Mercer back into reality. On the count of seven, Mercer caught Ronnie's eye, and nodded positively. Wally was the first to atone.

'Blimey, take back all I said, mate. I think the kid's cracked it.'

'Gutsy little bleeder, ain't he? As far as I'm concerned, the fight doesn't start until the second round.'

Mercer was already up on his feet by the count of nine, leaving the ref to shake him down back into a fighting posture. For his part, Harrison was now eager to capitalize on his early advantage, and moved in for the kill. Coming in square on, gloves held low, he'd clearly underestimated Mercer's resilience. A well-placed jab stopped him dead in his tracks, forcing him to cover up. The short time that remained of the round belonged to Mercer. Gaining a second wind, he was constantly on the move. Using the ring wisely put him in a position to dictate the fight. Firing at will meant Harrison couldn't enforce his earlier fight plan. Suffice to say, nobody was more pleased to hear the bell signalling the end of the round than Mercer. On walking back to their respective corners, the two eyeballed each other in a mark of respect.

A shattered Mercer slumped down on his stool. Ronnie swiftly took control of the situation, while Wally retrieved his mouthpiece from the canvas. 'Save yer breath, mate. You've taken his best shots and got up off the floor. Right nah, his corner have got more problems than you have. Believe me. Mentally, yer stronger, and he knows it. Keep dominating the centre of the ring, but avoid mixing it.'

Squeezing the last of a sodden sponge to the nape of his neck, Wally offered up the water bottle. The bell sounded as Mercer stood up raring to go. Slipping his mouthpiece in, Ronnie shouted, 'Be first, son.'

His well-worn advice appeared to be rubber stamped. The will to continue to carry the fight to Harrison showed in his performance. Constantly on the move, bobbing and weaving, he represented a smaller target. When he was compromised, two- and three-punch combinations enabled him to score at will. Going into the third round, Mercer had created a fight pattern by sheer doggedness of character. Frustration that he hadn't taken Mercer apart was costing Harrison dearly. Time and time again, he left himself wide open when coming forwards. Needless to say, he was punished for his ignorance. With two rounds to go, Ronnie now had Mercer slightly ahead on points, mainly due to his work rate, which was more than he could have hoped for.

Apart from the knockdown to his credit, Harrison hadn't stopped chasing shadows all night. Slowly, he'd managed to get back into the fight, but at a cost to his fitness, although he still represented a threat should Mercer get careless. From a trainer's point of view, Ronnie had his own version of events. Up to now, he'd considered Mercer's performance as something special. To get off the floor and carry the fight to someone of Harrison's calibre spoke volumes. From a spectator's view, the first seven rounds showed *par excellence*. From the very first bell, the crowd had been partisan in Harrison's favour, but Mercer had generated a fighting spirit they readily absorbed. Their appreciation for an under-card bout was worthy of a bill topper.

The penultimate round, Harrison shaded as his experience came into play. Having said that, the bell this round sounded sweeter to his ears than it did to Mercer's.

'Well, you've got three minutes to make it happen; don't stand still for a second. Be selective, make every punch count!' There was nothing more that Ronnie could add, as the bell went sounding the final round. It was left to Wally to have the final word.

'According to my reckoning, there's nothing in it, mate; it could go either way.'

Centre ring, the two gladiators touched gloves and prepared to give it their all. Fitness-wise, Mercer had the edge. Harrison's obvious experience was never given the chance to shine. A drop in standards from either one of them could now influence the result. Mercer once again opted to come forwards; slipping a right-hander, he worked away at Harrison's body. It became short lived, as his opponent claimed him. The ref duly prized the two apart; the crowd were on their feet now, and the atmosphere was electric. In their corner Ronnie and Wally were calling the shots, urging Mercer forwards. This time, it became Harrison's turn to level. Feinting a jab, he caught Mercer high on the temple from a chopping right. There was no way it would prove effective; the sting in the tail had been left behind in the gym.

Ronnie's earlier pre-fight assessment regarding Harrison's concern at the weigh-in had now proven to be right. 'Over trained' would be his personal summing up later on in the day. Shaking his head, more in frustration than pain, Mercer continued to harass his opponent. Toe-to-toe, the pair slugged away at each other, right up until the final bell went. For the last time, the ref prized them apart, as they continued their own private war. Finally leaving off, they stood and glared at each other.

Finally, it was left to Harrison to break the deadlock. Throwing his aching arms around Mercer's neck, he used him for a prop. It was as much as the pair could do to keep their balance; both men had given it their all. Nobbins from around the ringside began to shower onto the ring canvas, as the fans showed their appreciation. The ref finished totting up his score card; full of intention, he motioned the two into the centre of the ring. Grabbing one arm apiece, he systematically hoisted them upwards to declare a draw. Under the circumstances, it was the only decision he could have been expected to have made on the night. As a result, more nobbins soon followed, and Wally jumped into the ring, bucket in hand. Meanwhile, a delighted Ronnie made a beeline across the canvas, eager to congratulate the two boys.

Harrison turned to Mercer. A look of respect showed in his bruised and bloodied face. Grasping Mercer's hand, he spoke through swollen lips. 'We'll do it again sometime; that was some fight.'

'Don't make it too soon, mate, but likewise,' he fired back. Acknowledging Harrison's corner, he fell into Ronnie's arms. A choking sensation caused a lump to appear in his throat, as a tide of emotion swept over him. His eyes welled up, as he lifted Mercer clear of the canvas, at the same time parading him around the ring. It represented the climax to a day the camp would never forget in a hurry. No more so than Mercer himself. In terms of the business, his career had only just started to take off. Five minutes later, the atmosphere in the hall resembled a wake in comparison to their dressing room. Wally was busy counting the nobbins, while Ronnie was further engaged removing Mercer's gloves and sweaty bandages. In short, it was time to catch one's breath, and more importantly to assess the overall night's performance. There'd be time enough for celebrating, on their return journey home to Stonewater.

'God! That's better,' remarked a relieved Mercer as Ronnie removed the last of his bandages. Instinctively, he flexed his fingers, should he have incurred any damage.

'Any problems?' enquired Ronnie.

'No, they're fine. I think I'll grab a shower now, won't be long.'

Watching him go, Ronnie felt compelled to offload the last

of his inner feelings. 'By the way,' he shouted. 'Thanks for tonight, son.'

Mercer half turned in his stride, replying, 'Couldn't miss, could I? We're a double act.' The trainer–fighter syndrome had finally gone full circle, his parting shot now cementing that exclusive bond they both shared.

Rapt in sentiment, Ronnie had become unaware of the dressing room door being opened to expose the head and shoulders of a stranger. Wally, meanwhile, was still engrossed in counting the nobbins and chose to ignore the sudden intrusion.

'Ronnie Callaghan?'

Wally looked up and pointed across in Ronnie's direction, as the stranger walked in. His larger than life figure seemed to take over what little room they had.

'I'm Ronnie Callaghan, do I know you at all?' he enquired.

'No!' the stranger replied. 'We've never met personally before. Sorry to invade your private space. I called round to congratulate your boy on the gutsy performance that he put up tonight. To come back like he did was a feat in itself. To be honest, he cost me a pony, Harrison being the pre-fight favourite. I obviously underestimated your stable. Oh, I'm sorry, I didn't introduce myself. The name's Cochrane, Charlie Cochrane, that is.'

For a second, Ronnie felt stunned into silence. The stranger's name had collided with his subconscious. Still in limbo, he proffered his hand, which was warmly accepted. 'Pleased to meet you. The kid's taking a shower at the moment. I'll let him know you called in. He'll think a lot of that.'

'He earned it. Anyway, it's the least I could do,' Cochrane continued. 'Now that we've met on a professional basis, I'd like to keep in touch. I run a big stable myself, and I also promote in a big way.'

'Yeah, so I believe,' Ronnie confessed. 'Please, carry on. I'm more than interested.'

'To be frank, I liked what I saw tonight,' Cochrane declared. 'In fact, if you're agreeable, I'd like to bear Mercer in mind or anybody else come to that you can put my way. I'm thinking in terms of future promotions, as we speak. For me, it's a breath of fresh air to see a professional outfit like yours.' He sighed.

At this juncture, Ronnie felt that he needed to take a step back. For the short time that they had spoken, things were moving too fast. His sudden air of uncertainty hadn't gone unnoticed. Even Wally had left off counting to listen in. Cochrane was quick to put him at ease.

'I must stress, there's no pressure, Ronnie. You may want to dwell on it before you make any decisions. Here's my card, should you want to pursue any business deals. For what it's worth, I took the liberty of approaching Tommy Russell earlier on. I got the feeling that he'd also be interested in what could be on offer. As for myself, my initial approach is somewhat different than most.'

'Yeah, in what way, Charlie?'

'Simple really! Good trainer, result, better the boxer.'

Ronnie wasn't about to disagree with that, as a rule of thumb. Deep down, he respected the man's integrity and his ingenuous approach towards the business as a whole, as well as quickly warming to his exclusive personality.

Cochrane felt content to continue. 'I've reason to believe you're based in Stonewater.'

'Yeah, for my sins.'

'Uhm, interesting that!'

'How come?'

'Are you familiar with a certain Terry Winters?'

Immediately, Ronnie's jaw dropped and not for the second time, as once again he felt speechless to continue, as a dormant suspicion came back to bite his arse. 'More than you'll ever know!' he managed to blurt out. The relevance of his answer, and their joint interest, somehow eased his unsteady composure, allowing him to continue. 'What's your interest in a lowlife like that?!' he demanded.

'Simply, as little as possible. It's obvious that we both share a joint grievance where he's concerned.'

'That's an understatement that would take too long to explain, Charlie. Although, I'd welcome your take on the asshole.'

'Surely, mind if I sit down?'

Ronnie nodded.

Making himself comfortable, Charlie picked up from where he'd left off. 'It seems to me that he's always had this cloud hanging over him, since he was granted a licence. Because I know for a fact he's got previous—'

Their conversation became curtailed, as the door opened, and Tommy Russell entered, accompanied by Mickey Gibbons.

'Not interrupting anything, I hope?' quipped Russell. 'I had a hunch I'd find you here.'

'No, no, not at all,' Charlie assured him. 'I'll be with you shortly. Now then, where was I?'

'Winters!'

'Right! It appears he had a colourful reputation up the borough before moving on. Knowing what I know now, I should have given the guy a swerve there and then. At one point, his licence was revoked on the strength of a ticket scam. Lack of evidence enabled him to retain his licence due to a technicality. I took the decision personally, forcing me to contact him, warning him off.'

Ronnie nodded in full agreement, but held back on one crucial point. That being said, he was in Slatteries the same night as Charlie made that damning phone call! 'Sorry, mate, I was somewhere else for a minute, please carry on.'

'Apparently, I got wind that Winters had approached a couple of my boys, regarding their allegiance to me. I think you get the idea? I just hope for his sake he doesn't make a noise on my patch again. Take it from me, he's going to upset the wrong person one day, and it's bound to upset his health, know what I mean?'

Small world! Ronnie could have said so much more on the Winters saga. There was no way he would allow the asshole to rain on his parade. The night belonged to Mercer. Everything else at this point seemed irrelevant.

'A word, Charlie.' Russell appeared keen to talk shop, which gave Ronnie an opportunity to slip away.

'Nice talking to yer, Charlie. Be lucky, I'll be in touch, mate.'

Cochrane nodded, thanking him for his time. Catching Mickey Gibbons' eye, Ronnie walked across, and entered into a post-fight conversation.

Their trip home became one of sheer pleasure. The traffic situation had eased, in contrast to the morning's grief.

It wasn't that long before the Blackwall Tunnel had swallowed them up. From then on, the road belonged to them. Dropping Mercer off on the way through, Ronnie once again reminded him of his professionalism.

'You've made yer mark now, son; think onwards and upwards. I want you back in the gym on Monday night… right?'

Mercer gave him a robotic look, and bade them all good night.

CHAPTER 16

EXPANSION

It would appear that Ronnie wasn't the only person getting results. A two-week induction period of intense violence within the ethnic ghettos of Docklands had literally plucked Rossetti from obscurity. Now that he had served his 'apprenticeship', Ricky Peters had become tolerant towards his blatant ignorance. Sooner or later, he envisaged that their merciless reign would run its course. He also knew that villainy was always going to be a temperamental pastime, whatever! If you came out of it unscathed, and managed to thieve a few quid besides, then you were lucky and somewhat exclusive. Working as a professional career criminal meant he was always going to earn a living. His two associates, on the other hand, lacked the all-important brain power to survive.

A mental picture of his two sidekicks came into play, causing a negative look to cross his face. There they were, an Iron Curtain gypsy, who didn't know whether he was Hungarian or Bulgarian, and a half-baked Wop with the added brains of a rocking horse! It took him seconds to sum his thoughts up. *Fucking losers! The pair of 'em!* His reasoning apart, the monetary side of the business was still lucrative. Utilizing selective hits had paved the way for an easier, grief-free lifestyle. Everybody could be seen to be earning, including Terry Winters. His share of the protection money was forwarded on a regular basis, and as yet he still remained oblivious to their exclusive scam. Even the Traveller had his cut reviewed. By using a seventies-style PO book he'd found in a builder's skip, Peters convinced him that his alleged legacy was in good hands!

The plain fact that the gorilla couldn't read or write remained only secondary. But then, Peters did have this Svengali power over him. On arriving back at Rossetti's that particular night, Peters handed over his cut of the night's takings.

'Nice one, Ricky. Tonight's run has to be the easiest we've had so far, I never even got a buzz.'

'If yer looking for grief, it ain't hard to find, Rossi. What's on yer mind?'

'Who knows, another patch maybe? I think we need to put ourselves about a bit, spread our wings, know what I mean? There's a hell of a lot of victims out there, waiting to offload their money our way.'

'Yeah, yer could be right, as it happens. I'll sleep on it.'

The obligatory grunt via the Traveller appeared to have rubber stamped his decision. Lingering by his front door, Rossetti watched them as they drove off into the dwindling night. Shivering slightly, he went indoors. Once inside, he removed his Crombie overcoat and slung it over the nearest chair. Gracefully, it slipped off and landed in a heap on the floor. He never even made an attempt to retrieve it; instead, he poured himself a large scotch. Plonking himself down in a chair, his mind floated over the evening's events. It became obvious there was a certain air of restlessness about him. Subsidising his pocket seemed to have lost the desired effect. The wedge on its own didn't seem to be fulfilling anymore. Even the scotch he readily threw down his throat had somehow lost the meaning of stability.

A few more drinks, and an hour later, he'd managed to convince himself his thoughts started and ended with the same conclusions. Predominantly, he wasn't hurting Winters, in a physical sense, simply because the man wasn't aware of what was going down! Dangerous ideas began to circulate in his clouded mind. The top rung of the ladder, as far as he could see, appeared to be far more accessible now than at any other time. Blinded by arrogance and greed, his insane beliefs had now led him to believe that his premature learning curve had turned full circle. Consequences no longer figured in his erratic equation. Complete and utter control of the rackets would mean he could put the ladder behind him. Little did he realize that his negative thoughts had become brain-locked.

He hadn't even considered that a takeover could prove to be volatile, including having to win over a number of opposition faces. A sudden subconscious image of a coup, with himself at the helm, appeared. He was dreaming, of course, but was he? There was nothing to say that his insane dream couldn't become reality! The last couple of weeks had undoubtedly been an education, even to him. He realized that what you lacked in brains, you made up for with muscle, a working combination 24/7. The power and esteem it could generate would more than satisfy his maniacal craving for recognition. For the time being, he needed to suppress his lust for vengeance.

In the past, fear had always been his Achilles' heel. Now, it was role reversal time; for once, it was his turn to give it out, and it felt good inside of him. It was as if his victims were bleeding him dry of the cancer he'd been burdened with. In one way, he felt reborn, but remained blind to the fact that as one cancer diminished, another tumour, terror of evil, had developed, and it was never going to go away. Destiny itself had become the prime root of this new illness and could be found growing inside of what brain he could muster at any one time. A couple of drinks later, he fell onto his bed fully clothed. He remained that way until the following morning. Whatever dreams he may have had were undoubtedly full of cynicism.

Rossetti was dozing off again when his landline rang. A liquid lunch on a late rise was a trend for alcoholics alone. Arrogant as ever, he put himself above that. His watch was saying late afternoon, but he still needed another shot to convince himself.

'Shit! If that's a fucking wrong number...' After lunging at the receiver, he gave out a venomous, 'Yes!' In a split second, his attitude went from a to z. 'Ricky? Sorry about that, I just woke up, what's occurring?'

'Lazy bastard! Listen... meet me... say in an hour, in the Rat and Trap. I'll explain later, got it?!'

The line went dead. Slowly, Rossetti replaced the receiver. Immediately, his mind began to play tricks with his imagination. His first instincts were cast in Terry Winters' direction. Had their scam been rumbled? It seemed to be the only possible explanation.

It was a cautious Rossetti who made his way to the office an hour later. He hesitated before entering the pub. It wasn't through fear, but the intrigue hammering away inside of his malignant mind. He felt a blood surge, as he entered. It took a few seconds for his eyes to adjust to the lighting.

'Over 'ere, Rossi.' In one corner sat Peters and the Traveller.

Acknowledging their presence, he walked across, full of trepidation. Peters motioned him to sit down. Leaning forwards, he stared deep into Rossetti's eyes, taking his time before speaking. The tone of his voice then suggested that something big was going down.

'We need to talk... review a few possibilities.' Short, sweet and to the point!

Rossetti stalled for time before replying, his intrigue now

competing on two chains of thought. Obviously, Peters' meet was either a threat or an olive branch – which?

For a second, his thoughts were put on hold, as a dark shadow seemed to blot out what light there was as the Traveller rose up out of his seat. In doing so, he firmly riveted one giant hand on Rossetti's shoulder that felt like a bag of cement to him. It was all he could do from wincing. Something that resembled a face then made a bad job of trying to smile. His mouth opened to form a hideous grin. The foul smell of garlic he exhaled wafted directly into Rossetti's face. The irregular stumps that once resembled teeth were something else! Grimacing, Rossetti felt obliged to turn his head away. *Christ!* he told himself. *If he had one white one, he'd have a fucking snooker set!* His knees began to buckle as the Traveller continued to exert more pressure onto his shoulder, forcing him down into the chair.

Peters stepped in and called the gorilla off. 'Relax, Rossi, he ain't had any exercise lately.'

'Yeah? You could have fooled me!' Rossetti exclaimed. 'So what's the SP?'

'I got to thinking about what yer mentioned last night… It's been bugging me ever since.'

'Me and my big mouth, eh?' replied Rossetti in a patronising manner.

'No! Not this time, Rossi. As it happens, I think yer could be on to a winner.'

'Fuck's sake, Ricky, you gonna tell me, or what?'

Peters wasn't going to be rushed; he had a definite air of purpose about him. Eventually, he leaned forwards, glancing both ways before replying. 'Expansion, my son… that's what!' He drew back to allow the words to sink in.

Rossetti groaned. 'Let's get this right! Are yer saying what I've been thinking all along?'

'Nah yer messing me about, Rossi. So I'll simplify it for yer. Basically, we extend the business to include another patch. Since last night, things have begun to move on a bit, know what I mean? We can make a killing and, even better, Winters is out in the cold on this one. All the wedge we rake in is down to us, full stop. Wotcha think?'

'What do I think? It can't get better than that, Ricky. Shit! I need a bleedin' drink. Bloody Champagne's in order, eat yer bloody heart out, Winters.'

Peters wasn't impressed by his sudden change in persona. 'Keep it down, Rossi. I've told yer before about mouthing off. As for the bubbly, forget it; it's a wooser's drink anyway; not only that, we've got it all to do yet.'

Clearly Rossetti was on a high, and he didn't want to come down just yet. A mental image of Winters being sucked dry rivalled a lottery win. Peeling a £20 note off, he placed it down in front of the Traveller, and nodded towards the bar. The gorilla stared long and hard at the note; he held it aloft, as if to analyse it, and this in turn caused his face to stiffen. Rossetti immediately sensed a situation could be on the cards, and glanced across at Peters for support. Peters evoked a wry smile and loosened his tie. But not before a raised hand realized a calming effect on the gorilla.

Rossetti was forced to watch spellbound as the Traveller methodically rolled the note between sausage-like fingers, almost as if he was rolling a cigarette. Picking up an empty Coke can, he placed one end into the outlet hole, and slowly pushed the note inside until it was completely gone. After placing the can in his open palm, he crushed it until his fingers overlapped, leaving no visible signs of metal, leaving it completely surrounded by flesh. From start to finish, his face remained totally drained of any form of emotion. Finally, he placed the unrecognizable residue on the table, staring vacantly into space as he did so.

Rossetti sank back into his seat, mouth agape, eyes bulging with fear, as if in a trance. Peters' shoulders rose and fell, stifling a meaningful laugh as he did so.

'Shit! I don't believe he just did that! It must have been something I said; at least it was Winters' money.' Rossetti tried to make light work of the situation, but it fell on deaf ears.

It was left to Peters to mark his card. 'I should have told yer before, Rossi, never, ever mention the word Champagne again in front of the Traveller. Unless, of course, you've got a shooter in yer hand!'

'I don't get the connection, Ricky.'

'Nah, you wouldn't, so I'll tell yer.'

Like it or not, Rossetti felt isolated, as Peters endorsed the Traveller's manic actions. Easing himself back into his seat, he listened intently, as Peters continued.

'A couple of years ago, or was it three? I can't be that sure. Anyhow, I happened to get involved while doing a heist inside a casino up west one night. From word go, it never really happened. Because there happened to be a timer set on the portable vault, it meant us going in earlier than we would have liked, just to get a result. As I say, it all went fucking pear-shaped; the gaff was heaving with punters when the old bill showed up. Even though we were mob-handed, we just lost it. I was luckier than most; my role was to clear the tills in the pay-out kiosk.'

The gorilla's almost non-existent memory went into overdrive, as he struggled to recall the night in question. Nodding in the Traveller's direction, Peters once again took up the story.

'He was minding me at the time. Trouble was he had his back to me when it all kicked off.' Pausing again to gain breath, he stared intently at the Traveller and added, 'You must remember it nah, surely?'

Rocking in his seat, fists clenched, he nodded his shaven head repeatedly in a grotesque fashion, grunting at the same time, in an animated way. Leaning forwards, he eyeballed Rossetti through pig-like eyes, boring deep into his face. Although the atmosphere inside the bar felt warm, his action caused a cold shiver to run down Rossetti's spine. To avoid any further intimidation, he swung round to Peters.

'So is that it, then, Ricky?!'

'It could have been, but some bleedin' joker decided to make a name for himself. Grabbing a Magnum bottle of bubbly, he whacked the Traveller over the head with it!'

'Fuck's sake! The geezer must have had a bloody death wish.'

'Whatever, but you know the Traveller same as me. He got up quicker than when he went down. Unfortunately for the other guy, the bottle he picked up happened to be empty. The poor bastard never stood a chance. The Traveller threw him inside the kiosk and began stuffing wads of £20 notes inside his mouth, until the bleeder turned blue.'

Slowly, realization began to set inside Rossetti's head, as he pieced together the connection to his own £20 note.

'Yeah! I know where yer coming from now, but what's with the Coke can?'

Peters sneered, before continuing. 'That, Rossi, is meant to be the geezer's head! The difference being, he used two hands instead of one when he squeezed! We found out later, the Traveller had stuffed almost ten grand's worth of £20 notes down his throat. He choked to death of course, which was just as well; he'd have wound up a fucking cabbage no matter what. Quite honestly, he done the geezer a favour really. So like I said before, Rossi, bubbly ain't on the menu, right!'

Nodding like a zombie, Rossetti stood up and faltered, as

he made his way over to the bar. Something had crossed his mind, causing his legs to buckle. A nearby table offered him a form of support, and he readily took advantage of it. His face paled, as his own private thoughts came into play.

Bloody hell! he told himself. *If he caused that much grief using an empty bottle, what the fuck would he have done if it had been full?!*

The barman happened to be hovering, and picked up on his demeanour. 'Well, that must have been funny, d'ye want to share it with me, Rossi?'

He declined the offer and slowly shook his head. 'Yer wouldn't believe me if I put it in writing, Billy boy. Although it's gonna take a few drinks for me to forget it.'

'Large ones all round, then, I presume, yeah?'

'Yer having a poxy laugh, ain't yer? Brandy and a scotch fine, but the gorilla's on Coke.'

'Weird, innit? I mean, I can't see somebody like him with a Coke in his hand!'

'Yeah, know what yer mean, but I can see somebody like me still breathing, more to the point!'

The barman walked away, scratching his head. *Maybe it'll come back to me later,* he told himself, and proceeded to deal with their order. A few minutes later, he offered up their drinks on a tray, and weighed Rossetti in with his change.

'You gotta problem, Billy boy?' asked Rossetti.

A questionable look appeared on the barman's face. 'Just got to thinking.'

'What?!'

'The big guy.'

'Yeah, what about him?'

'Just an observation, I guess. I bet that underneath all that muscle he's all heart!'

Rossetti nearly choked as he attempted to keep a straight face. 'Billy boy! You'll never ever know, will yer?'

As he got back to the table, Peters remarked casually, 'You took yer time, Rossi.'

'Sorry about that, poxy bar staff, a bit slow.'

'Yeah, know what yer mean. That Billy has always struck me as being a divvie! Right! Let's talk some business.'

As per usual, it fell to Peters to get things moving. Systematically rolling his brandy glass between his palms, he eyeballed them both in turn. It was noticeable that even the Traveller appeared to be getting restless by his prolonged silence, and it now started to rub off onto Rossetti, who was beginning to harbour a few negative thoughts. Peters suddenly looked up. Raising the brandy glass to his mouth, he hesitated for a second, and not before a hidden conclusion creased his thoughts. Throwing it down in one gulp, he shuddered slightly, as it bit the back of his throat. Licking his lips, he placed the empty glass down on the table, and lowered his eyes.

The gorilla folded his massive arms across his chest, at the same time making contact with Rossetti, who seemed to be miles away. The pair were then rapidly brought back into the world of reality as Peters took on a serious tone. 'Now, you both listen, and listen good!' He pointed his finger in the air, as he emphasized his point. 'What I've got in mind is a whole new ballgame. You can forget all about last month, and Winters' poxy pocket money. As from now, we go freelance... long term. I fully intend taking over the rackets on the Docklands manor... totally!'

Rossetti was wide awake by now, although struggling to take in Peters' ambitious plans. But one facet remained planted inside his brain: his use of the word 'totally'! Never sounded sweeter, as Peters hammered it out. His blood count surged, only this time for a purpose he could favour.

'You're something else, Ricky, d'ye know that? You bloody

well mean it, don't yer? I mean, this changes everything.' Just then, his thoughts took a step backwards, as the odious smell of decaying teeth wafted into his air space from the Traveller's direction, as he attempted to smile, causing Rossetti to cringe. 'Well.' He paused for a second. 'Well, almost everything!'

By now, Peters had a heavy duty buzz about him. 'Take it from me, Rossi baby, we're going all the way, okay? Saying that, it means getting other faces involved. I realize it can either work for yer or against yer. But don't worry, I've got that covered; we ain't short on insurance.' Breaking off, he acknowledged the gorilla and winked. 'Plus the bottom line is we get the lion's share of the proceeds… whatever.'

Rossetti issued an air of brief negativity. 'Winters ain't gonna take this little lot lying down, is he?'

Peters wasn't interested in a third-party viewpoint. 'Yeah, well, fuck the guy, I've had a bellyful of him lately. Time I'm finished, the asshole will be history; he don't even rate a threat, Rossi. What he doesn't know, and you'll love this bit, is I've got half of his little firm on the payroll, when we make our move.'

'I gotta hand it to yer, Ricky, you've done yer homework on this one. I'd love to be a fly on the wall when he gets his!'

'Sooner the better, Rossi, but for your part, and I'm warning yer nah, I don't need any poxy hang-ups. There's still a lot to do; you fuck up once, and yer out… understand?!'

'I get the SP, Ricky. I just want to be there, know what I mean?'

Meanwhile, the gorilla busied himself with drinks, as the two got their heads together.

Peters was laying it on the line. 'This is where it all starts to get hard, Rossi. Up to nah, we've had it on a plate, and bloody gift wrapped with it. In the past, we created an understanding backed up with muscle, and it worked. Okay, so you get

161

aggravation once in a while, but you kick a dog nah and again, and it does what it's told… right? Not only that, the firm as a whole needs to believe in us; if we put a foot wrong, they'll be over us like a bleedin' rash. So we tread carefully from nah on.' Peters continued to state his case in no uncertain terms. 'The last thing we want is old bill involvement.'

'Yeah, same as that! By the way, how did you come by this latest hit?' Rossi enquired.

'Funnily enough, it was handed from one of Winters' firm. I just happened to have been earwigging at the right moment. The guy happened to mention a restaurant that'd only been in business for a few months, so I made a few enquiries of my own.'

'Any downside?'

'Nah, wouldn't have thought so, except to say the owner hasn't been approached for protection yet. So we're going in blind, plus we've gotta funk Winters ain't already made a move in that direction.'

By now, the Traveller was beginning to feel out of the conversation, and motioned towards his empty Coke can.

'Gotta thirst, then, mate?' Peters asked him. Rummaging in his pocket, he produced some loose change. ''Ere, it's yer birthday, Traveller.' And promptly handed the shrapnel over.

The gorilla gave him what he took to be a smile of thanks. Rossetti likened it to his worst nightmare. Turning to Peters, they continued where they had left off.

'This restaurant, Ricky, what part of town is it located in?'

'It's a refurbished gaff takeaway at the bottom of Marine Walk.'

'That's in the heart of 'Balti land', ain't it? From what I can remember,' Rossetti stated.

'You seem pretty sure of yerself, Rossi.'

'Yeah, I am! And with good reason. When yer happened to

mention the old bill previously, I remembered that the central police station is only two streets away.'

'Exactly! That's why we can't afford to fuck up.'

'Right! So what's the set-up?'

The untimely arrival of the Traveller interrupted their banter, as he placed a fresh round of drinks on the table. For once it seemed the gorilla had got it right: a respite was on the cards. Since entering the pub, a lot of verbal had gone down; now wasn't the time to get it wrong. Rossetti's scotch tasted like Champagne, on a par with what SP had emerged. But he drew the line at disclosing his body language, as far as the Traveller was concerned. Sipping at his brandy, Peters motioned them both forwards, lowering his voice, as he spoke.

'I've decided that we go for it Saturday night, about 11.30. They've got a licence up to midnight, so I can't see it being that busy. Last orders for a meal is about eleven o'clock.'

'Surely we can't just walk in and take the gaff over, can we? We'll get bleedin' mullered!' emphasized Rossetti, with arms raised high.

Peters was quick to quash any doubts in his mind, and fired back, 'Asians are no different from anybody else, when it comes down to money. Don't yer think I know that?'

Sensing a needle creeping in, Rossetti backed off. Peters continued where he'd left off.

'That's why we do it nice and private, Rossi.'

'Sorry, but you've lost me, Ricky.'

Peters shook his head, and swigged his brandy again. 'This is how it goes, so listen and learn. There's an access slip road at the bottom end of Marine Street, which takes yer to a private block of garages, situated at the rear of the restaurant.'

At this, Rossetti's face lit up. 'I'm beginning to like this, Ricky.'

'Yeah, but that ain't all, that's only half of it yet. At the far end of the block there's a service path, which leads directly to a door. This doubles up as an emergency fire exit to the restaurant. Behind that door is a small room partly used for storage. It's bloody dark as well, which will be in our favour. So we can afford to offload the wheels at the far end somewhere. Nobody will ever know that we're there. Nah this is important: at precisely 11.25 you and the Traveller make for the door after dropping me off.'

'Drop you off? I don't get it, Ricky!'

Peters forced a smile. 'I'm doing it the easy way: I'm going in from the front. As soon as I'm inside, I ask to see the manager, I convince him that I'm old bill, plain clothes, of course, and yes, Rossi... I'll be carrying a bent warrant card.'

'Yer a bit short for old bill, ain't yer, Ricky?'

'Maybe, but I've got a fucking big mouth to make up for it. The guy won't know what day it is. Anyway, I'll shoot him a story like we've had a report about a possible break-in at the back of the restaurant. I simply get him to open the bloody door, and bingo, youse two walk in; that's when I tell the manager his fortune. Depending on how he reacts, I can either make him an offer or we go for broke, as a one-off.'

'He's bound to kick up, then what?'

'If he's stupid enough to do that, then it's all down to persuasion.' Raising his hand, he pulled back his jacket top, exposing the butt end of a revolver strapped to his body.

Rossetti swallowed hard, and wiped his brow before replying in a shallow tone. 'Christ! Ricky, you don't fuck about, do yer?'

Peters was unrepentant. 'Yer never know when it's on yer, Rossi. Take it from me, the minute I get the shooter out, the geezer will be only too pleased to cook us a five-course meal!'

'Please God yer right, Ricky.'

The Traveller caught his eye as he spoke and evoked a sickly grin.

'Reckon he likes you and the idea, Rossi,' said Peters.

'Blimey, I wouldn't want to argue with that! By the way, is the shooter loaded?'

Peters just smiled and refused to comment. They remained at the Rat and Trap for another hour, backtracking their game plan; it was crucial they get it right. Saturday was still two days away, but there was still some groundwork that required checking out. It was agreed that Winters' possible claim regarding their private hit would be left in the hands of Rossetti, as he was better placed within the firm to have access to any leaks without unsettling anybody. Peters' role consisted of checking out the side of the restaurant for alarm systems, etc. In the event the hit went sour, on parting company, Peters suggested that they keep a wide berth until midday Saturday, when he would contact, Rossetti at his flat. He knew too much to disagree, and readily sanctioned the idea.

After hailing a cab, Rossetti asked to be dropped off at the Miami Club via the bookies. He had a winning ticket to cash in. There was a private card school going down at the club, and he wanted in. At least he had his stake money, so he had nothing to lose. Couple of minutes after getting in the cab, a deep tiredness crept over him. The subconscious is an unknown factor, although Rossetti's, by default, was more sensitive than most, as it took a grip on his twisted mind.

The vision of an extended ladder filled his mind, growing in stature as it swept over his body like a tsunami. The top rung seemed to have a mind all of its own. It appeared to be calling his name, over and over again. Lifting his head upwards, he tried to respond. It was never going to happen. The vision as a whole began to fade, yet his conscious wouldn't let go as yet. Strangely enough, although his eyes were shut, in his mind they were wide open, as he strained to forge a link with the ladder. Like a dimmer switch, the light in his head faded and then glowed brightly, as he heard a demanding voice yet again, repeatedly calling him from the top rung. He could just make out the image of a figure climbing upwards. For some unknown reason, it stopped halfway even though the legs continued to keep going. A voice in the background began screaming at him to get higher; suddenly, the image started to slip backwards. Faster and faster went the legs; the situation remained hopeless.

Without warning, the rungs supporting the feet appeared to shatter out of sight. For a brief second, the figure hung in space, as if suspended like a puppet. In desperation, arms fully extended, the image reached upwards once again. The urging voice rose to a crescendo, as the bottom half of the ladder disappeared into oblivion. An eerie silence followed. Through the haze, he could just make out a pair of hands, feverishly grasping out for the security of a rung. At the same time, the tones from a partisan voice shattered his nightmare.

'Wakey! Wakey. You alright, guv?'

'I made it, you know!'

'I expect you did, in your dreams. You had me worried for a minute, you and yer poxy ladder!'

By now, Rossetti's demeanour had gone full circle. Shaking his head, he exclaimed, 'Shit! Where the hell am I?'

'The Miami Club, guv, that's what yer asked for.'

'Damn! I must have dozed off.'

'Yeah, you could say that!'

'Stupid, I know. But did I mention anything?' His obvious concern lay with the upcoming hit.

'No!' the cabbie replied emphatically.

'Good! How much do I owe yer? Ah forget it, here's a tenner; keep the change.'

'Cheers, guv, by the way, I reckon yer made it after all.'

Rossetti scratched his head, muttered something inaudible and got out. Ten minutes later found him heavily involved in a card game he could have done without. A couple of hours later, disillusioned and pissed off, he left to go back to his flat.

Twenty-four hours had elapsed since his vision had taken him over. But it still remained firmly imprinted on his mind. Time and time again, it had tirelessly reappeared in his subconscious to haunt him. Least of all when he didn't need it, Saturday being no exception. The timely interruption from his mobile kicking off offered some relief to his addled sanity. Instinctively, he knew it had to be Peters at the other end. In the event, he was right. The message itself was brief.

'Yeah! It's on for tonight. I'll pick you up at 10.45, and one other thing: keep off the poxy scotch!' was all he said. Time left to kill left Rossetti with plenty to dwell on, but staying indoors wasn't even an option.

'I'd have more going for me if I was bleedin' well banged up,' he muttered to himself. Grabbing his coat, he decided that a few frames of snooker might be a means to some sort of normality.

CHAPTER 17

A BAD ARRANGEMENT

Ronnie had known about it for the last hour or so, and he hadn't stopped dwelling on it since. Sitting at the kitchen table having a cup of tea, he couldn't contain himself any longer.

'You sure yer doing the right thing, Mickey? I mean, Docklands of all places. I thought we'd both agreed to give it the elbow, until things had died down a bit.'

'I hear what you say, Ronnie, and believe me I know you mean well, but I can't help circumstances. My girl doesn't live over there out of choice. Not only that, she's been raving about this curry house that opened up recently. By all accounts, it's supposed to be the business! I'm really looking forward to it.'

'I realize I can't make yer change yer mind, mate, but watch yer back. That little asshole Rossetti has got a nasty habit of showing up when he ain't wanted, know what I mean?'

Later on, Mickey was in the shower when he was distracted by Ronnie shouting, 'Get yer finger out, mate, it's nearly eight o'clock.'

The bathroom opened, and a bedraggled Mickey appeared. 'God! Is that the time already? Blimey, Joan has booked a table and I can't be late. Do me a favour, mate, as soon as I leave, give her a bell, and let her know I'm on me way over… thanks. It'll stop her worrying.'

'Bleedin' good job yer jabs are quicker than the time yer take to get ready! Go on, oppit, and have a good time.'

Mickey didn't need telling twice. 'I'm out of 'ere… see you later.'

Closing the door behind him, Ronnie smiled to himself, and proceeded to turn the hand of the clock back twenty minutes. Still chuckling to himself, he buried his weight in the comfort of his armchair. Less than five minutes later, his early morning start at the market caught up with him, and he soon dozed off.

Elsewhere, Mickey Gibbons hung onto the doorbell. In no time at all, his girlfriend, Joan, opened up.

'Sorry I'm late, did Ronnie phone to let you know I was running late?'

Joan was quick to reassure him. 'Phone call?' she queried. 'I've had no call, and who said you're late? If anything, you're early.'

It took a few minutes for the penny to drop. 'Bloody Ronnie, he's done it again; that's the second time I've stood for that one, he's done me up like a kipper!'

They were both still laughing about it when they departed her flat. Saturday night and Canal Street was heaving; parking, they feared, could be a problem for punters and holiday people alike. Nearing the end of China town, Joan suggested a 24/7 supermarket to ease their parking problem, although it would have meant a further ten-minute walk back to Balti land. Eventually, they arrived outside the curry house.

'You sure this is the place, Joan? Looks a bit upmarket to me.' Mickey decided to air his views, but Joan got straight to the heart of the matter.

'Well, it's fairly obvious to me they've spent a lot of money refurbishing the place. I do know that the food they serve up comes highly recommended. Incidentally, the table's in your name.'

'Good enough for me, Joan, let's do it!'

Once inside, they made themselves known, and settled in for a pleasant evening… or so they thought!

CHAPTER 18

THE HEIST

Rossetti was on an all-time high. Just for once in his torrid life it seemed as if he'd become the flavour of the month! Having bought himself in on a private card school, the afternoon now belonged to him. Every single card he played appeared to have the Midas touch, and the company he'd cleaned out were glad to see the back of him. That did more for his temperamental ego than the large wedge he'd accumulated. Any hidden doubts were swept to one side, as he reflected on the good times to come. On leaving the Miami Club, he grabbed a bite to eat, and shortly after made for his flat. He had an hour left to come down before Peters' arrival. Washed and changed, he glanced at his watch, nodding to confirm his preparation schedule. According to his timing, he had six minutes of freedom left, before he was back on the street once again.

'Think I'll have a scotch while I'm waiting,' he convinced himself. The size of his newly found wedge strewn across the table seemed to have given him a personal licence to win, as he carried his thoughts forwards. *Another decent wedge again tonight, and I'll have the best little earner this side of Docklands,* he thought. The 'win some, lose some' syndrome didn't figure in his makeup. After downing his scotch in one, he let himself out of his flat. The cool evening air felt good as it washed over his skin, making him feel alive. The Rossetti of old was dead! Long live the king! They don't have their problems, do

171

they? What did he know anyway? Get today over; tomorrow's another day. His self-indulgent meandering came to an abrupt halt as Peters came into view. Rossetti felt instantly drawn to the car, as if it were a magnet. A bitch on heat in comparison would have come a close second.

Peters acknowledged him, and eased himself over in the passenger's seat to let him in. 'Yer looking like you've had it off, Rossi,' he stated. It was a personal observation, well noted. Although, the smugness Rossetti had given out had inadvertently set a seal of confidence allowing him to milk the moment. Calmly, he placed the lever into drive and released the handbrake. They were on their way. Briefly, an awkward silence followed.

Glancing across at Peters, he stated confidently, 'I only back winners, Ricky… and tonight, I'm feeling bleedin' lucky!'

'Full of it, ain't yer?' Peters fired back. 'But there's nothing wrong with that!' However, Peters still felt slightly uncomfortable with Rossetti's newly induced persona. A judgment or on the spot decision that needed to be made came via your head and not on the strength of somebody backing a few alleged winners. *I only hope he knows what he's in for, if it all goes fucking pear-shaped!* he told himself.

For the time being, personalities were put on hold, as he gave Rossetti some directions.

'In case yer forgot, Rossi, we're heading for Marine Terrace. It's a no-entry from Canal Street, so you'll have to double back, and cut through Seaman's Grove at the bottom end.

Rossetti soon allayed his doubts. 'Don't worry, Ricky, I'm on the case. By the way, who are the victims?'

'Outsiders! A consortium from out of town; the lease is on a franchise basis. The guy up front is a Rushjak Patel.'

'Well, Mr Smith!' Rossetti stated sarcastically. 'Let's

hope you've taken a nice few quid tonight,' and booted the accelerator.

'Let's get to the gaff first, Rossi, and slow down a bit, will yer? It ain't a fucking race.'

On entering Marine Terrace, Peters pointed out the access slip road leading up to the rear of the restaurant.

'Drive to the end of the forecourt and do a U-turn, Rossi; I want the nose facing the bloody exit. Oh, one other thing: dim yer lights and don't slam the poxy door when yer get out.'

The Traveller leaned forwards, and placed one hand on Rossetti's shoulder, squeezing it slightly.

'Yeah, I get the bleedin' message, Ricky. Just tell the gorilla to back off, will yer!'

Abandoning the car, they furtively made their way up the service path, serving the shops to the rear of Marine Terrace. Litter lay everywhere, and any light that prevailed was deeply overshadowed by the surrounding buildings. The Traveller encountered a refuse sack that had taken root, causing him to stumble. A torrent of Bungarian abuse followed, as he righted himself.

'For Christ's sake, keep the bloody noise down,' Peters hissed. A few yards on he stopped, and allowed his eyes to adjust to the odd pockets of light escaping through the ventilation grille, in situ in the emergency-cum-service door. Running his eyes carefully over the door, he checked to see which side the hinges were hung. The Traveller could be excused, but not Rossetti. If it were left to him, they'd probably wind up with a mouthful of metal, merely by standing in the path of the door, as it opened in their faces. 'Right! Check yer watch, Rossi. I make it 11.20.'

'Same as that!'

'Okay, you know the SP, wait 'ere until the door opens, and keep shtum. Like I said, I'm going in through the front. I'll give Patel a story, and funk he swallows it. The bent warrant card I've got ought to convince him. If and when he opens up, play the old bill routine till yer get inside. But don't shut the bleedin' door. Oh, and in case you've forgotten, don't stand to the right of the door, otherwise you'll wind up with a fucking headache when it opens, okay? Give me ten minutes when I leave yer for me to convince Patel I'm kosher. If the door doesn't open, then do a runner, and we'll meet back at yours.' Turning to the gorilla, he grinned before continuing. 'By the way, you've got a night off tonight, mate.'

Sighing, or something similar, the gorilla cocked his blitzed head to one side.

'Wotcha mean by that, Ricky?' demanded Rossetti, who began to look concerned.

'He knows what I mean, Rossi. Simple really, nobody gets mullered tonight!' A genuine sigh of relief followed, as Peters left them to their own designs. Once again, Rossetti checked his watch, as the gorilla stood by the door, making sweeping movements with his massive arms.

Thick bastard! he thought to himself. 'Don't worry, Traveller, I'll sort it.' After he grunted, Rossetti pointed him in the right direction.

For his part, Peters was glad to see some decent light at last. The scene in the street was another league. Everywhere he looked, people thronged the pavements like ants on a mission. Their presence would became his salvation.

'Soon lose myself in this crowd if I have to do a runner,' he told himself. Clearing his throat, and steeling himself, he entered the restaurant. The interior, he quickly noted, consisted of cubicle compartments for customer privacy. He could also make out a small drinks bar, which was positioned at the far end of the room. For the time of the night, the pace appeared to be busy, judging by the flow of waiters. With a purposeful air, Peters approached the bar, while at the same time absorbing as much of the interior layout as possible. His keen sense of observation picked up on an open passageway to the left of the bar. The ladies' and gents' toilets were situated to the right of the bar, and one 'Staff Only' door could be seen clearly marked. He imagined this would lead to the manager's office, and the fire door to the rear of the restaurant, where Rossetti and the Traveller were waiting. For once, his chain of reasoning appeared to be flawed into thinking that the fire door was an independent entity. What he couldn't have known was that it linked up with a rest room, which lay behind the 'Staff Only' door.

A member of the staff then approached him, as he got as far as the bar.

'You wish to pay your bill, sir, or a drink maybe?' he asked.

Peters deftly brushed his enquiry to one side. 'Oh, no! I'd like to speak to the manager, Mr Patel, and it's urgent.'

The waiter studied him briefly, with raised eyebrows. He seemed to be somewhat bemused by Peters' brusque manner. 'Who shall I say—?'

'The police! Local constabulary, by the way, I'm DC Wellar.' Producing the bent warrant card from his pocket, he waved it in front of the waiter's face. It was good enough to convince him that Peters meant business.

'I'm on my way, sir.' Turning on his heel, he flew.

It seemed like a minute or two, but Peters appeared to be showing signs of agitation. *Christ's sake! Where's the guy gone to, fucking Bombay?!* Patience wasn't exactly his forte. When the waiter finally appeared, he had an accomplice with him. The penguin suit and carnation buttonhole gave an instant clue as to his standing.

Obviously the manager, Peters swiftly deduced, and elected to make the first move, as the minutes were slowly draining away. 'Mr Patel, I believe, sir? I'm DC Wellar.' Once again he flaunted the warrant card, and hastily returned it to his pocket. 'I'm sorry to have to trouble you, sir, it's purely a routine enquiry. But we've been alerted by a phone call suggesting that you may have an intruder to the rear of the property. With your permission, I'd like to check it out, sir.' Peters was in full verbal flight by now, leaving Patel unable to say a word, as he continued his routine. 'We're aware there has been a spate of burglaries in the vicinity over the last couple of weeks, that's why we're forced to follow any likely leads that may arise, even if it means checking your fire door for security's sake.'

Peters had gone for the jugular with his last request. Patel never stood a chance, leaving Peters to reel him in like a wriggling fish. Consternation was written all over his face. Turning to a nearby waiter, he spoke rapidly to him in Indian, and hastily dismissed him.

'Please, to follow me, sir, if you will.' Beckoning, he stepped out from behind the bar. Peters didn't need to be asked twice. Together, they made their way to the rear of the building, via the two-way door. On passing the office, Peters paused, as he spotted a door to his left.

Wonder where that leads to? he asked himself. The answer to that particular question would come from another situation later on. Having made their way through to the storeroom, Peters glanced at his watch, and allowed himself a tentative smile. Up until now, the whole charade had taken only seven minutes. Momentarily, his thoughts were interrupted by the manager, Patel.

'This is the only access door to the rear of the building,' he explained.

Peters bit his tongue, but the pain it caused didn't stop his inner frustration. *I already know that! Just open the fucking door, will yer, you asshole!* he told himself. It just wasn't happening. Peters immediately imposed an authoritative approach.

'If you don't mind, sir, I need to know if the security door is fully operative.' Patel seemed reluctant to make a move, possibly for reasons of his own. Time and patience were running out fast for Peters. So he quickly decided to take matters into his own hands. Turning the key already in the door, he forced the locking bar upwards, at the same time causing it to fly open. Things had moved a bit too quick for Patel, and the need to keep him sweet still remained vital. Peters quickly reassured him of his intentions. 'Just a precaution, sir, although I will need to check with my two colleagues waiting outside.'

From out of the gloom, Rossetti and the Traveller appeared. 'Anything to report, Summers?' Peters asked Rossetti, and winked.

'Looks like it could be a false alarm to me,' he replied casually.

'Good. If that's the case, you'd both better come inside, and we can all leave by the front door, if you don't mind, sir?'

With the Traveller lurking in the background, it wasn't even an option. Patel realized he was outnumbered, and his choice seemed to have been already made up for him. Once they were all inside, the Traveller pulled the door to, careful not to close it, as Peters ushered Patel into his office on a pretence of examining his fire certificate. Later, Patel would wish he'd never got out of his bed that morning.

As soon as the office door was closed, time was of the essence. The last thing they needed would be from a nosey member of staff creating problems. Acting quickly, the Traveller grabbed Patel from behind, and picked him up like a ragdoll, using one hand to smother his face.

'Right! Stick him in the chair, Traveller, while I tell him his bloody fortune!' Peters was getting busy. Up to now the firm had won an Oscar between them. But the night was yet young. From out of his pocket, Peters produced a pre-written statement on a piece of prepared paper, which he readily thrust in front of Patel's face.

It read as follows: 'Do as you're told and nobody gets hurt. You get on the intercom to the bar. Whoever answers, you tell them you're not to be disturbed for an hour or so. Nod if you understand.'

In a split second, Patel's world had been forced upside down. His mind couldn't begin to cope with the situation. Sheer terror filled his eyes, as he vainly tried to make some sense of the written demand forced upon him. By now, he was struggling to get breath into his lungs.

'Ease off, Traveller, I reckon he's got the bleedin' message.'

The gorilla moved his hand away from Patel's mouth, causing it to drop in total anguish.

'I take it that's a yes?' prompted Peters in a decisive tone.

Any form of resistance remained futile. Justly so, Patel intended walking away from the situation thrust upon him with a clean bill of health. After all was said and done, he was only the manager. As far as he was concerned, the intruders could have what they wanted. Having said that, he did have one last trump card he could fall back on, should he need to use it. It consisted of a push button alarm set in the underside of his office desk. In time, it would be invaluable, but at the moment, common sense would remain a way to a means. Peters, meanwhile, continued to interrogate him.

'Nah, yer not that stupid to know that we're not just 'ere for the bleedin' curry!' Peters was getting busy, and Patel was pissing him off by not moving from his chair. 'I reckon the asshole wants some encouragement, Rossi. Shall we give him some?'

It wasn't his intention to be un co-operative, but fear itself had left him legless and rooted to the chair. It was left to the Traveller to make his mind up for him. Ambling across to the office desk, he picked it up bodily, and placed it in front of Patel. Rossi, meanwhile, was busy ripping out the leads connected to the outside phone lines.

Peters found the receiver to the intercom on the desk top, and gave Patel a threatening leer. 'Just make the call, sunshine, and talk in English, right? Then we talk some business together!'

With hands shaking, Patel duly obliged by making the connection to the restaurant bar.

'That wasn't hard, was it nah? So where's the keys to the safe? And move it!'

From out of one of the drawers, he produced a ring containing various sets of keys.

'Good! Nah open it. Give him a hand, Rossi, yer know what to look for.'

Patel's head had by now cleared enough to know that the alarm button was indeed an option. At the last moment, he reneged, knowing that twenty stone of gorilla was watching his every move.

Rossetti, being what he was, had inadvertently overlooked the lead to the intercom, now made barely visible by the Traveller having removed his desk. But for Patel, getting himself into a position whereby he could operate it was never going to be easy. Rossetti thought it was his birthday as he removed three well-stocked money pouches and a quantity of loose wads from out of the safe.

'Don't bother counting it, Rossi, it looks like a bleedin' Van Gogh from 'ere. Not bad for a night's work, eh?'

★

Back in the restaurant, a young couple were discussing the events of the evening over coffee. Their body language spoke volumes, as their intimate conversation rang out with intermittent laughter. Clearly, it would become a night they would both remember in time to come, and for more reasons than one! Breaking off, the young man made his excuses to leave, and headed off to find the toilets.

★

Meanwhile, back in the manager's office, Peters made a hasty decision by deciding the heist would end as a one-off hit. Managers come and go; consequently, he didn't relish the thought of spending the next months breaking them in. The heist itself had resulted in being a nice little earner, and he quickly put Rossetti in the picture.

'You're the guvnor, Ricky, suits me fine, but what we gonna do with him?' He pointed at Patel.

'Tell yer what, use some of that phone lead to tie him to the chair; that should keep him quiet for five minutes. The Traveller and me are on our toes, so give me the keys to the wheels, and I'll have it running... be quick about it.'

The pair disappeared, leaving Rossetti to secure Patel. It wasn't necessary, but he stuffed a hanky inside of his mouth, just for the craic. Standing back, he said, 'I never did like fucking curry anyway!'

His remark sensed a spark of being in Patel's brain, tipping him over the edge into reality. Raising one leg, he located the alarm button, and booted it with all his power. Rossetti found himself instantly rooted to the spot, as the bell kicked in.

Back in the restaurant, the young man had left the toilet and drew level with the staff room door. It was slightly ajar, and he picked up on the ominous wail of the alarm sounding off. The memorable moments that had once made his evening complete vanished from out of sight as his body took on a fresh slant. Pushing the door to one side, the noise grew ever louder as he entered the staff room. He could see another main door on the back wall of the building, with a sign that read 'Fire Exit'. Approaching the door, he could hear what he thought were raised voices above the alarm. Throwing open the door, he found himself in a passageway. The light showing at one end convinced him that the exit door was partially open.

Without any warning, a figure appeared from the office end, running at great speed towards him. Any action on his part became noncommittal by taking the full impact as their bodies collided. He felt powerless to dictate terms and as a result found himself forcibly thrown to one side. In an attempt to stay upright, he lunged at his aggressor, and managed to claim hold of his jacket sleeve for a means of support. The sheer weight and the impetus of the two combined bodies proved too much for his own good. Almost immediately, the sleeve to the jacket came away in his hand; at the same time, the alien figure turned his head round to face him. Above the noise of the alarm, a stunned silence came over them, as they confronted each other. The hunter was now on his knees, and the hunted remained standing over him, minus his sleeve. With mouths agape, they continued to stare at each other in total disbelief, while dumbstruck. As if in unison, their singular brains turned full circle, systematically arriving at reality. Like an action replay, the young man on the floor slowly pressed home his claim.

'Rossetti!?'

His assailant fired back simultaneously, 'Gibbons!?'

That was the last he heard or saw, as a well-directed brogue shoe met flesh and bone. It smashed into the side of his head with sickening speed. The force imploded inside of Gibbons' skull creating an immediate paralysis to his arms and legs. Millions of tiny lights flickered and glowed in a blanket of pain and combined nausea, before finally dying away. A surge of darkness overtook his useless frame, causing him to slump backwards into a heap. He was unconscious long before the floor rose up to meet him.

'What the fuck kept yer, Rossi?' Waiting outside, Peters was desperate to leave.

'You ain't gonna believe who I've just tangled with!'

'No! Try me?'

'It can wait. Let's get the fuck out of 'ere.'

Peters booted the pedal. In no time at all, the mayhem they had caused was history. As they reached the Canal Street junction, two squad cars and an ambulance were pulling up outside of the restaurant. Nothing strange about that, you might say, just another consequence arising from a night out in Docklands!

CHAPTER 19

THE AFTERMATH

An hour later following the restaurant incident, two frustrated cops were having a hard time in gaining access to a particular flat, the other side of town. For the third time, the elder of the two rang the doorbell and waited for a response. It wasn't forthcoming. Shrugging his shoulders, he turned to his colleague for support.

'I just don't get it! I can see a light on in the lounge; somebody has to be in there.' How was he to know that the light had been left on for Mickey Gibbons' convenience?

'Could be he's out the back,' suggested the younger of the two.

'I wouldn't have thought so, it's a bit late.'

'Give it one more go, we've got nothing to lose.' He was determined to get a result.

What they didn't know was that Ronnie Callaghan was a hard nut to crack. There were three things he excelled at: selling flowers, training fighters and sleeping. Unfortunately, the latter had begun to run its course. Sleepy eyes flickered open in protest. Groaning, he moved his head, which was set at an awkward angle. He rubbed the affected part to relieve the tension, when the clock on the wall caught his eye.

'God almighty! I can't believe I've been out that long.' The constant droll of the doorbell finally brought him back into the land of the living. 'What the hell is going down?' he exclaimed loudly. Struggling to his feet, he peered through his side curtain. The shadow from two figures became apparent. Slowly his eyesight began to adjust. 'Can't be Mickey,' he mused. 'He's got his own key.'

By now, his mind was racing, as the incessant ringing ceased. Through the glass-panelled door, the two coppers appeared to be larger and threatening. It was almost as if circumstances were trying to tell him something. In a split second, any coincidences were dismissed as the obvious solution hit him.

Raising a clenched fist to his mouth, he bit hard down on his knuckles. 'Mickey! Mickey!' he moaned. 'Please God, no!' As if in a trance, he turned his attention to the door, and opened it slightly.

'Mr Ronnie Callaghan?' said one of the cops, and waved a warrant card at him.

'Yeah! Yeah, that's me, how can I help yer?'

'Sorry to trouble you at this hour, sir, but we need to talk. Can we come in?'

Ronnie ushered the pair through to the lounge. Turning round, he confronted them before they could speak.

'It's about Mickey, isn't it? He's in some sort of bother.'

The two cops looked at each other, as if slightly mystified. The elder of the two then took the initiative. 'I'm sorry to have to inform you, but Mr Gibbons has been involved in a robbery over at Docklands. We have good reason to believe he lodges here.'

'Yeah, I can certainly verify that! But a robbery? You gotta be joking, the kid's straighter than a bleedin' Roman road!'

'What I'm trying to say, sir, is that there's been an accident. I think you'd better sit down, and I'll fill you in with the details.'

At this point, Ronnie was struggling to take it all in. It

was 1.30 in the morning, and with a brain registering zero, it was fast becoming his worst nightmare. 'I blame myself... I warned Mickey that if—' Stopping short suddenly, Ronnie took a verbal step back. His outburst could be taken as a disclosure regarding certain facts surrounding Terry Winters. The last thing he needed right now would be a question and answer time. Whatever his grievances were with Winters, it was crucial he kept them under wraps, at least for the time being.

The officer was quick to pick up on Ronnie's omission of self-guilt. 'Nobody's blaming you, sir, it's a question of wrong time, wrong place.' Having put his case in perspective, he continued with his previous line of enquiry. 'I have to tell you, sir, that Mr Gibbons has been transferred to Stonewater General, as a result from a confrontation that occurred in a restaurant. From what we understand, it would appear he suffered a head injury. The hospital intend keeping him in for observation, it seems, for an indefinite period. I'd like to add that we can only presume at this stage that his involvement came about through no fault of his own. This was later verified by the manager.'

'How bad is Mickey? I need to get over there.' Clearly Ronnie wasn't thinking rationally. But who could blame him for that?! When grief looms and yer own are in trouble, it goes deep and starts to get personal.

The officer had already read his mind. 'If I was you, sir, I'd get a good night's sleep, and make your way over there tomorrow morning. As things stand, he's not in any immediate danger, from what I can gather. He owes his wellbeing to his obvious fitness. His girlfriend happened to mention some sort of tie-up with the fight game.'

Straight talking had now taken its toll on Ronnie's demeanour. His shoulders eased through lack of tension;

outwardly he appeared to be calm. Facing the two officers, he thanked them for their role in dealing with the situation. Standing at the front door, he lingered until they had pulled away, before finally closing the door and locking it. He paused at the foot of the stairs, as a delayed surge of anger rose up inside of him. He gazed upwards; the top riser seemed to be a million miles away. His head began to spin in a semi-controlled state.

Diligently, he forced his weary limbs upwards, each step becoming a reminder of what lay ahead. Set alarm… phone Siddie… contact hospital… arrange visit. There was no point continuing; he'd run out of steps. With so much shit circulating in his head, he literally fell into bed mentally drained.

★

It was just after 5.30 am the following morning. Siddie Levy hadn't even finished dressing, when his landline unexpectedly sprang into life.

'Rachael! Rachael… phone, I'm not dressed yet!'

Somewhere, a voice replied in a similar vein. 'I'm in the toilet already.'

'Get off your fat tukhus and answer it. It has to be important!'

Moments later, muttering away to herself in Yiddish, Rachael made her way downstairs and snatched at the receiver. 'Do you know what hour this is?'

A small silence prevailed. Her cold manner went clean over Ronnie's head. 'I hear what yer say, Rachael, it's necessary—'

'Ronnie!' She cut him off in an instant, as his voice became apparent.

'I thought it was miscall. Is there something wrong you should phone me at this hour?'

'Bear with me, Rachael. Life could be better, but I don't have the time to explain right now, although it's paramount I talk to Siddie. Can you arrange a meet say for 8 o'clock in Toni's this morning? That way, I'll give him the full SP. In the meantime, I've some stock arriving; could he sort it out with Granite? Give him my keys to the lockup... thanks, Rachael.'

Always the actress, she went to pieces. 'Oy vey! These problems, I should need this grief.'

By now, Siddie was dressed and standing at arm's length away as she spoke.

'Is there anything I can say or do that would help?'

'Nothing, Rachael, nothing at all. Except to say don't over worry yerself... right? I'll be in touch... be lucky... bye.'

The line went dead. She was still holding the receiver a minute after Ronnie had hung up.

'Rachael, you okay? You look as if you've seen a ghost already. Who the hell was it anyway?' After taking the receiver from her, he replaced it on the handset.

She turned to face him, hands aloft. 'Ronnie! It was Ronnie!' Settling herself down on the tread of the stairs, she began babbling away to herself in Yiddish.

'I don't like the sound of it, Rachael, give me a story, any story.' She shook her head in despair. Apart from the message and the meet, there was no other indication as to the problem. It was finally left to Ronnie's track record and Siddie's awareness to corroborate a story. Half an hour later, and a mind full of consternation, Siddie made his way to the market. His journey, habitual as ever, seemed to take that much longer than usual, but then he did have a lot on his mind.

★

Priority was Ronnie's unforeseen dilemma; his gut instinct kept pulling him down a one-way avenue, and Winters was at the other end. *Please God, I'm wrong*, he told himself. *But whatever is going down, I swear it ain't kosher!*

On entering Toni de Angelo's, Ronnie produced a £5 note, and offered it Siddie's way. It was quickly waved to one side. He remained adamant.

'No, I'll sort it, grab a table.' Placing the coffees on the table, Siddie sat down, and begun to rub his hands together in a fetish manner. Selling and listening he was good at! At the moment, he demanded a hearing, and looked to Ronnie for guidance.

'Right! Where to start?' asked Ronnie wistfully.

'At the beginning is as good a place as any, mate.'

Stern-faced, Ronnie related the facts as they stood. Meantime, Siddie's face remained impassive, knowing that his turn would come later. Pausing now and then to sip his coffee, Ronnie concluded by stating that Mickey's condition was in no way life threatening and he would be contacting the hospital later on that morning.

'I should have been a rich man,' Siddie erupted. 'Already I'm a fortune teller!' It was just his way of saying, 'I told yer so.' Although this time he broke with tradition, as his voice took on a ring of sympathy. 'How could anybody be that unlucky? I feel for the kid. One minute sanity… and the next, who knows? Please God, the kid got through it. A head injury, you say? That's not good at any time. You can't blame yerself, my friend. Nobody can control fate… luck, maybe. This has to be an omen; from now on, Docklands is history. I truly felt there had to be an element of Winters, judging by yer call this morning.'

'Strange you should say that!'

'Go on.'

'Well, the last thing I said to Mickey as he walked out of the door was a word to the wise concerning Rossetti.'

'Huh, I've said it before. The guy's a schmuck! People like him just don't go away. You can almost imagine the possibility of a link to Mickey's injury.' Siddie could never have known that he was stating the obvious.

They left it that Ronnie would contact him within the hour. Half an hour later, Ronnie's prediction had turned full circle, as Siddie's mobile went off.

'Hi, it's Ronnie.'

'What news?'

'Some good, some bad.'

'I'll settle for the good already.'

'Thankfully, Mickey is out of danger, as it goes. Apparently he took a right kicking to the side of his head, so they're keeping him in for observation. At least for a couple of days. As for the bad, it would take too long on the phone.'

'Listen, my friend. Come round mine tonight, and share dinner with us. We can talk in comfort... yes? Anyway, I'm sure that Rachael would love to see you again.'

Ronnie wasn't about to pass an offer like that up. 'Yeah, why not, go for it, Siddie.'

'Good! Shall we say 7.30?' They exchanged their goodbyes, leaving Siddie in an unsettled frame of mind. It was evident by his sombre mood that Ronnie's version of the events had the distinct aroma rising from a past and now present problem rearing its ugly head! Zapping his mobile off, he gazed around the market, as if to justify his own version of events. The lack of punters and a half-empty money pouch spoke volumes. 'God! What a morning. The business should be that bad!' He had to be right; there was nobody around to contest it.

★

That evening, Ronnie showed up as arranged clutching a box of chocolates, which Rachael readily accepted. In turn, she reciprocated by making a fuss of him.

'Sit yerself down, mate, she'll drive yer mad.' Siddie got him out of jail, as a touch of embarrassment crept in.

With a sigh of relief, Ronnie plonked himself down in an available armchair. The strain attached to the last twenty-four hours had finally got under his skin. He did his best to stifle a yawn, apologising profusely. 'Guess it's been one of those days, and it ain't gonna get any better either, know what I mean?'

Instantly, warning lights flashed inside of Siddie's head, making him eager to digress. 'The hospital. What happened when yer got there?'

'I'm still in the dark really, mate. It's all about tests, and more bleedin' tests.'

'At least they're on the kid's case, you were saying?'

'Where was I? Oh, yeah. Apparently internal bleeding could be a factor.'

'Did you manage to talk to Mickey?'

'Hardly, but you ain't gonna like this, it's getting to be a damn nightmare.' Ronnie began to show signs of emotion, and sighed deeply before continuing. 'Mickey only managed a few words, which I couldn't really get my head around, although I swear "Rossetti" was one of them! He did manage to slip me a note on the QT before I left the ward. The old bill were hovering around at the time, so it wasn't until I got outside that I realized the full strength of what it contained.'

After producing an envelope from his pocket, he thrust it at Siddie.

''Ere, see what you make of it.' Ronnie's breathing became intense, as Siddie revealed the contents. It took only a few seconds to digest, but the effect it had on Siddie became twofold, struggling as he did with disbelief and anger. One word... one name. It was almost tattooed onto his brain. Between gritted teeth, he managed to force the name out.

'Rossetti!'

Ronnie's reaction became rubber stamped. 'Yeah! Yer read it right, mate. Mickey ain't spoofing; he knew who was on the end of the kicking, alright. You could make a book on what that bastard's involved in. I just feel for the kid; he didn't ask for any of this shit. Of all the poxy restaurants in Balti land he could have gone to!'

'C'mon, Ronnie. You can't think that way. Sooner or later it was going to come on top. You should be so lucky it wasn't you.'

They both nodded simultaneously, as Ronnie took up a fresh stance. 'So where do we go from 'ere? Knowing what we know now, Mickey has placed Winters in the frame. So now we're talking unfinished business. I should imagine that gutless little bastard Rossetti is running around with a right little firm. There's no way he could have pulled a job like that off on his own.' Taking a deep breath, he continued to press home his claim. 'Before this all kicked off, I could live with the fact that Rossetti was always gonna be a born loser, shouting his mouth off once in a while, but this latest episode changes everything. The whole damn rotten thing moves up another league. As if that ain't enough, there's the other asshole Winters on the loose as well. You can't tell me he doesn't figure in this somewhere? The way I see it, the guy has got a foothold in some sort of a scam over in Docklands. Remember Charlie Cochrane? South London boy I mentioned. We met at Mercer's last outing in Bethnal Green.'

'Yeah, come to think of it, the name does ring a bell.'

'Well, he marked my card as far as Winters is concerned. According to Charlie, he's got more bloody past form than Shergar had, and that's saying something! It seems he's upset a few faces from up the smoke; no wonder Stonewater is convenient for him. The devious bastard has got more front than Rossetti by putting himself about on our manor.'

Siddie, unsurprisingly, appeared to take Ronnie's damning portrayal of Winters personally. But that's what friends are for. To agree when not to disagree was one bet the bookies wouldn't give you odds on, especially when it came down to their exclusive friendship.

Drumming his fingers on the table top, Ronnie attempted to level with Siddie. 'Just occurred to me: I wonder what the press boys make of it all. It's bound to get a show tomorrow; should make interesting reading. Although I can't see them knowing any more than we know. Oh, which reminds me, I must phone Joan… Mickey's girlfriend, she could hold some possible answers.'

'You say Mickey can't help yer with any more information?'

'Not yet anyway. He's far too ill. Although it looks as if the old bill ain't aware of Rossetti's involvement as yet.'

'In that case, it'll pay yer to keep shtum for the time being; wait until yer settle down before yer decide on any action. Just don't get ahead of yerself. I can well understand yer feelings, as far as that schmuck Rossetti is concerned, but your priority right now is the kid! Mickey needs a sense of security, which means you!'

'You're ever the guvnor, Siddie. I dunno what I'd do without yer.'

'All I'm trying to do is to make some sense out of this mess. What yer don't know ain't gonna hurt yer. So, as I say, don't push too hard.'

Just then Rachael appeared in the doorway, interrupting their conversation.

'For you, Ronnie, I cook your favourite. Come sit up at the table.'

Siddie shook his head and sighed. 'What is it with you, Callaghan? I don't even get this treatment.'

Any further thoughts, good or otherwise, were shelved for the time being, as food became priority.

'Rachael, that was the business.' Patting his stomach, Ronnie pushed his empty plate away and relaxed back in his chair. 'Nobody does salt beef like you; that was as kosher as it gets!'

After gathering the empty crockery together, she made for the kitchen, talking to herself as she did so.

'Schmaltz! That's all I ever get, schmaltz.'

'Was it something I said, Siddie?' For a second, Ronnie appeared concerned.

Siddie fell about laughing. 'Don't look so serious, mate. Rachael was only winding yer up.'

A more than relieved Ronnie replied, 'Women, eh? I'll never get to understand them. No bleedin' wonder I ain't married.'

Before leaving that evening, he told Siddie his intentions regarding the next couple of days. Because of Mickey's predicament, the market wasn't an option. Therefore, he intended spending time talking to Mickey at the hospital. He also thought it could prove beneficial as far as Rossetti's movements were concerned. The gym itself was in good hands, Ronnie having contacted Wally Churchill earlier in the day, along with Frankie Lyons who readily took on the trainer mantle for the time being. Tommy Russell had also been informed, so it was a case of business as usual.

Driving home from Siddie's that night, Ronnie's concentration became somewhat hazardous. One name in particular kept nagging away inside, refusing to let go. He constantly shook his head in a vain attempt to break the spell, but it remained like a malignant tumour. Slowly, it crippled what sensibility he had left; the harder he fought it, the worse his reasoning became. Unknowingly, it was beginning to reflect on his driving performance as well, which had now become nothing short of erratic. He realized he needed to take some form of action. Spotting an empty bay ahead, he slewed the wheel over and the car screeched to a halt.

Blindly, he adjusted the handbrake, and allowed his head to rest on the steering wheel. It was a vain attempt to ease the tension he felt building up to the back of his neck. Unfortunately, it wasn't working for him. On looking up, he caught the reflection of his face in the interior mirror. It was noticeable that beads of sweat had begun to form on his brow. The palms of his hands were also sticky; with a mind of their own and out of control, they slid off the wheel! Close by, a defective street lamp appeared to join in and mock his misery. The loose-fitted strip light flashed on and off to the beat off his tormented mind.

Closing his eyes to shut it out proved futile. It was almost as if his brain had become mesmerized, with no let-up in sight. His blood count rose to pound away incessantly inside his head, over and over again. Without realizing it, he'd begun to shout out in unison, desperately seeking an escapism from his dysfunctional mind, before finally exploding into a dramatic verbal climax.

'ROSSETTI! ... ROSSETTI! ... ROSSETTI! NOOOO!' Clenched fists came crashing down onto the dashboard in blind fury. Suddenly, his demons were gone. Slowly, his eyes flickered open, and the tension he invested had now melted away into obscurity. His thinking became stable, and an inner calmness prevailed. In sympathy, a wave of pure relief swept over his frame. Leaning back, he allowed himself a moment's respite to catch his breath. Shortly after, a solid mood of self-criticism began to function.

How could I let a nonce like him get to me? It all ends here! I owe it to Mickey as well as myself. As from now, I'm on yer case, Rossetti. No more backing off; in future, I'll be the one doing the chasing!

His demons, it seemed, had evaporated out of mind and out of sight. It was a rejuvenated Ronnie who continued his journey back home that night.

CHAPTER 20

CONNECTIONS

On his way over to the hospital the following morning, Ronnie stopped off to grab a morning paper. He noticed that the local rag carried the brunt of the story regarding the robbery, in contrast to the tabloids, which came as no surprise to him. The amount of money involved didn't rate as highly as the personal damage incurred by Gibbons and the manager of the restaurant alike. Casting his eye quickly down the press column, he scanned the print in the event there just might be some fresh evidence that he hadn't been party to. It was quite clear that the manager of the restaurant had been the only source of information, which in turn was of little or no use whatsoever to the local police. The only genuine lead they held was the description of one of the felons: 'A gorilla look-a-like inside a man's body!' A perplexed look crossed Ronnie's face as he read it. But, to be fair, he'd never met the Traveller, as yet!

By staying in the background, the manager was unable to provide a viable description, but when it came down to Peters, the image of the Traveller firmly planted in his mind seemed to cause a mental block. The report went on to say that the manager would possibly have to undergo counselling as a result.

'God almighty! What a bleedin' mess,' Ronnie told himself. 'I'll read the full report later.' Stuffing the paper under his arm, he crossed the road and entered the hospital. Nothing untoward had changed since yesterday, and any form of conversation was still limited to the odd single word. The intense swelling to the lower part of Mickey's face was consistent with the murderous blow delivered by Rossetti's ill-placed kick.

His face was badly bruised, and the jawbone obviously broken, which gave way to sheer frustration more than pain. For his part, Mickey appeared to hold back on the trauma he'd been subjected to, for reasons of his own. As a result, a nod one way or the other served as a means of communication. The grapes supplied by Siddie ended up on the bed next door. How was he to know that Mickey was on liquids?! Within a few minutes of Ronnie's presence on the ward, a police officer entered, and made his way across to Mickey's bedside. Recognition set in, as he approached. He soon realized that he was the same officer who had relayed the news of the robbery in the first place.

'We've met before, haven't we? Sorry about the circumstances being the way they are.' Ronnie accepted his hand of friendship, and shook it warmly.

'Nice of yer to drop by, appreciate it.'

'Least I can do. I experienced the same situation myself once, so I know what the kid's going through. Is there any improvement as yet?'

'Far too early to say, as yet. Guess it's all about time.'

The officer nodded, and continued, but this time in a serious mode. 'We'd love to get our hands on the animal responsible for this mess.'

'You and me both!' Ronnie echoed. 'Five minutes on a one-to-one basis would give me a lot of pleasure.'

The officer shrugged his shoulders in a negative manner before replying. 'You know I didn't hear that! But do know where you're coming from. Well, best be off. If and when Mickey can come up with anything, a name… description… whatever, you can always contact me on this number.' After handing Ronnie his card, he went on his way.

As pleased as he was to see Ronnie, it became obvious that Mickey was on a downer. His further reluctance to pursue any line of events led Ronnie into believing things had taken a step backwards. Naturally full of concern, it was left to the ward sister to induce him into thinking otherwise.

'It's all part of the healing process,' she explained to him. 'But I have to say, he's got this fighting quality about him, you understand?'

Ronnie completely misconstrued her statement into thinking she was talking shop. 'Yeah, the kid's got class, alright. I'm sure he'll wind up going all the way.'

The sister gave him a blank look, and walked away shaking her head.

Three days later, Gibbons was released from hospital, on the understanding he undertook light body training only after he'd been given a clean bill of health. Having said that, Ronnie needed to contact the BBBC as a matter of course, so that his medical history could be logged. For their part, the local police had made no headway with their own investigations, and to all intents and purposes, the case had died a death.

As for the criminal fraternity, crime itself had become their chosen oyster! It seemed they couldn't put a foot wrong. In more ways than one! As they had planned, so they had reaped, along with the muscle they managed to purloin from the Terry Winters regime. The robbery itself became just a stepping stone to unlimited scenes of crime and corruption. Peters' strategy had withstood the test of time. And his prize was at the helm of well-organized hit and run gangs, who were oblivious to whoever stood in their way. The fear that they generated enabled them to run riot from one end of Docklands to the other! In the space of a month, full control of the rackets came under Peters' monarchic jurisdiction. On a par, Rossetti had proved to be a formidable henchman in their relentless surge of destruction, culminating in a vast web of fear and terror.

The police, as a whole, were powerless to act. Any probe on their behalf ended at a wall of silence. The multi-ethnic society that cohabited the Docklands, as a whole, dealt with the unexpected within the realms of their personal culture. Should an outsider become a problem, they quickly formed an integrated system of solidarity, which proved invulnerable. In a moralistic world, it could work! Corruption breeds corruption, so everybody wins. Everybody, that is, except the police. But even they shared a slot on a par with Winters.

Peters' sudden and successful rise from obscurity created an enigma in Winters' side. The loss of muscle was strangling any standing that he'd nurtured within the criminal underworld. The extent of his downtrodden firm of misfits was beginning to rub off on his so-called 'reign supreme'! In no time at all, he'd become the butt of many a joke bandied around by the fraternity. 'Shortest Winter in living memory' appeared to be the most prolific. The added loss of revenue he could live with. Even crime had its bouts of recession. For his part, money was never going to be an issue. Offshore banking had taken care of that! But on a more personal level, he did have exclusive rights to an Achilles' heel that, when exploited, readily brought him to his knees... pride! It contained ninety per cent of his being, which he carried around with him 24/7.

For a token short in stature, his eternal lust for ambition had always remained on a high! Unfortunately, the chip on both of his shoulders you couldn't give away! Right now he was festering. His pride had been severely dented, and someone was going to have to pay for their intrusion. Sitting at his office desk in Slatteries, he stared long and hard at a list of names in his notepad. Breaking off briefly, he gainfully helped himself to a cigar from out of a solid gold case, and proceeded to light it, although, with some difficulty. Noticeably, his eyes had never strayed from the list of names on the pad. The level of intensity his face afforded was synonymous with revenge. Grabbing a pen, he began to doodle, as he digested the list of names. Drawing long and hard on his cigar for a minute or so, he left off and averted his gaze upwards. The gesture suggested that he'd made a decision.

Removing his cigar, he used the pen to underline three specific names, as a sinister expression crossed his face. Pausing, his face tightened; he then nodded, as if to justify his selection. Reaching inside his desk, he removed a personal address book. Running his finger down the side of the index, he stopped at the letter 'M'. Flicking the appropriate page open, he studied its contents, letter by letter, name by name! Seemingly satisfied, he closed the book reverently and replaced it back in his desk drawer. Reaching for his phone in a business-like mode, he lost no time getting through to an offshore number.

*

Winters' office door had been left ajar, so the caller didn't bother to knock before entering. Continuing to push the door wide open only confirmed his suspicions.

'Strange, he must be in the karzy,' the man muttered to himself, and placed a package down on the desk top. In doing so, his roving eye caught the attention of a used sheet of note paper, which lay by the side of the phone. It seemed to draw him in as his curiosity got the better of him. Glancing back over his shoulder, he checked to make sure he was alone.

Some of the names he noted on the list he could identify with. Three in particular screamed out for attention. The fact that they were underlined gave them credibility. In one corner, a six-digit number set aside from some scribble seemed to suggest a connection between the two. His intrigue finally got the better of him, as he swiftly jotted down the numbers on a nearby notepad.

The names themselves were never going to be a problem, when it came down to recalling them. Four weeks of manic outbursts from Winters had instilled them inside his brain. Although his allegiance lay with Winters, there's no honour amongst thieves where loyalty is concerned.

'Might do meself a bit of good 'ere. Could be onto a nice little earner, if I play it right.' Wearing a smug look, he pocketed his copy of providence, and silently left the office, making sure that he left the door as he found it. Heading for the snooker room, he whispered three names to himself, in a tone of conviction. 'Peters! ... Santini! ... Rossetti!' Smiling broadly, he disappeared into the snooker room.

CHAPTER 21

WARNING BELLS

Fumbling with his door key, Rossetti finally found a clue, and it fell inwards taking him with it! A twelve-hour sting of clubbing lay behind him. With more luck than judgment, he managed to hold his balance, as he slammed the door shut behind him. In a semi-comatose state, he made for the end of his hall. A cocktail consisting of scotch, pool and cards had become a prescription he'd written out himself! Combined, of course, with a licence to print money. His tawdry life was now one long round of self-indulgence. The last couple of weeks had seen his torrid existence turned around, akin to a rollercoaster that never seemed able to stop. Sleep had just become a word, serving a double purpose. The ladder of success was alive and sweet, and he relished in its entirety. No more for him the nightmare of a ladder destined for disaster.

'I am the fucking king! … Long live the king!'

The scotch he readily imbibed said it all, as he stood swaying in front of his mirror, venting his sick esteem. His reflection seemed to beckon to him, as he continued to sway. Fortunately, a close-by phone table checked him, as his body rolled forwards. Reaching out, his hand enabled him to make contact with the answer phone. Glancing downwards through bleary bloodshot eyes, it occurred to him that somebody had left him a message. Dazed as he was only led to his curiosity, as his enquiring digit hit play.

'Hi, Rossi, it's me… Jackie Baines… we need to talk, I'll get back to yer!' It took him a few seconds for the name to register. Slowly, it dawned on him, and what's more, the caller had hit a nerve.

'Jack fucking Baines! What's a bloody loser like him want with me?' he pondered. The fact that Baines ranked only as a gopher in Winters' regime gave him credence to cast a shadow on its relevance. Options now began to run wild inside his fuddled brain, causing him to dig deep for answers. It resulted only in his issue playing havoc with his sanity. The amount of wedge he'd managed to offload during the day couldn't even buy his body two minutes of sensibility. Finally, he broke it off. Shrugging his shoulders was his idea of dealing with the situation. He was beginning to have second thoughts.

'Can't be that important… unless…' An evil glint appeared in his eye, as his warped and sicko mind kicked in. 'Unless the little bleeder is working on Winters' behalf, saying that times are hard, could he have some of the action back.' Deleting the message, Rossetti broke into a maniacal burst of laughter. A mental picture of Winters grovelling on his knees was the only positive reaction he'd manifested all day. Two scotches later, and he was laughing, prior to passing out in his armchair.

The following morning, just after eleven o'clock, a drink-sodden Rossetti was leaving his flat when his phone rang. Hesitating, he allowed the dialling tone to expire, and the recorder to kick in.

'Shit!' he exclaimed vehemently. Grabbing the receiver off the hook meant he was cut short, as the caller reacted. Almost immediately, his body stiffened, as the now familiar voice made its plea. Déjà vu set in.

'Jack?'

'Yeah!'

'It's Rossi, what's occurring?'

'Something I picked up on, I thought you might be able to use, know what I mean?'

'So what's in it for you, then, yer little scrout?'

'Leave it out, Rossi, yer know me, I go with the bloody tide. At the moment, I've inherited the shit you used to get, the only difference being, it's better quality!'

'Yeah, is that right? I fucking feel for yer. So what's the SP?'

'I came across a list of names on a pad in Winters' office. Strangely enough, yours and two others were pencilled in.'

'So what yer saying? I ain't exactly on his bleedin' mailing list these days, yer know, so anything else?'

'Yeah, amongst some scribbling, I came across a six-digit number. I just wondered if it meant anything to yer, that's all.'

Rossetti was losing it fast. Even the scotch he'd downed was losing patience. Sobriety had been given a wakeup call.

'A number, yer say? Fucking well try me!' After grabbing a nearby pen, Rossetti listened hard and fast, jotting down each digit in turn as Baines spelt them out.

'0… 1… 5… 3… 4… 7.' Once again, Baines repeated the numbers, and finished by saying, 'I got the impression there could have been more, it just seemed to tail off, know what I mean?'

'Thanks anyway, I owe yer. If a spot comes up, I'll bell yer.' Placing the receiver down, he once again ran his eyes over the six-digit number. A look of concern began to invest in his face. He judged that there was a distinct familiarity regarding the first five. Something was obviously bothering him. His booze-sodden brain wrestled for conclusions. Moments later, a wave of coldness consumed his useless body, causing his heartbeat to increase in sympathy. Recognition had finally set in, as he realized that the first five digits held the key to the answers he desperately sought.

'Fuck's sake!' he shouted through gritted teeth. Despair racked his nerve ends, as it all became clear to him. A look of combined fear and hatred consumed his frame. There was no mistaking the sequence that the digits were set in. He knew it to be the dialling code for Jersey; that in itself had caused his demeanour to fold. But worse was to follow. Whenever there was a contract to be arranged, Winters would always fall back on that particular code plus digits. The full number itself was exclusive to him alone. But amongst the firm, it became second knowledge that there was a hitman at the end of the line!

Rossetti attempted to bolster his pathetic image with an outburst of verbal ranting. 'You want a war, Winters? You can have a bleedin' war! But trust me, I'll finish it. How easy is that!? You may ask. Standing in the safety of your own setting, and mouthing off!' Surely, even he couldn't be that dumb to realize its futility. Consequently, his raving ceased, as quickly as it had started. The thought for the day could have read, *You want to be Mr Big? Then you play your part to the full! No half measures.* In the real world, he wouldn't have got out of the trap. Full of apprehension, he bowed out of his flat with his tail between his legs. Once outside, the full impact of Baines' phone call proved to be a lesson in disguise. In the light of day, it became obvious to him that any personal recrimination didn't exactly hold water.

'I mean, how the hell do yer wage a war with the unknown?' he tried to convince himself. 'Besides, it's all about me; Peters and Santini ain't gonna come out of this smelling of poxy roses!' Passing the buck was breath wasted. Whatever way he played his malignant thoughts, there was no escape. His track record was a cross of his own design. Although, on the downside, it was good enough for him to become a nominee in an exclusive club of three! As per usual, negative reasoning kicked in. 'Ah, what the hell. Ricky's bound to sort it once he knows the SP.' Gaining a false sense of confidence, he hailed an oncoming cab.

'Where we going then, guv?' The driver needn't have bothered to ask him. The minute Rossetti got in his cab, something jolted the two per cent of brain that was allegedly working. It fired back in response to his present mode of thinking. An inner voice filled his head, and common sense took a backseat, as the voice changed to a laugh of contempt before resuming.

Who the fuck is this Peters guy anyway? What makes him so bleedin' special? He ain't God! Lost in a world of fantasy, he'd become oblivious to the cabbie's request.

'You sure yer need a cab, guvnor? You look as if yer could use a good night's kip!'

Yawning deeply, Rossetti shook his head before replying. 'Yeah, yer right, bang in order, but that's my problem. Drop me off at the Paradise Club, will yer?'

The cabbie did his best to smother a laugh. Their paths had crossed on many an occasion, although Rossetti wouldn't have known. Tonight was a first for the cabbie; at least his fare was half sober.

'Bloody Paradise?' The cabbie jested under his breath. 'The nearest he's gonna get to that is a forty-eight-hour bar.'

'You say something?'

'Yeah, I was thinking it's gonna be a nice day.'

'Wish I could say the bleedin' same; yer never know what's round the corner, know what I mean?'

'Glad you said it and not me, mate,' retorted the cabbie.

Five minutes after paying him off, Rossetti was ordering his first scotch of the day. 'It don't matter which way yer wanna look at it, Winters has got the upper hand. Okay, so we've got the muscle, but how the hell do yer deal with a geezer like Winters?' Seated around a table in a private room at the Paradise Club, Rossetti was emphatic while running scared. 'Yer bleedin' paranoid, Rossi. One poxy phone call from a fucking loser like Jackie Baines, and yer throw a wobbler.' Peters wasn't having it. 'I mean! Baines... c'mon, what does he know?'

'It's what he saw that matters, Ricky.'

'Right! So how d'ye know it ain't a wind-up?'

'Simple, there's no way he could have known that the digits he gave me were the Jersey code.'

'I'm still not convinced, Rossi. What d'ye make of it, Tito?'

Tito Santini was the new kid on the block. His exclusive style when dealing with a threat became the epitome of evil. Less than a month ago, he would have willingly removed any part of Peters' body just to fulfil a sadistic moment of extreme pleasure. 'It's the sheer buzz I get out of it,' he would tell you. His many victims were left in no doubt as to his potential. Ninety per cent were still living; the rest died of shock or gangrene! 'Win some... lose some, I ain't perfect, I can only get better.' Chilling words indeed! But they bore him the respect that he carried as a means of survival. Within the trade, Tito 'the Butcher' Santini had a reputation second to none. As number one blade man installed in Winters' regime, his expertise with a knife assured that his status carried the added bonus of fear and terror.

His unexpected career move became Winters' loss and Peters' gain. The inducement of self-rule proved to be an offer he couldn't refuse. Sole charge of administering misery in the Italian quarter fell onto his shoulders. Ruthless at dealing with the downtrodden victims of his own creed put him in a bracket apart. Consequently, his evil reputation soared to a new dimension. Even the Traveller was wary when in his company. His newly found psychotic channel of thoughts aimed in his direction proved to be a temporary cover for Rossetti. Santini had become a new toy to meddle with. For the time being, the pressure was now exploited elsewhere. Rossetti glanced across at Santini with sole interest, as his fellow countryman deliberated, before replying to Peters' request as to a possible threat from an alien source. Their origins were compatible, but the bloodline ended there! The only point they readily agreed on was a God-given right to inflict pain. Santini turned towards Peters, with a look of conjecture.

'I'll go along with yer, Ricky, on this one. Personally, I don't think Winters is capable of making a war.'

Rossetti jumped in quick to drive his point home. 'More reason why he's involving an outside interest. You know as well as I do, Ricky, it ain't about the wedge and territory anymore. You've fucked with his pride, and that's what he can't handle. Up to know, that joker Callaghan is the only person to put one over him, but even he's living in promised land.'

Giving out a look of contempt, Peters replied in an outburst of fury. 'Winters! ... Callaghan! ... Names, just fucking names. I don't need this shit. I toppled him once, I can do it again!' Halting for a second, he wiped his brow before continuing. 'Any aggravation coming our way on the strength of what you've told me, Rossi, I swear to God I'll bury the bastard.'

Santini seemed unmoved at Peters' singular vendetta. His cold and callous eyes fixed Rossetti as if anticipating a response. It caused him to squirm in his chair, as a chill of fear ran down his spine.

The Traveller, seated nearby, picked up on his uneasiness, and gave him a sardonic glare. His body language had been a complete giveaway. It became clear that Rossetti was now way out of his depth with the company he extolled. He'd just witnessed a side of Peters that was new to him. Suddenly, he felt vulnerable; up to now, it had all been a game. A few smashed skulls and money over was small time. It rated only the middle of the ladder. His mind once again reached out for the top rung. As before, it came away in his hand, crashing down into oblivion.

'Shit! You say something, Rossi?' Santini was leering at him, or maybe he just smiled that way?

'Nah, just thinking out loud about Winters. As it happens, the stupid bastard won't know what hit him, if he decides to push it.' His statement had more than a ring of realism about it and Rossetti prayed it wasn't that noticeable. But he knew that from now it was time to up the ego.

Their meeting as a firm had been the last chapter in his learning curve. Welcome to the big time, Rossi. As from now, it was put-up or shut-up!

CHAPTER 22

AWARENESS

'You sure yer up for it, Mickey?'

'I feel fine, Ronnie. A little stiff maybe, but I'll soon get back into shape.'

'Amen to that!'

'The run won't do me any harm, that's for sure. Besides, I'm beginning to forget what the inside of a gym looks like.' Having had the benefit of a few days to mull it over, Mickey Gibbons had decided to resume light training. The BBBC had now sanctioned his wellbeing based on a stringent medical report regarding any past effects from his alleged accident. As far as he was concerned, the incident was now dead and buried, as was any investigation on offer by the local plod. Selfish or otherwise, the events of Mickey's unforeseen involvement with Rossetti were still firmly locked away in Ronnie's mind. When Rossetti had delivered his kick for freedom, it had developed into a two-fold effect. From Ronnie's viewpoint, he'd taken the blow for Mickey as well. The mantle of pain and frustration rested entirely on his shoulders.

In the extreme, it would have been unacceptable if the act had been carried out by a total stranger! But this was no ordinary low-life perpetrator; they were talking about Rossetti! And Ronnie was hurting in such a way that his judgment came into question on occasion. He had good days and bad days, as a result, making it a habit of his own making.

His lounge window was open, and the warm gentle heat of the evening air wafted in off the street.

'Ideal,' he told himself, and allowed himself a smile of contentment. This had been the climax to one of his better days. Although, deep down, he had a gut feeling it could be borrowed. The inevitable bad ones were always available on ice, waiting for the right moment to wreak untold havoc!

CHAPTER 23

OUTSIDE FORCES

Just over an hour's flight away from Stonewater, the heat in Jersey took on a different vein. Even ice, it seemed, had a mind of its own; the tendency to melt at a given temperature could be seen causing a certain individual to curse the world at large. After replenishing his glass of Sangria, he reached across for the ice bucket, only to discover that even the sun had a way of manipulating people. In this case, it meant dragging the bottom half of his semi-tanned body from out of the blissful coolness of the water belonging to an exclusive oval-shaped garden pool. The highly detailed stone-built villa situated beyond complemented the privacy of a designer garden. The overall layout to the grounds was specifically based on total security. Electronic controlled gates to the front of the property opened up onto a short gravel drive. The remainder of the boundary could be flanked by a six foot high perimeter wall. This in turn was backed up by a solid mass of foliage, consisting of poplar trees.

Positioned to the right of the villa, at the bottom end of the drive, a huge detached double garage incorporating living accommodation above made up the additional estate. The token Rolls-Royce along with the Ferrari, housed within the garage, were a symbol of the owner's status. The property as a whole was set at the Rocque end of St Clement's Bay, above Plat Rocque Point, where the A4 coast road meets the B37 to

Grouville. It was well isolated, as was its owner in terms of social contact. It became imperative that his cloak and dagger style of existence was maintained for more reasons than one!

As a highly sought after hitman, Enrico Maniela had led a colourful and far-reaching career. The only son of a South American diplomat married to an English society lady was the start in life he could only have dreamt about. As it was, fate had other ideas in mind. Constantly on the move, and the humdrum of the social life, led to a decision to have him boarded out. From then onwards, the seeds of an impending life full of cold-blooded sequences were sown. He was never going to accept a push button strict regime form of life. In time, 'loner' and 'misfit' became references aimed at his social progress.

On arriving home one day, for the beginning of an intended six-week mid-term break. Fate again stepped in with tragic consequences. His mother and father were mercilessly gunned down in cold blood in his presence. The assassin's motive in itself was classed as political, but for a witness aged sixteen the impact arising from the deed would have far-reaching implications. Like two ragdolls, their bullet-riddled corpses lay strewn in front of him. He stood and witnessed their obsolete life blood forming an ever increasing plush red carpet of convenience, in contrast to the white granite chippings that made up the forecourt to their summer retreat. As if in shock, he stood gazing down at their discarded forms that minutes ago once represented a sense of high importance. The scene became instilled within his mind, wrapped in warped satisfaction. Two grotesque shapes that were once capable of breathing life to the full fascinated him, body and soul.

Twisted and contorted flesh did nothing to stir the form of emotion from within his seduced mind. The speed of it all impressed his sicko mind. It was at that moment in his life that he realized his chosen calling in the years to come!

'Blown away, like a feather in the wind' concluded his sadistic summing up of his parents' untimely deaths. In time, on a face-to-face basis, he was never in a position to relate his strategy, as the hunter in question. His own unfortunate victims were never placed in a visual setting whereby they could see him. Those who did, on the odd occasion, managed to suffer only more torment. His emotionless face would be the last image they witnessed, as the bullets of fortune tore into flesh and blood.

His philosophy was simple: 'If it's in the way, then I will remove it!' And he never wavered. Playing God, and the additional satisfaction of getting well paid for it, was one thing. But the final analysis ruled supreme. But for all his egotistical power and money, there was nothing he could do to stem the heat of the sun from melting his ice! Cursing under his breath, he hauled himself from out of the pool; clutching the ice bucket, he headed off towards the villa. The semi-glazed terrazzo patio was hot underfoot, causing him more discomfort. Glancing skywards, he cursed even louder for its untimely presence before disappearing into the villa.

He may have had Enrico Maniela listed on his dual passport, but to his clients past and present, he was referred to as 'Buffy Manilla'! New Scotland Yard and Interpol alike were also aware of his pseudonym, plus a personal trademark he'd take great pains to leave at the scene of every contract killing. The change in name style was foisted onto him through grim circumstances relating to his debut hit! Having left his intended victim for dead, he recalled a moment of egotism getting the better of his judgment. It almost proved to be his downfall. The victim in question was chosen from his erratic past, coinciding with his newfound career. 'I'll class it as a dress rehearsal,' as he would tell you. The fact that it concerned an ex-school principal from way back meant that they shared an affinity together.

The two bullets that he contemptuously emptied into the principal's chest, by rights, should have been sufficient to claim an immediate result. When the police finally found the corpse, it soon became apparent that the victim had not died instantly! 'STUBBORN IN LIFE UNTO DEATH' became his eternal epitaph. He was found lying face down on his desk top. Blood pooled everywhere. His right arm, outstretched, and resting on a size A4 brown envelope! On closer examination, it appeared that the lettering on it, which was written in his own blood, told them that he'd attempted to name his murderer, indicating that they were known to each other.

As a result, the services of an expert graphologist were called into play, with a view on a second opinion, to define the almost completed word. The conclusion he arrived at, in his view, spelt 'Manilla'. Thus the police accepted his decision. On that evidence, the tabloids had their own version of the outcome. The combination of the envelope type and colour led them to the headline, 'BUFFY MANILLA MURDER'. Without realizing it, they had inadvertently given Enrico Maniela the perfect pseudonym as a cover to go alongside his self-imposed licence to kill! As a macabre gesture, a similar envelope could be found placed in the vicinity of his late victims' bodies. Faceless and dangerous, he was allowed to continue plying his trade to whoever could afford his credentials. Thus, the infamous Buffy Manilla came into existence!

Replacing the refreshed ice tray back into the fridge, Maniela became aware of a security bell sounding off. It only added to his existing annoyance. 'Damn! Privacy!… I pay for privacy!' he yelled. Slamming the fridge door behind him, he made his way to a small central control room off the hallway. On the wall, a dozen CCTV cameras could be found situated. A flashing light on a mounted display grid was indicating the location of the bell. Pressing a particular button brought the appropriate camera into play. It quickly revealed a figure at the entrance to the drive, sitting astride a motorbike. His initial reaction was one of concern, until he recalled a particular phone call some forty-eight hours earlier.

'Uhm,' he muttered. 'Could be what I've been expecting,' he then assured himself. Picking up a nearby roving mike, his following instructions were short and to the point. 'Do not touch the gates! Identify yourself, you are under surveillance!'

The figure then spoke into a recording grille set into one of the stone-built pillars containing the gates. 'Inter Island Courier Services, special delivery for Mr Maniela.'

An instant look of recognition crossed his face, confirming his needless concern. The trade heading given out was a name he'd been well accustomed to in the past. Based in St Helier, they had proven to be more than useful when dealing with his many clients. The gates swung inwards, giving access to the biker. Maniela could be found waiting for him at the front of the villa. He readily took possession of a flat package, which he duly signed for, ensuring that his signature comprised Maniela and not Manilla! With the messenger off the premises, he turned his attention to the alien package.

With the aid of a solid gold letter opener, he deftly slit the large envelope open. Swiftly he removed the contents. A nearby roll-top bureau served as a desk, and he placed the contents on top. Pouring himself a drink, he began to familiarize himself with a set of three mug shots, including a street map/index, and a blown-up location plan representing Docklands in Stonewater. A letter of introduction and various useful snippets of information were also found in situ. From out of a pose of intense concentration, he found time to pause for a second, as he thumbed his way through the enclosed SP. His face creased into a forced smile of satisfaction.

'Well, Mr Terry Winters,' he exclaimed dryly. 'It would appear that you have done half the intended work for me. I congratulate you.' Sipping his Sangria, he removed a folder from out of the bureau. Gathering all the information to hand, he placed it all in the folder. Three specific names were carefully written on the front for future reference. 'SANTINI! PETERS! ROSSETTI!' In that order! He then placed the folder inside a slot marked 'V', presumably the initial for 'victim'.

There seemed to be no escape from the heat of the night. What ice he did have left in his glass had long melted. This time around, it didn't appear to have upset his demeanour. There were far more important things on his mind to contend with. Leaving the villa, he made his way back to the sanctuary of his pool. The Sangria, he noted, tasted sour in contrast to the sweetener Terry Winters had come up with as an interim payment to fulfil his latest contract. Saying that, there would be a couple of issues to iron out. Least of all being a personal request to eradicate Tito Santini first, with an additional rider.

The preference itself was irrelevant to Maniela's future planning. Three deaths in as many days could be bad for business! The police involvement alone could prove highly dangerous where his security was concerned. No! He intended to carry out the contracts by the book! Santini by request, leaving Peters and Rossetti to his own designs.

'What's the rush anyway?' he told himself. 'It's all money in the bank.' Slowly, he eased himself back into the solace of what the pool had to offer.

CHAPTER 24

SETTLING IN

Mickey Gibbons was beginning to have second thoughts, or maybe it could be the heat of the evening that was getting to him.

'D'ye mind if we stop for a breather, Ronnie? I seem to be way off the pace.' Ten minutes into their run to get to the gym, and things weren't going to form. His lack of exercise and the humidity had taken their toll. As usual, Ronnie was on hand to sympathize.

'No problem, mate. The subway is only minutes away, if yer can hang on for that long?'

'Blimey! I didn't realize that spell in hospital would affect me as much as it has. I feel absolutely out of it!'

'Yer only human, mate, just pace yerself. Wally's opening up tonight. So there ain't no hurry up.'

Without incident, and sweating profusely, they eventually arrived at the gym, fifteen or so minutes later than they had intended. Big Tommy Russell disengaged himself from a small crowd of disciples, and made to approach the two, as they made their way to the dressing room.

'Ronnie!' His larger than life voice boomed across the gym floor. 'We need to talk... catch up time.'

A week away from the gym, and even Ronnie was paying the price. He was dripping with sweat and a one-to-one with Russell wasn't on the cards right now. Adjusting his stride, he looked across in his direction, and yelled, 'Yeah! I'm bleedin' back, ain't I?'

'What you say? Can't hear you.'

'I said I'll get back to yer later. I need to get changed.'

Russell, it appeared, got the point at last. 'Yeah, you do that!' he acknowledged with a shake of his hand. Turning on his heel, he rejoined the company of the side line devotees. The peace and quiet of the locker room were far removed from the business end of the gym. Ronnie sat down and reflected on his thoughts for a second or two.

'Funny, yer know.'

'What is?' Mickey enquired.

'Well, just got to thinking, it's the longest period I've ever been away from the scene. And yet, when I walked in 'ere tonight, I felt like I ain't been away at all.'

Mickey shook his head in a positive manner. 'I'm not surprised, Ronnie, you are the bloody gym!'

'Blimey, I wouldn't have given it a thought, but thanks for that!' Ronnie towelled himself down, and Russell's earlier request came home to roost. Well aware of his shortcomings, it could mean only one thing: business! On reflection, it was his way of saying, 'I need a second opinion on a deal that I've already sorted!' Shaking his head, Ronnie smiled derisively, saying, 'Silly old bastard, he ain't changed one bit.' Chuckling away to himself, he finished changing, and the pair made their way back into the gym. At the last moment Ronnie pulled Mickey to one side. 'Don't strong it tonight, just do yer own thing, and remember, quality not quantity gets results. I'll get Frankie Lyons to work with yer, as far as yer groundwork goes. So relax and enjoy, yeah?' Ronnie left him to his own devices, and made his way across to the ring. In doing so, it meant bypassing Dave Molloy working out on the 'big boy' punch bag.

As the two neared, Molloy broke off and confronted him. With nowhere to go, Ronnie found himself forced to listen to what he had to say.

'Look… I just wanna say… good to see yer back. The gym don't seem to be the same when you ain't around.'

The spontaneous turnaround in Molloy's attitude left Ronnie feeling speechless and searching for an answer. Meanwhile, Molloy continued.

'That business we had words over, some time back' – the reference he made had now hit a raw nerve, as he honed in on Molloy's alleged idea on sparring – 'I was bang out of order that night, I know that now. I just needed to be told. I'd like to think we could sorta start all over again… yeah?'

Ronnie found himself struggling to take it all in. The honesty of the man, in his book, couldn't be faulted. At least he owed him a straight answer.

'What d'ye say?' Molloy got him out of goal by extending a gloved hand.

Without hesitation, Ronnie shook it warmly, nodding vigorously in reply. 'I hear what yer say, and we can work it out; besides, I'd rather work with yer than against yer. Know what I mean? Now get back on the bag.'

Molloy didn't need to be told twice. The big boy rocked as he took leather to canvas. Ronnie continued on his way, as the bag fell and rose in his wake.

'I always knew he could bang a bit. Bleedin' good job it won't be my fecking chin, though.' He stifled a look of relief. Wally Churchill was at the ringside, overseeing Eric Mercer, who was engaged in shadow boxing. He looked up as Ronnie approached.

'Good to see yer back, mate, and Mickey of course. Nasty old business that!' It became evident that Wally wanted to pursue his line of thought, and Ronnie seemed powerless to stop him. 'Strange, though.'

'What's that, mate?'

'The old bill.'

'What about them?'

'You'd have thought they'd have got the bastard responsible by nah. Stonewater ain't exactly the flaming smoke, is it?'

Ronnie felt he had to concur with reluctance. There was so much he could have said, instead of bottling it all up inside. Not only that, it made him feel bad about himself for having to sidestep Wally into thinking otherwise. 'Eric's looking the business, mate, you've done a bloody good job on him in my absence.' Talking shop would be one way of avoiding a steward's enquiry. Up to now, the evening session had been a revelation. The mere thought of Rossetti forcing him to break his silence didn't figure in his reasoning.

Wally readily took the bait on offer, and filled him in with Mercer's progress. 'I can't believe the turnaround in the kid since the Harrison fight. He's got this tendency of wanting to come forwards more often. I gotta say, it suits him. It's more noticeable when he's sparring.'

'Well, it seemed to work for him in the actual fight, so yeah, give him a complete makeover, Wally. He's the guy throwing the leather. If he feels comfortable coming forwards, then exploit it. I'll leave him in your capable hands. Right now, I've got some unfinished business to sort out with Tommy… okay? In the meantime, no let up. Push Eric all the way, concentrate on durability.'

'No problem, mate, sorted!'

Just then, Tommy Russell sauntered across to them both, as they finished talking. Ronnie decided to get in first.

'I was just coming over to see yer, we can talk in the office.' Winking at Wally, he left him to concentrate on the job in hand. Russell motioned Ronnie to take a seat, but Ronnie declined his offer. In doing so, he put Tommy on the back foot to start with. 'So what's so important it can't wait, then, Tommy?' As a double act, they tended to work off each other's weaknesses, but Ronnie never forgot his lines, or his cues, come to that!

'I've had a phone call—'

'Don't tell me,' interrupted Ronnie. 'I bet it was from Charlie Cochrane.'

'Callaghan! You're a bleedin' witch. How the hell d'ye figure that one out?'

'Intuition, mate. Seriously, though, I had half an idea he'd get back to yer before long. You can thank Mercer for that!'

'I got to say, he strikes me as the sort of guy you could do business with.'

'You wanna rephrase that, Tommy?' His answer had now left Tommy squirming, as he quickly realized Ronnie was on his case... full stop. 'Never kid a kidder, Tommy. So what's going down?'

'Charlie looking to promote a show on our doorstep.'

'No kidding, What, here on our doorstep?'

'Yeah, and he's looking to us to fill a couple of slots on the bill.'

'What sort of dates are we looking at 'ere?'

Russell got the impression Ronnie was hedging. 'We don't have anything pencilled in as such, yet.'

'We?' Ronnie was quick to cut him short, in the event that a promise became a contract. 'You can forget Gibbons for a couple of months... okay, so there's Mercer, of course, and Molloy.' He had a sudden cause to hesitate. 'Which reminds me we need to get our heads together over Molloy, if he's gonna have any sort of commitment in the near future.'

Russell evoked a look of concern, fully aware of their outstanding relationship.

Continuing, Ronnie stated his case. 'If push comes to shove, I'll do what I can for the guy, especially knowing

what I now know. But I ain't gonna be fucked about...
understand?'

Russell's face lit up a smile that threatened to swallow his
ears. In contrast, Ronnie wore an expectant look as he fronted
him. A sustained silence briefly followed, as the two finally
made four, sealing his mode of expectation.

'You've bloody well gone and done it! Ain't yer!? You've
already done a deal!' Seconds later, they both fell about
laughing.

CHAPTER 25

UNDERCURRENTS

They say, 'If you've met one, you've met the lot!' Maybe? The trouble with Baines was Baines himself! He ranked as your typical stereotype-classified loser. But he did have an edge on his counterparts. For a diminutive little guy, he did have one exclusive aspect going for him. And that was having a bigger mouth than the majority. Suffice to say, it tended to overtake his mind, body and soul on occasion, and was something he'd never been able to come to terms with! 'Putting it about' became his idea of keeping abreast with the world around him. Furtive and living in the shadows of a crime-ridden society gave him the benefit of access to certain unsolicited information, which he readily fed off. On terms of ability, his success rate was second to none, ears and eyes constantly working on overtime for that odd snippet of SP, even a moment of contact, which he could exploit as a means of getting by.

Strangely enough, money itself was never a motive for his fixation. It became purely personal, acting like a fix as it so often did. Ninety per cent of what he allegedly knew was accepted by the fraternity surrounding him as being one part verbal diarrhoea. The other ten per cent was crap anyway. Although, he did at one stage manage to mark Rossetti's card for him. That should have been the end of the story. But no, like a parasite, the information he'd unwittingly disclosed remained locked inside his addled brain. He now found himself on a high, and the impulse to divulge his actions in public was building into a climax of his own making. I mean, you wouldn't begrudge a man five minutes of self-imposed glory... would you?

If only he'd kept the phone call to Rossetti under wraps, then nobody would have been any the wiser. But this was Baines at his best! The world was his stage, so listen in, everybody... and they did just that! Anchored in the Rat and Trap, with a wino as a companion, plus a three-hour boozing session behind him, wasn't the time and the place to give it large. If he'd had a mike in his hand, the effect would have been the same. Blinded by the booze and the impulsive urge to let the world know of his paltry existence, didn't cut any ice with three members alienated to the Terry Winters' fan club sitting on an adjacent table, well within earshot! The wino sitting opposite Baines appeared to be on another planet, lost in an unknown galaxy somewhere, completely off his face, oblivious to the verbal ranting aimed in his direction.

'Rossi listens to me! I tell him everything I know... I'm good for the word... he'll look after me, you see if he fucking don't! And that's only a start.' The verbal spewed out of his mouth, as he voiced his delirium. Finally, a welcome curtain came down inside his sodden brain, as he finished. It seemed to ignite a small spark of what sensibility remained. 'Fuck you, cider Johnnie! I'm talking to myself... I'm out of 'ere. Rossi will listen to me. I've got another lead on that bastard Winters he can use.' Rising shakily to his feet, he somehow shuffled out the bar, and into the coolness of the night air. The wino didn't even bother to look up.

Once outside, Baines' body reacted like a shot of plasma, as his next verbal fix kicked in.

'Gotta get hold of Rossi... he needs to know what I got.'

225

Steeling himself, he headed for the nearest call box, situated at the far end of the harbour basin.

A short while after he left, the three heavies who had witnessed his suicidal outburst ended their own personal discussion. Nodding their heads in unison, and looking grim, they left the pub as one, carefully shadowing Baines from behind. Stopping short of the call box, Baines attempted to clear the demons running riot in his head. Rossetti, or so he thought, was his only remaining salvation, if he were to rid himself of the verbal tumour eating away inside of him.

By now, he was cursing with utter frustration. 'Pick the sodding phone up, will yer, Rossi!' Over and over he repeated himself, before finally depressing the call bar. His thoughts were now on a sponsored walkabout. 'Time! I need fucking time... there is no time... Rossi... where are yer?' He was almost screaming, as the demons mocked his futile attempts to contact him. Through semi-glazed eyes, his watch said 11.35. The time seemed to strike a hidden chord. 'Club. Yeah, that's where he'll be, at the bloody club.' After removing his wallet, he rummaged around and managed to find a contact number on an old membership card. His thinking became more stable, as he punched the required digits home.

Watching and waiting in the background, the three heavies bided their time before making a move. They could almost hear Baines' sigh of relief as he made the desired contact.

'I need to talk to Paul Rossetti... it's urgent!' Blasting the message out was causing a connection problem.

'Who did you say? Try talking slower, will yer?'

'Rossetti! Paul Rossetti!'

'Hold the line, I'll get back to yer.'

Baines, meanwhile, drummed his fingers on the side of the kiosk in anticipation. 'C'mon... c'mon, Rossi. Where the fuck are yer?'

'Hello!'

'Yeah!'

'Rossi wants to know who's calling.'

'Tell him… just say 'the mouth'… he'll know.'

A few minutes later, Rossetti appeared on the other end. 'Wotcha got for me, Jackie? It had better be kosher, I'm in a card school, and I'm on a roll… know what I mean?'

'Rossi… Rossi, it's about them digits I give yer the other day. Did they mean anything to yer? I need to know.'

'I wish to fuck they hadn't! But yeah, I worked it out for myself.'

'The thing is Rossi, I overheard a phone conversation this morning, concerning an outsider, whatever that means. Winters was happy, though, when he put the phone down.'

'Conversation, yer say?' Rossetti started to get fidgety; the script was all too familiar.

Baines then continued where he'd left off. 'I don't know the full SP, but I got the impression he was talking to a geezer from Jersey of all places. What's all that about? I just thought yer needed to know, because I heard your name mentioned in the conversation.'

Rossetti's heartbeat accelerated, at the same time causing him to wince at what he already knew to be valid. 'You did right to mark me card, Jackie. But that's the end of it, it goes no further than you or me… you understand what I'm saying?'

Baines hesitated before replying. Something or somebody had caught his eye in the booth mirror. Fear tore his body apart, as an alien hand clamped tight over his mouth. The receiver was snatched from his grasp, left to swing wildly; in a split second, he found himself forcibly ejected from out of the booth.

'Jackie… Hi, Jackie, you still there?' At the other end, Rossetti's patience was getting thin. He was wasting his time even trying. 'Bleedin' tosser! Probably pissed anyway, I'll give him a mouthful when I see him next.' Cursing Baines and the rest of the world at large, he returned to his card school.

The following day, the *Stonewater Gazette* ran with their own story.

Bleary eyed, Rossetti bent down to pick his paper off the mat. He almost joined it, as a wave of nausea swept over him. Devoid of sleep, pot-less and living on a liquid diet had once again caught up with him. Unfolding the paper, he glanced at the headlines. The look of sheer horror reflected on his face resembled a double take, as he stood transfixed, unable to grasp what his distorted mind was trying to take in. Slowly, his eyes opened in sympathy with his clouded brain. He found himself lowering the paper briefly, before scanning it once more, just to reassure him of its contents.

'The poor bastard! Well, we all know whose fucking orders he came under!'

A certain phone call sprang to mind, as he considered a likely motive to the victim's untimely death. By now, he was wide awake. The headline read as follows.

'MURDER VICTIM'S BODY FOUND IN HARBOUR BASIN'

The report further went on to say that the body of a man had been officially identified as being a resident of Docklands who went under the name of Jackie Baines. The motive for the murder itself had yet to be established. Robbery had been ruled out, as all personal effects were found to be intact on the body. Although, a gangland vengeance killing was a possibility. The police could confirm that the victim's body had been badly beaten prior to entering the water.

'Ricky. Yeah, it's Rossi. Have you seen this morning's *Gazette*?'

'Yeah, bit of a turn-up. Looks like the mouth got his, alright! Finally ran out of something to say.'

'Not from where I'm standing, he didn't.'

'Wotcha mean by that?'

'I actually spoke to him last night, after you left the club. I got involved in a card school; that's when he phoned me from a call box. This was about 11.45, give or take.'

'Did he come over with anything useful?'

'More than enough. Although, I got the feeling he could have said a whole lot more, but the line suddenly went dead on me. I assumed he'd hung up on me.'

'So on the strength of what you do know, what's occurring?' A short silence followed before he continued.

'Poxy Buffy Manilla, that's fucking what!'

Peters appeared to be unmoved by his explanation. 'So what's new?'

'It proves to me that Jackie was clueless over those digits he passed on to me. But since then, the information I got out of him last night was kosher, bloody gilt-edged even.'

'Maybe, but that ain't enough to muller the poor bastard… is it?'

'Difference is, Ricky, he's fingered Winters. So now we all know what's going down!'

Peters was once again adamant. 'One thing's for sure, Rossi, Winters ain't gonna stop at nothing, but what he did to Baines was bang out of order. And now this Manilla geezer is on the fucking loose. Could be time to cut a few ties, I'm thinking.'

'But we've come too far, Ricky. Besides we're better off mob-handed. That way we get to flush the bastard out. No, I ain't running on the strength of that asshole Winters calling the shots.'

'Yeah, it makes sense, yer right, Rossi, but it does mean

taking a low profile for the time being. The word's out on the street anyway, so from now on we play it to suit… right?'

'Oh, what about Santini?'

'Leave it with me, Rossi. I'll contact him in the morning, and give him the SP. It shouldn't affect the firm staying busy.'

Rossetti appeared keen to pursue Santini's viewpoint in person. 'Tell yer what. Why don't we have a run over to the Latin quarter tonight? Get off the manor for five minutes. Do us all good. The Athenium Club is a half-decent meet. What d'ye say?'

'I like the sound of that, Rossi. I'll pick you up at nine o'clock tonight.'

Feeling partly relieved, Rossetti placed the handset down. The thought of meeting up with a few faces lifted a level of pressure away from him. It became short lived, as his eyes came into contact with the morning paper he'd slung to one side. A combined inner feeling of sudden fear, frustration and revenge took over his body. His blood count rose, as the headlines seemed to pull away from the front page, screaming out at him in defiance to take it all in. Through a veil of red mist, the word 'victim' slowly disappeared, only to be replaced by his own name, as his torment came to a climax.

'NOOOO!' He shouted long and hard, shutting out his manic version of hell. But nothing was going away. Like a magnet, it seemed to draw his body forwards. Suddenly, he lunged at the paper in a burst of mad frenzy, feverishly tearing away at it, ripping it into tiny shreds page by page and laughing hysterically as he did so, attempting to balance his moment of depravation. Slowly, his actions eased, as normality took over. In contrast, his skin felt cold and sticky, as the sweat of fear kicked in to replace his deranged torment. Shuddering, he made his way through a defunct mound of newspapers, and headed for the bathroom.

Head bowed and brow beaten, the sanity arising from a ten-minute shower was the only respite on offer. The Baines murder weighing heavily on his mind and the rest of the day to dwell on it resulted in Rossetti's devious life having to take a backseat for once. His rollercoaster ride of notoriety over the last week or two had begun to look slightly flawed, in more ways than one, and it wasn't going to take an Einstein to work it out for him. Baines' demise had done him a favour in retrospect; a steward's enquiry was now on the cards. It worried him enough not to venture out of his flat, at least until Peters and the Traveller had arrived to pick him up that evening.

When you're not used to thinking straight, the answer that you crave above all else appears to be over your head in more ways than one. In Rossetti's case, they had become sky high! As a result, his train of thought pointed only one way. So had his conclusion come too late to be realized? On his terms, it was quite simple really: remove Winters – the cancer – and you eradicate Manilla! In his singular manic world of evil parallels, it was probably the best option his brain would allow.

'Yeah, I like the idea, why the hell didn't I think of that before?' The added fact that he was eighty per cent sober would have told him the answer to that. Knowing Winters' movements like he did at least gave him an edge; it could prove invaluable when dealing with a game plan. The heinous task he'd set himself hadn't really sunk in, as yet. But due to the exceptional circumstances regarding Manilla hovering in the background, it did at least give some credence to his mode of thinking. One minute it was a passing whim; suddenly, it became a reality. There was nothing left to him to question anymore. 'I'll happily blow the bastard away; he owes me the pleasure.' The adrenalin surged through his body, as he re-enacted his vision that had now become his prime objective.

Peters, he noted, was running late. Some twenty minutes in fact.

'Shit! I don't need all this. C'mon, Ricky, pick up the poxy phone, why don't yer!' The sudden change in his temperament was blatantly showing its hand. The last forty-eight hours had been a turning point in his erratic relationship with Peters. As a sidekick, their self-styled form of allegiance came under question. Even though they had formerly agreed to stand firm, the seeds of doubt once more crossed his mind. Although, the mere thought of being out in the cold with Manilla on the loose gave him a sense of isolation. He knew the rules like everybody else. Whenever certain circumstances arose, then number one figured highly!

'Honour amongst thieves' went out with pink socks! For once, he'd convinced himself that his judgment was right.

'Self-security, that's the game. I need to get tooled up; a shooter means a mark of respect, and people need to know where I'm bleedin' coming from.' A shooter, in this case, was only a phone call away at any given time. Having the bottle to use one was another league. Words encouraged words, all from a gutless self-appointed villain. The thought of possessing a handgun was enough to tip his ego over the edge of fantasy.

The plain fact that it happened to be Peters and the Traveller did nothing to undermine his personal undertaking to once and for all grasp the top rung of his beleaguered ladder of success!

'Make the most of it; pretty soon you'll be waiting for me!' Just then, the familiar wailing sound of a car horn outside brought him down to earth. 'So much for his poxy phone call, then!' he cursed. Muttering away to himself, he exited his flat and got into the waiting car. 'Problems, Ricky?'

His newfound alter ego went down quicker than the *Titanic*! 'Problems? Nah, nothing that the Traveller and me can't handle. Why, have you, then? Got problems, I mean!'

Once again, Rossi found himself out of his depth, and decided on a more patronising approach. 'Sounds like yer might be getting some grief from a bad client.'

'Heh, it was looking that way until the Traveller educated him. Now the geezer's wound up with a fucking headache for a week.'

Inwardly, Rossetti admired Peters for his direct line of approach. For a little man, he had a big case going for him. 'He'll chew you up, and then spit you out in corned beef tins!' somebody had once remarked.

'So where's the grief… Balti land?'

'Yeah, as it happens. That's the third kickback I've had this bleedin' week. Poxy Asians, they want the protection, but they don't like paying for it.'

'Mind you, he always gets a result, doesn't he?'

'Who the fuck you talking about nah?'

That's when Rossetti realized he'd pushed Peters too far. 'Santini!' he gushed. Without thinking, he'd inadvertently sidestepped Peters for one of his own. His actions had resulted in putting Peters in the shade without trying and in a devious way. There was no kidding Peters; he was to fly for that. Rossetti's war on words quickly died a death, as Peters fired back.

'Well, Rossi, maybe. But it takes a Wop to know a Wop, and his reputation, of course!'

Rossetti found himself forced to cave in to superiority, and glossed over the situation. Smiling, he raised his eyebrows.

'I say something bleedin' funny, Rossi?' asked Peters.

'Nah, yer right about his reputation. Knowing you, yer on a bloody winner before you've opened yer mouth!' What he didn't say was, 'That image is gonna be me in future. It's already been discussed; nothing and nobody is gonna stand in my way!' Yeah, dream on, Rossi!

Apart from the odd grunt from the gorilla, who was nursing a badly bruised knuckle, nothing more was said until they pulled up outside the Athenium Club. Rossetti was the first to alight from the car. He stood up and looked around the dimly lit vicinity surrounding the frontage of the premises. Without prompting, an uninvited vision of Manilla took over his subconscious, as he continued to stare into the misty, foreboding gloom of the night. 'Wouldn't be fucking hard for him, would it?' he told himself.

There was a feeling of expectancy hanging on the night air, which even he couldn't shut out. *Better get used to the idea*, an inner voice kept telling him. *As from now, this is how it's going to be, constantly looking over your shoulder!*

Peters had picked up on his meandering. 'You're quiet, Rossi. We going in… or what?'

A mantle of uneasiness crept over him, as he acknowledged Peters' remark. It caused him to shiver slightly before replying. 'Yeah, of course. I just got this poxy feeling—'

'About what?!' Peters cut in.

'Tonight… I can't help thinking it's gonna be one of them poxy nights. Know what I mean?'

Peters declined to answer. Inwardly, he was registering the same conclusion.

Basically, the club was no different than a hundred other drinking venues, the only difference being the criminal element, who were widely known to patronize its hallowed walls. There were three main rules the main body instituted listed as follows: 'One murder limited to one member in any one year… removal of said victim's body… damaged or blood stained décor to be made good!' Nobody, it seemed, ever turned up with their wife or mother!

With the Traveller leading the way, they swiftly entered, and made a beeline for the lounge bar. There to greet them was Santini. Peters quickly declined the offer of Champagne, and pointed towards the Traveller for a reason! Devoid of any inner feeling, Santini's face remained impassive.

Cold bastard! Peters thought to himself. Electing for privacy, they made their way into an ante room to discuss business in hand. Making themselves comfortable, Santini pressed the drinks bell. Seconds later, a nearly dressed waitress with legs up to the back of her ears appeared, and proceeded to take their orders.

Peters, being himself, took the initiative by deciding to talk shop. 'Well, Tito, you've made quite a name for yerself, since yer involvement with the rackets. I'm impressed.'

Santini sneered, or maybe he was smiling? 'There ain't no secret, I don't even have to work at it. The firm I got around me understand how I operate. And they in turn run the punters.'

'I gotta say, it seems to work for yer. So you haven't had any grief, as yet?'

Santini dismissed the question out of sight. Shaking his head slowly and methodically, his bloodless face evoked a sardonic leering grin. He replied, 'Only because I rule by fucking fear!' Easing himself back into his chair, he raised his arms to emphasize his point. 'I gift it to them for nothing, and they know not to fuck with me, you understand? So, yer see, gentlemen, "Butcher" Santini, he gets results.'

The Latin blood they both had in common gelled as Rossetti voiced his opinion. It suited his ego to have an ally in the firm, and was quick to patronize him. 'You got my vote, Tito, when yer gave Winters the elbow. His loss is fast becoming our gain.'

Santini shrugged his shoulders before replying. 'Loss... loss, yer say? Huh, so I'll deal with it. What difference?' He stopped short as the waitress appeared again. Santini signed the tab, and looked up. 'You were saying, Rossi?' he asked, in a nonchalant manner.

'It ain't that simple, there's—'

Peters waved him down, and cut in. 'The fucking point is, Tito, you're on a shortlist of three, coming from an outside interest. The interest is called Buffy Manilla! All expenses paid… money no fucking object! … Surely I don't have to spell it out for yer?'

That blossomed into the start of a cold and lengthy silence. Any reaction, big or small, would have meant something. Meanwhile, Santini's posture remained ice cold. Any thoughts he may have been harbouring on the subject seemed to be on an arrogant hold. As usual, Rossetti was getting impatient, and threw a withering glance Peters' way. Shrugging his shoulders, without sounding off, was the best he could muster. At length, Santini downed his glass, and commenced to state his case.

'Gentlemen, I suggest to you that we are dealing with two problems here.'

His arrogant attitude finally pushed a heated Peters over the edge, as he intervened. 'Fucking Manilla on his poxy own is grief enough, Tito! So what are yer trying to lay on us now?'

Once again Santini appeared totally unmoved by Peters' outburst, choosing instead to wave a nearby waitress over.

'This guy ain't for real,' Peters muttered.

'Repeat order, please… and more ice.'

Even Rossetti's patience had now stood the test of time. 'Manilla!' He spelt the name out in no uncertain terms. 'We all agreed on that point, so are yer now saying Winters is the other fall guy? Because I don't see it that way. For the simple reason he happens to be on the bleedin' manor. All this shit about "I can deal with it", that's total bollocks!'

'True! But you just made the point, Rossi, like I've been saying. This Manilla guy has got two sides: the one we know about and the one we don't!' There was no denying Santini his logic. But then you wouldn't deny a faceless hitman his characteristics either, under the circumstances. He was still taking a low-key attitude as far as Manilla was concerned. It was almost as if the guy had a date with death and failed to show up.

'Riddles! Poxy riddles. All this double talk ain't getting us anywhere.' Peters was again pushing for some form of action. 'Where the fuck are yer coming from, Tito? All this crap, yer know the guy, and then yer don't.'

Santini wasn't about to bite on a level of criticism. 'Okay, let's start with you first, Ricky. As Rossi rightly stated, we're all agreed that Manilla is under orders working on Winters' behalf as far as any contract goes.'

'And the second?' Rossetti voiced. But this time with a ring of allegiance, reiterating Peters' call for action.

'The second, gentlemen, and this is crucial because it's the one point you've all failed to pick up on…' He was in the chair, and he knew it. Lording over the proceedings was good for his image, although Santini wasn't ready for a curtain call just yet. Peters and Rossetti, at this point, together shared a look of indecision again, as Santini fiddled around with his glass on the table top. Stopping abruptly, he glanced up, and gave out a sick oily grin, before stating emphatically, 'Habit! The guy is a creature of habit!' Thumping the table repeatedly with a clenched fist, he spelt out his convictions.

Santini's show was going to need more evidence to convince Peters. 'The asshole has been blowing people away for the last ten years, so I'm told. Yeah, that is one fucking bad habit.'

'Let the man finish, Ricky. Anything we don't know is a win.'

'Nah yer thinking straight, Rossi. Listen and learn. What SP I do know, I managed to glean from the old bill. As you say, it's all we've poxy got to work with.' The meet had come alive unexpectedly. A glimmer of mutual reasoning appeared to be on the cards, as Santini began to deal some aces.

'Christ! I could use another bleedin' drink; do the business, Traveller.' Peters looked hot under the collar as he thrust a nifty into the shovel-like hand of the gorilla. 'Carry on, Tito, you were saying?'

'Two words I will say: airport and flowers! Together, they form a habitual part of every contract Manilla has carried out on the mainland.'

A sustained silence followed, as they digested the impact of his statement. Peters appeared to be half interested, without committing himself. 'Fucking flowers! How d'ye figure that?'

'This is the bill's version. On half a dozen of his contracts, a carnation buttonhole was found at the scene of the crime, apart from his usual trademark, a buff manilla envelope. The guy has to be an eccentric asshole anyway, and the bill reckons he always wears the buttonhole out of sympathy.'

'And the airport, how does that fit into your equation?'

'That is the easy one. He always uses Shoreham airport in Sussex, hour and a half's flight from Jersey. How convenient is that? Once he's landed, there are no security restrictions, plus he's only fifteen minutes away from the motorway!'

'I gotta agree, too bloody simple! So where do yer suggest we go from 'ere?' Peters retaliated, although, having stated his case convincingly, Santini wasn't quite off the hook just yet, certainly not in his book anyway.

Suffice to say, Santini then picked up where he had left off. 'Given what we know, and the fact that the asshole is faceless, I suggest we get a couple of the firm down to Shoreham a bit lively. He shouldn't be too hard to winkle out. In which case, they can stick a tail on him and keep us informed of his movements… sorted!'

The night undoubtedly belonged to Santini. Full agreement was unanimous, and the remainder of the evening flowed into the early hours and beyond. For some, it was intended to be a never-ending pattern. Although, one particular person amongst them stood out alone. He could never have known it at the time, but his club membership was beginning to lose its expiry date!

SECONDS OUT

CHAPTER 26

DEATH ON DEMAND

The electronic gates closed gently behind him, as he fanned the accelerator. The booted tread of the wide tyres spontaneously gripped the dusty surface of the short access road eventually leading to the main highway. In doing so, it caused a mini shower of loose gravel laced with gasoline fumes to disperse in the wake of the Ferrari. On meeting the A4 coast road, the driver turned left heading for St Helier, and the A2 interchange to Beaumont, prior to turning off again for St Peter and Jersey airport. For the driver, it was a comparatively short journey, which he'd made many times in the past. But not always for pleasure. Today, Enrico Maniela, alias Buffy Manilla, found himself on a mission of work operating on the mainland. The only hiatus between departing and the return journey would be conducive to murder!

In no time at all, he'd parked up in the private owners' car park. From the boot of the Ferrari, everything that was required to ensure the operation went smoothly he removed methodically. Purely out of professionalism, he double checked the small amount of luggage he'd previously allowed himself, before closing and locking the car. Turning his full attention to an adjacent hangar, a satisfied look crossed his face. He readily noted that a Piper Cherokee monoplane was having a final crosscheck prior to use. Without delay, he crossed the turf and, armed with his luggage, headed for the plane. This was his *pièce de résistance*. It went with the job of course, along with asking price. On one particular occasion, a curious bystander speculated its worth and on how Maniela could afford the luxury of owning a private plane.

He had replied coldly, 'It was murder at first, and then after that, it just became a habit!' The real meaning to his line of enquiry was completely lost in self-ignorance, as the perpetrator walked away shaking his head. For Maniela, this was life at the top. And every aspect surrounding it was allocated. The cockpit door was already open for use, so he lost no time in getting underway. The mechanic on hand acknowledged his desire to get airborne, and promptly removed the wheel chocks. He was satisfied that his seat harness felt strapped tight, and an instrument check quickly followed. He depressed the starter control button, and the engine spluttered and finally roared into life.

The aileron movement proved positive, and he double checked the fuel consumption. As he thought, there was enough gasoline for six flying hours. Donning his headphones became a matter of course. In seconds, he'd made contact with the control tower with the intention of submitting a flight plan, which included landing directions at Shoreham airport in Sussex. Given control clearance, he now had the tarmac at his disposal. A last-minute check over enabled him to set a flight course heading north. Thirty minutes into the flight, he glanced at his watch. It was just after 8.30 am.

'Perfect timing. I just hope Mr Winters has got his facts right at his end,' he mused. 'Think I'd better contact Shoreham for landing advice, and my predicted time of arrival,' he added.

On consideration, it was just as well. Another twenty minutes or so would see him in mid-Channel. The air space, he noted, especially for the time of the day, appeared to belong to him exclusively; suffice to say, he made good headway.

Reaching inside of his flight bag, he removed an outline map, illustrating the south coast, which he studied for a short while. Slowly, a dormant idea began to take shape within his flexible thinking. Concluding his thinking, he spoke out loud.

'Yes! Why not? It can't make that much difference; besides, I'm well in front of my schedule anyway.' Pausing to open up a contact line with Shoreham control, he nodded decisively to justify his belated decision. Just then, his contact came through, and he explained that his previous flight plan would be terminated, in preference to Lydd airport in Kent. Ten minutes later, and the habit of a lifetime blown away, his plane crossed mid-Channel. Banking steeply to the right, he set out on an easterly flight path.

Meanwhile, back at Shoreham, two pissed-off heavies sat waiting in a car for somebody they were never going to meet in a lifetime!

For his part in the charade, it was just another day at the office for Enrico Maniela, as far as he was concerned. Having landed and paid his ground fees, he wandered off into the reception bar, deciding to order a coffee. He sat on a bar stool, and his upper body became mirrored in the glass panelling, which formed the backdrop to the bar.

Catching a glimpse of himself made him start. His hand instinctively flew to his lapel to hastily adjust a loosely hanging carnation buttonhole.

Just then, his coffee arrived and the incident became history. Time was still on his side, as he lingered for a pre-arranged Hertz hire car to be delivered for his disposal. Fifteen minutes later, and fully refreshed, saw him mobile again. He reckoned that in less than an hour he would converge on Stonewater and reality. The information he held via Winters had proved to be invaluable on the day. It would safely enable Maniela to fulfil his contract with the minimum amount of grief. It consisted of a three-tier operation, as he recalled, with one Tito 'the Butcher' Santini heading the bill. In his case, there would be a personal rider clause attached, to include the maximum amount of pain prior to premeditated death!

As far as personal security went, Maniela insisted on zero association when dealing with prospective clients. Any monetary transactions were commuted by an exclusive contact number and offshore banking. Operating under a mantle of mystery afforded him the element of total supremacy when dealing with a hit. Living within the auspiciousness of the twilight zone enabled his reign to form a passport to success. Thinking low-key, a two-star commercial hotel in Stonewater provided him with a decent enough base to work from. After signing the register, using a pseudonym and a bent address, he made his way up to his bedroom. He made himself comfortable and his thoughts began to dwell on the only thing he was good at... murder!

★

Less than a mile away from Maniela's hotel, Tito Santini and half a dozen of his firm were grouped around a table, set in the lounge belonging to a luxury flat. This, in turn, could be found situated on the fifth floor of an exclusive block of buildings. Private parking went with the territory, alongside the use of a personal integral lift, sited at one end of each lounge. Their sordid banter was riddled with violence, as the night's uncompromising schedule of hits was allocated. Monday night within the Latin quarter became retribution time for the few restaurateurs willing or game enough to take on the corruption of Santini's evil regime. The weekend takings were the bait on offer as an alternative to wrecked premises and maimed bodies.

Briefly, their heated conversation ground to a halt, as the in-house phone kicked off. Santini reached out for the receiver, and raised it to his oily mouth. His chilling personality bordered on contempt, when he eventually spoke.

'Tito?'

'Make it fucking quick... I'm a busy man right now!'

'We need to talk.'

His initial intention meant slamming the receiver down. At the last moment he raised it once again, as recognition set in. Peters, it seemed, was on the other end of the line. The ongoing friction between the two stemmed from day one of Santini's induction to oversee the Latin quarter. Strangely enough, it would appear that even Peters had a shred of feeling locked away somewhere in his puny frame.

The man's a fucking animal, treating his own like he does. Easing himself back into his chair, Santini broke the silence. 'Ricky! You gotta problem?' His wilful approach to the call was Santini at his best, undermining Peters' austerity as he did. Question for question gave him an added advantage when it came down to pecking order. Big mistake! He hadn't figured on Peters' reputation as the mouthpiece.

There would be no way he was going to buy his line of approach. Besides, he'd witnessed too many faces like Santini take a fall from power in his time! Peters put it to him, selecting his words as a mental weapon.

'Problem?! I got insurance for that sort of thing. You seriously need to get smart to survive. The way I see it, a threat only becomes a fucking threat if yer don't remove it! At this moment in time, there's two of yer poxy team down at Shoreham... for what?! They've been there nah for two fucking days, and the word on the street tells me that Buffy Manilla has been in the country for twenty-four poxy hours!'

Santini was visibly shaken by Peters' damning statement,

deciding instead on a different stance. 'I can't argue with that! I'll up my security this end. There's still a chance we can flush him out.'

'Contact is the best option as it goes, Tito. Stand on me, I know what I'm bleedin' talking about. I'll bell yer tonight at your place again… say around 10.30. Just watch yer back, be lucky.'

The line went dead. Santini felt a wave of pressure sweep over his body; removing a silk hanky from his pocket, he mopped his brow. On reflection, it was never going to be the best conversation he'd had for a long time. Peters' verbal superiority had virtually given him an education in survival. And right now, it was causing his flagging ego to plummet into a rock bottom abyss!

'Yer looking worried, guv. The call, some sort of problem?' One of his henchmen had picked up on his body language.

'Problem? Yeah, yer could say that! Peters was on the phone. He reminded me about some outstanding trouble that needs sorting… Billy!' He motioned with a nod towards one of the firm. 'As from now, yer on surveillance out the front of the building. Anything that doesn't feel or look kosher, I wanna know about… understand?! The rest of yer know what yer gotta do, so move it.' His cold eyes narrowed, as he spoke through gritted teeth. 'Don't stand for any old crap! I want fucking results, and I don't give a shit how yer get 'em. I want to see yer all back 'ere tomorrow morning at eleven o'clock… right?!'

Waiting until the firm had dispersed, he poured himself a drink, consisting of a large gin from a tailored bar situated in one corner of the lounge. He rammed the ice pick home in the bucket, finally placing it to one side on the bar top, as he carefully removed a couple of cubes to refresh his drink. For some reason or another, he inadvertently failed to replace it back into the bucket. 'No big deal' some would say. In Santini's case, it would become a costly oversight, given time! After walking across to the balcony doors, he pulled a drape to one side, and studied the street below. With little to go on, apart from Peters' take it or leave it option and an alleged buttonhole, it would take a shrewd man to make a book on his long-term chances of survival!

Swigging his gin, he visually observed his insurance taking up a position on a strategic corner, right in full view of the building. The effect from the gin seemed to have loosened his tongue, allowing the first symptoms of fear to lick over his palate. 'That bastard Manilla is out there somewhere, I can almost smell him!' he told himself. Crossing himself, he threw back the remaining gin in his glass, and grimly made his way to the front door of the flat, which he was careful to lock, taking his time as he did so.

★

Less than a mile away, in the confinement of his hotel room, a figure began to stir. Enrico Maniela, alias Buffy Manilla, had now started to emerge. He proceeded to rub his eyes, at the same time reaching out to inject some form of life into his limbs. Still lying on his back, he glanced up at the ceiling above him, endeavouring to collect his current thoughts. The hour or so of respite had done him good, and he now felt wide awake. The time, he noted, was just coming up to 4.30 pm.

'Just right!' he muttered, and elected to take a shower. Twenty minutes later and fully dressed, he stood in front of his mirror to check himself over. Satisfied, he removed a small leather-bound address book from within his jacket pocket. The one particular contact number it contained was paramount to his game plan. Obtaining it in the first place, you could call a *coup de grâce* in anybody's language! The fact the number was ex-directory and it belonged to Tito Santini appeared to be justification in itself. The expression 'money can't buy the gift of life' also applied on Terry Winters' terms, whereby he could foreclose on it to order.

Everything and everybody has a price, when it all comes down to money! And Winters used his wisely to overcome disloyalty. Allowing for the phone call he intended making, prior to vacating the hotel, he'd allowed himself thirty minutes to get across to Santini's residence. This would include a brief stop-off at a gents' public convenience. Now, with the address book open at the appropriate page, Maniela picked up the bedside receiver, and an open line to the reception desk.

'Yes, sir, can I help you?'

'I require an outside line please.'

'What number do you require, sir?'

Maniela duly obliged and waited for the connection to be made. He didn't have long to wait.

'Your number is ringing, sir.'

'Thank you.' With baited breath, he waited as the ringing tone sounded. 'Sweeter than the nectar from a rose'; quoting a line from an ode, he afforded himself a charismatic smile, and continued to listen. Crucially, the contract as a whole depended solely on his call proving positive. It seemed like an eternity between the tone ceasing and the connection. A disgruntled voice at the other end appeared to be unimpressed. A succession of gins during the day had left their mark.

'Who the fuck is this?!'

Maniela had time to draw on a breath of relief, before finally replying. 'I apologize for troubling you, sir, I'm trying to contact a Mr Waites.' Biting his tongue, Maniela waited for the inevitable response.

'This happens to be a private number... go to hell!'

Slowly and deliberately, Maniela replaced the receiver, laughing coldly as he did so. Stopping briefly, the corners of his mouth dropped as he sneered in utter contempt, before saying, 'I'm sure you will, Mr Santini, I'm sure you will!' After grabbing his car keys and a medium-sized plastic bag, he swiftly vacated his room, ensuring the door was locked behind him. The purpose of his call was all the proof he required ensuring his victim's whereabouts. After turning the key in the ignition, he pulled away from the hotel, set on a route he'd engrained in his mind. A certain buzz seduced his body, allowing an adrenalin surge to flow through his body. In twenty minutes or so he would be sharing an appointment with death!

Two streets short of his intended destination, he pulled the car over into an empty bay and parked up. Leaving the car, he made his way to a nearby gents' toilet, carrying a plastic bag. Minutes later, he emerged wearing a three-quarter-length work-soiled overall jacket. The cheese cutter cap and false moustache were an added touch. In no time at all, he found himself at the block of flats where Santini was holed up. He then drove to the rear of the block. It soon became apparent that without a gizmo to affect the crash barrier the underground parking zone had become a no-go area, forcing him into having a rethink. Fortunately, a parking space became available in an adjacent side street.

Breathing a sigh of relief, he hastily parked up. Time was of the essence. After locking the car, he made his way to the front entrance to the flats. In one hand he held a clipboard containing a bent delivery note and a Moody ID card. In the other, he held a small package. Perception was ninety per cent of his business; it developed into an inborn trait he'd matured, way back from his primal initiation. Turning the last corner, his acute suspicions were readily confirmed, as Santini's insurance eyeballed his every step before he entered the building.

The in-house porter took his time before making an appearance. Once again, Maniela pressed the service button on the reception desk for attention. This time with meaning. As a result, the reluctant figure of the porter appeared; his eyes, Maniela noted, were nearly on his chin. *Good result*, he told himself. Maniela looked upwards as if in prayer, while a smug look creased his face. Circumstances were boding well for him up to now. At least he could start to relax.

'Parcel for Mr Santini!' Thrusting the clipboard forwards, he waved it under the porter's nose, causing him to blink.

'Who did you say?' His line of authority was doomed before it had even materialized.

'Twenty-four hour parcel and document service, sir, for a Mr Santini!' Presenting his ID card from a distance, he held it at an oblique angle obliterating the porter's line of vision.

Through sleepless eyes, the porter made a token gesture of approval, before replying. 'I see, I'd better check to see if he's available... bear with me.'

Maniela found himself forced to bite his tongue. He could quite easily have said, 'I'll save you the trouble!' But why spoil an illusion? The porter turned his back and negotiated the intercom. Straining his ears, Maniela attempted to pick up on his conversation. Credentials became a topic, as the ominous charade was played out in full. Finally, Maniela got the nod he'd craved.

'You can use the visitors' lift, mate. You want flat two on the fifth floor.'

'Thanks for your help.'

Once inside the lift, he breathed easier, closing his eyes as he ascended. His inner thoughts ran like quicksilver, one overlapping the other in a crazed sequence of events. He appeared to be unaffected by it all, and allowed a self-satisfied expression to light his face. For him, the moment had now become personal, and justly so, enabling him to activate his premeditated routine. His right arm instinctively dropped down to his side. He could feel the handgun burning a hole in his pocket, just crying out to be used. From out of the poacher's pocket inside the overall, he produced a .44 Magnum Blackhawk, equipped with an in situ silencer.

By now, the lift had reached the fifth floor. Moving swiftly, Maniela shadowed the weapon under his clipboard, whilst his other hand contained the alleged parcel. His mood was electric, as he emerged from out of the lift. Complete and utter self-satisfaction had now become a reality, and the climax was just minutes away. Shortly, another contract to add to his ever increasing CV would manifest itself. Pausing briefly, a poignant distant scene became mirrored in his subconscious: an image of his late parents' lifeless bodies, etched his sadistic memory.

'It's my duty, you know, you do understand, don't you?' He spoke as if surrounded by a human awareness. Leaving off, he continued to walk on down the corridor to flat number two. His eyes instantly lit up. 'How convenient,' he muttered. The door to the flat appeared to be slightly ajar, as he called out, 'Mr Santini? Parcel, sir.'

His would-be victim made himself known in seconds, by appearing in the doorway. Everything about the man fitted into place with Terry Winters' blessing: immaculately turned out, in a well-tailored, lightweight suit, and sporting an open-neck silk shirt. His swarthy looks were a giveaway. This indeed was Tito 'the Butcher' Santini. At last, they were face to face. Santini seemed to be edgy, and it soon became evident.

'Make it quick, I'm just on my way out. Where do I—?'

His intended victim froze! Maniela forced the weapon into his lower ribcage, as he removed the Magnum from underneath the clipboard. Swiftly, he tossed the parcel and clipboard into the flat. With one hand now free, he closed and locked the door behind him, waving Santini back into the lounge. Santini immediately backed off, but found himself forced to stop, as the edge of the bar top met his back. It became an all too familiar setting for Maniela; the stage was his, and he revelled in the power it instilled in him. As an extra in the cast, Santini wasn't even aware of his lines.

Whimpering like a baby, he made a pathetic attempt to use money as an inducement. It quickly fell on deaf ears, as Maniela shook his head and laughed confidently.

'You must know why I am here, Mr Santini. I come here courtesy of Mr Terry Winters. I'm expensive, and the man who spends... wins! In one respect, you're lucky, it would seem.'

'Lucky! ... How? Please... please, take the money.'

'I can't do that! Besides, I'm under orders to ensure that you receive preferential treatment.'

Santini in desperation read into his statement from the wrong angle. 'You mean I get to—'

His plea ended abruptly as Maniela shook his head. 'It means, my friend... you don't get to die straight away.'

Sweat poured down Santini's face, his whole body convulsed in stark and he wrung his hands in a desperate begging attitude. 'Manilla, God! No... don't do this to me... anything, I'll give you anything.'

Taking a pace forwards, Maniela lowered the Magnum. 'You still don't understand, do you? I'm the one who gives.' Slowly, he fondled the trigger; suddenly, there came a pffft-like sound from the gun, as the silencer kicked in and the fatal bullet exited the barrel. The mask of extreme pain registering on Santini's bloodless face was indescribable. His left kneecap exploded in an outright burst of splintered bone and defunct flesh! The rush of blood that followed formed a backdrop to the gaping hole that was once a working leg. For a man devoid of feeling, every injustice he'd ever incurred had now come back to haunt him, as once again he repeatedly begged for his useless life. Grovelling on the floor in a sea of blood, he raised his right arm and placed it on the bar top in an effort to right himself.

Maniela casually strolled across to where he lay straddled against the bar. His eyes fell onto the ice pick, left there by Santini himself earlier on in the day. Grasping it in his left hand, he brought it crashing down through the back of Santini's hand, pinning him to the bar top as he did so! Gurgling and choking on his own vomit with pain, Santini appeared to be beyond redemption. His useless body hung down like a sodden rag, as the ice pick took the weight of his terminal suffering. Maniela stood over him, staring long and hard at his victim, the past sequence of events highlighting the inner fascination of his trade. To be an accomplice to somebody's premeditated death was payment indeed.

His singular thoughts crumpled as without warning Santini's body arched and slewed around. His free left hand reached upwards, in a last ditch attempt to make contact with the cuff of his jacket sleeve. As a forlorn gesture, it fell way short. Once again, bloodless eyes gazed upwards, forever pleading to end his misery. Unfortunately, Maniela wasn't quite ready to oblige just yet. After slipping out of his overall, he quickly discarded the hat and moustache. From his jacket lapel he extracted a carnation buttonhole, which he placed under his victim's nose as a macabre gesture. Methodically, he then moved it from side to side as if imitating the beat of a musical metronome, every movement representing a second in time.

For Santini, time had just become irrelevant. It was to be his last sensation to smell, as a 10mm neat, round, burnt hole suddenly appeared in the middle of his forehead, blackened by cordite and ringed with a trace of blood. The kick from the Magnum jerked Santini's head backwards as if kicked by a horse, then whiplashed forwards in a split second. His sightless eyes remained open. By now, they were almost thanking him for his inevitable one-way ticket to hell! The back of his head was missing primarily, and whatever Santini had in the way of brains could be found decorating two walls and half the ceiling way beyond his distorted corpse.

'Nasty!' remarked Maniela coolly. 'But effective!' Moving swiftly, he produced a brown A4 manilla envelope from out of his pocket. Stopping off, he looked around for a convenient place to rest it. In doing so, he brushed against Santini's jacket sleeve and exposed a tailored arm sheath. 'I thought as much,' he muttered. Taking his time, he removed a half-sprung stiletto dagger. It seemed to give him added inspiration, as it served to pin the envelope to Santini's chest. The buttonhole he managed to wedge inside of what remained of his mouth, in the hope it wouldn't fall out at the back!

Casting his eagle eye over the grotesque scene before him, he stood back to admire his work. There was nothing more that he could do; time to make a move. By his reckoning, Santini had been given the grace of fifteen minutes' bonus of extra life!

'I'm slipping,' he reprimanded himself. 'Far too generous, but I've more than earned my money.' Checking that the door to the flat was still locked from the inside, he left by the personal integral lift to gain access to the private car park in the basement.

Thus far, he hadn't put a foot wrong, and his luck seemed to be holding out. There wasn't a soul in sight, as he made his way through the car park, up the ramp and then to ultimate freedom. The thought of being back in Jersey the following day, and giving it large around his pool, was indeed a bonus. As for Peters and Rossetti, they both needed to grab what fresh air was on offer, before it became rationed!

Without doubt, Maniela was now on a roll, having terminated the first leg consisting of a contract treble. For the time being, a spontaneous phone call would now take precedence. It would appear, according to Maniela, that Terry Winters' birthday had come early this year and, as such, wasn't aware of the fact! He just needed a gentle reminder from Buffy Manilla to give him the welcome news!

CHAPTER 27

A DEATH TOO MANY

Rejecting his cup of stewed tea, the porter frowned and checked his watch for the second time in five minutes. With seven hours of shift under his belt, even boredom had become obsolete. His wage didn't rise to the heights of having to think, should a problem arise. But as they say, 'There's always one!' The foyer itself had been as busy as a poxy doctors' surgery for the last couple of hours. So he did have an excuse. Nevertheless, something appeared to be bugging him. Slowly it dawned on him: Maniela's appearance had given him food for thought. Stubbing his cigarette out made his conjecture conclusive.

'It doesn't add up: the guy has been gone nearly twenty minutes by my reckoning. Bloody long time just to deliver a parcel!' He wore the look of a much worried man, and he felt even less pleased when he replaced the intercom receiver. Nobody, it seemed, wanted to pick up the receiver in flat two on the fifth floor!

For some unknown reason, his thoughts took a negative swerve. *Maybe the owner went out? What about his car? No way, it hardly moves during the day, and then there's the chauffeur of course. I would have seen him come in.* Backwards and forwards, his thinking rebounded without reaching a viable conclusion. He then decided to approach his dilemma from another angle, by focusing his mind on Maniela acting as the delivery agent. *There's no way the guy could have left the building without me knowing, I'm convinced of that!* From a rational point of view, he was clearly right. But somebody needed to tell him about the exclusive force confronting him. Right now, he was stuck with a situation that was way over his head.

The thought of personally checking the flat out, as a last resort, appeared to be the obvious solution. He was armed with a pass key and the fifth floor beckoned. To be honest, he should never have got out of bed that day. It just wasn't happening for him. The key he was using seemed defunct!

'Shit!' he exclaimed. 'I don't need all this.' His concentration lapsed, as he realized his attempt was getting him nowhere fast. 'Bloody lock! Why the hell won't it budge?' Then it dawned on him. 'Damn! Why didn't I think of that before? The door must be locked from the inside.'

Fair comment, nothing wrong with that, except it still didn't explain the absence of two people, seemingly having vanished into thin air! Job's worth immediately reared its head, as 999 came into play. Having explained the situation as he knew it, the porter replaced the receiver, and waited nervously for the police to arrive.

The two plain clothes officers took their time, before finally turning up. Another thirty minutes would have seen their shift out! Producing their warrant cards, they made themselves known.

'Detective Sergeant Hadlow and DC Mullins. Your call suggested a disappearance, sir?'

'You tell me, mate! The only thing I can be sure about is that it's all happening upstairs; best I take you up there.' The porter immediately ushered the pair upstairs, filling them in with what additional information he thought relevant. Once outside the threshold, the sergeant took over.

'Right! From what you've told me, sir, we don't have any

alternative by the sound of it. I suggest we carry out a forced entry; that should tell us something. If you're agreeable of course?'

The porter shrugged his shoulders in mock defeat. 'It's not for me to say, guv, you fill your boots.'

The attending DC was a little on the short side of legal, as coppers go, although nearly as wide. Suffice to say, the door appeared to have his name on it. His second attempt proved to be a no-contest, as it buckled inwards under his weight, leaving the porter cringing at the damage incurred. The sergeant turned to his sidekick; a look of doubt clouded his face.

'This had better be worth it,' he said dryly.

Cautiously, the two coppers entered the lounge, closely followed by the porter. In comparison, they might as well have walked into a brick wall! As they all stood rooted to the carpet, the insidious sight that met them would haunt their memories for some time to come. Horrified, they ventured closer towards the murder scene itself. The sergeant was the first to speak. His past experience came into play, as his initial observations came home to roost. In the past, what he already knew about Buffy Manilla had been only words on paper. Utter disbelief etched his face. The hallmarks were all there to be seen; this was no illusion! He knew there and then he was sharing a ringside seat to a performance by a murderer whose name he could spell backwards, but never seen in the flesh! With one hand gripped tightly against his forehead, and narrowed eyes, he gazed down on the misshapen form of abused flesh and bone that was once Tito 'the Butcher' Santini!

With his loose arm, he waved the other two back, at the same time, speaking in a melodramatic tone of voice. 'Oh my God! What a bloody mess. Poor bastard obviously upset you know who!'

The young DC felt keen to venture closer, as the porter, wearing a mask of horror, wretched unashamedly. 'What's with the envelope, sarge?' he asked.

'It's a long story, Mullins. But for the time being, this one is for the big boys. Get on the blower immediately. I want SOCO, forensic... the full Monty up here. When he's finished throwing up, you can tell the porter nobody leaves the block; get on to it now! Meanwhile, you can forget you're off duty, and I suggest if you're going to throw up as well, you do it outside. There's enough damn mess in here as it is!'

Within ten minutes of making contact with HQ, the block and surrounding periphery became classed as a no-go area. In the event, Santini's insurance was long gone.

Two murders in less than a week became a statistic you couldn't sweep under the carpet. The local press boys were having a field day. The macabre touch of Buffy Manilla gave them an added licence to print and to reprint!

'GANGLAND MURDER TO MODERN-DAY RIPPER' featured highly in the dailies, while the tabloids chose to run with 'DEATH OF THE ITALIAN JOB'.

The community as a whole was all affected one way or another. That aside, the ethnic ghettos of Docklands were on a roll, it seemed. Hostilities had ceased to reign overnight! A tendency towards racial acceptance appeared to be the word on the streets. The profound effect of the murder was also felt deeply, none more so than by Ricky Peters himself.

'Rossi? Yeah... it's Ricky. Shit! What a week. Nothing to show for it.'

'I ain't surprised, the amount of old bill on the manor. You sound really pissed off, what's going down?'

Peters' negative attitude marked a side Rossetti was unfamiliar with. 'Tell yer the truth, I'm pulling out... me and the Traveller, that is. I don't mind admitting to yer, but that fucking Manilla is something else! The job he done on Santini was a bit special. Makes yer wonder if the guy was on crack at the time.'

There were many versions doing the rounds, the least of which sent out a grim reminder to the once ambitious. The writing was on the wall for all to see. And Peters knew it.

He continued. 'I ain't a bleedin' martyr, Rossi. The only cause I got is for fucking living!' His reasoning showed through as he went on. 'What with him and Winters, I—'

Rossetti cut him short. 'He's really got to you, ain't he?'

'Yeah! Him and the Traveller both. He actually fired back at me yesterday; that tells yer something.'

'Blimey. So where was yer thinking of going, then?'

'About as far as I can leg it. That asshole Manilla will be out looking to get some more holiday money soon. I fancy giving Manchester a whirl. It had to end sometime… fancy it?'

Rossetti held back before replying. 'I'll have to give it a swerve. I've still got one more bit of bleedin' grief to sort out before I leave Stonewater.'

Peters was on his case almost immediately. 'You ain't gonna let Winters drop, are yer?'

'No! The bastard's got it coming to him. Besides, it's personal, Ricky.'

'I figured that much. Just make sure yer do it on the QT, and cover yer tracks. Oh, I nearly forgot. There's a safety deposit box in town with yer name on it. I'll forward you the key and the SP. The box contains a nice few quid to tide yer over. Anyway… be in touch… be lucky.' He rang off, leaving Rossetti to ponder on what the future held in store.

CHAPTER 28

TIME OUT

'Jesus! I can't get my head around this latest murder. You take that other guy… Baines, or whatever his name was. That was bad enough, but this gangland killing business is a bit naughty. D'ye reckon the two killings are linked?'

'Possibly. Just over a week apart, makes yer think that way, doesn't it?'

Ronnie Callaghan and Siddie Levy were on a coffee break in Toni de Angelo's, while engrossed in conversation. The topic of murder could be found on everybody's lips. Joe Public, given time, could manage to absorb two unfortunate victims. It was the method of execution that riveted their interest. Ronnie cupped his hands between his head, deep in thought.

'The more I think—'

'I know exactly what's going through yer mind.' Siddie, sharp as ever, honed in on his case, which reminded him to say, 'You still think Rossetti's involved in all this grief, don't yer?'

'You can't disclaim it out of sight, mate, can yer?' retorted Ronnie. 'One thing's for sure: even if he isn't, I bet he knows a man who is!'

At this point, Siddie decided to keep shtum on the matter, as an act of diplomacy. Deep down he knew that Ronnie had got it right. Feeding him with logical bullets would only aggravate his unintentional desire to career off on a one-man mission of utter madness.

Given time, and the frame of mind, he felt convinced that someday it was going to happen. Knowing what lay in Ronnie's court, nothing he could say or do would change that! Since Mickey Gibbons' brush with Rossetti, his attitude had developed dramatically. 'It's like working with a time bomb, Rachael,' Siddie would explain. 'Please God, he doesn't get hurt.'

Ronnie was more than incensed, and it began to show. 'Five minutes with the gutless bastard, it ain't a lot to ask... is it? I'll make him wish he'd never been bleedin' born. I've had it with the nonce all my life!'

Siddie sensed that Ronnie was about to go into one, but found himself forced to take a backseat, as he pressed home his feelings.

'Satisfaction! Just him and me, you couldn't better that.'

This time, Siddie got a result as he cleverly smoothed the situation over. Pushing his empty cup to one side, he stood up, and pointed in the direction of their stalls, arms flailing, set wide in a gesture of longing. 'Money! Money! Money! Can yer do better than that, my friend? C'mon, we're keeping the punters waiting.'

Having firmly convinced him, they hurriedly exited Toni's. On the way over, Siddie glanced upwards as if in prayer, breathing a sigh of relief as he did so. This time he'd managed to get Ronnie out of goal, but at the same time realized that he was fast running out of time and, more to the point... ideas!

CHAPTER 29

EVER DECREASING CIRCLES

Elsewhere in town, Ronnie's nemesis began showing signs of restlessness. Rossetti picked the receiver up, hesitated slightly, and then proceeded to make a call. A mood of self-confidence, laced with expectancy, seemed to be in favour. Elsewhere would have told a conflicting story. Ever since Peters' sudden whim to pull out, the manor had become a graveyard, as far as the criminal fraternity were concerned. 'I've seen more action in a nun's knickers!' was one particular heavy's answer to its sudden demise. As a solo act, Rossetti felt compelled to go back to his previous shallow existence, consistent with ducking and diving, as a means to get by. But that's not to say he didn't have foreseeable plans in mind. Safe in the knowledge that Buffy Manilla had vacated the mainland had inadvertently given him the golden opportunity he'd craved: to bring down Terry Winters. Nothing else held any importance. It was destined to be, the one act that he was committed into carrying out, before finally moving on to God knew where.

He became alerted to the fact that the dialling tone had ceased. Hesitantly, he uttered one word. 'Sedgeman?'

A few seconds elapsed, before a voice replied. It stank of suspicion, he noted. 'Do I know you?' His reply gave nothing away.

'Ricky Peters put me on to yer. I thought maybe we could do some business together, know what I mean?'

'Business? That depends.'

'On what exactly?'

'How do I know yer kosher?' Rossetti was fast becoming pissed off with Sedgeman's lack of co-operation.

'You'll have to trust me, although wedge I'm holding says I'm good for a deal. So if it ain't you, then I'll find some other fucker, please yerself.' His brusque manner held the key, as Sedgeman folded.

'You looking for anything specific?' The breakthrough was made, enabling him to relax his tone.

'I'm totally in your hands as it goes. But given the choice, nothing bulky and no extras would do the business!'

'Okay, I'll see what I can do; call me back in twenty-four hours.'

Considering the current crime climate, obtaining a shooter at such notice was more than he could hope for. Completing the deal the following evening now found him in possession of a .38 Cobra Colt (or 'snubbie') compact snub-nosed, ideal for short-range work, plus a dozen rounds of ammunition, all original ID completely obliterated. Sedgeman, for his part, had moved mountains in twenty-four hours. Rossetti still had his to climb! The prompt removal of Santini was one thing. Having to live in the aftermath of his unholy demise could be seen now causing Terry Winters personal repercussions. With the slick removal of Baines as well, Slatteries had become a second home to the local plod.

Winters' precarious track record was beginning to lose its credibility, as law and order began to cause untimely ripples in his once illustrious empire. Regulars from the old bill were becoming commonplace, forcing him to close the snooker hall. Apart from a couple of loyal heavies and himself, the place appeared deserted. Ricky Peters put the situation in perspective when contacting Rossetti, speaking as he was from a club in Manchester.

'The little bleeder might have won a battle, but he ain't won the fucking war!' From a strategic viewpoint, the old bill's recent intervention had become Winters' loss and Rossetti's gain. The lack of bodies would provide him with the space he could readily capitalize on.

The prospect of venturing close to his intended target looked better by the minute. Choosing the right moment would be something he needed to work on. As a result, obtaining a pattern of his movements would be his prime objective. As he was drunk with desire to oust Winters, his torrid life of gambling and booze consequently shuddered to a grinding halt! Four painstaking observations from a safe distance produced an ongoing sequence of events, from which he drew some speculative intelligence. It emerged that the two heavies he retained on his payroll made a point of checking out anytime between six and seven o'clock of an evening. Alternative business interests further afield meant that his office was in constant use up until nine o'clock most nights for Winters' benefit. As a secondary observation, Rossetti discovered that the light from his office could be clearly seen from outside of the building when in use. Adjacent to Slatteries, the open ground that made up the car parking area fell short on security. But the two surrounding derelict warehouses on the two sides offered ample cover after dark.

Downing his scotch, Rossetti's face evoked an evil mask of satisfaction. The fruits from his last four days of labour had finally ripened. It would soon be time to reap the harvest of death. Relaxing in the front room of his flat, he toyed with the empty .38 Cobra, constantly aiming it at an imaginary target. The wall clock came into view, as he traversed the pistol round in an arc. The time was just after 4 pm. Spontaneously, he let fly. Throwing his head back, he began to laugh, childlike at first, steadily increasing, allowing it to get stronger and stronger, as he wildly picked off false targets in a crazed frenzy.

From a shrill, his voice intensified into a peak of manic intensity. A huge blurred image of Winters suddenly manifested itself in the ceaseless crossfire. By now, his distorted body and mind were at fever pitch, acting hysterically, as his trigger finger worked tirelessly to remove the figment of his lurid imagination. The charade ceased as quickly as it had started. His limp body slumped back into a nearby chair, allowing his head to loll forwards. The pistol almost fell from his grasp, induced by the sweat exuding from his sodden palm. Struggling to regain his composure, he reverently placed the tool of death down on the table in front of him, still obviously mesmerized by the power it instilled. For the first time in his unco-ordinated life, any hidden phobias were swept to one side, as his world of inborn fear became obsolete.

In a few hours' time, the climax to his murderous quest would become a reality, fuelled by a transfusion, synonymous to egotism and elation. After draining his glass, he lost no time in refilling it.

*

Meanwhile, from another source, another set of misplaced circumstances had also begun to evolve. For one person, it would entail a personal vendetta. But an unrehearsed intervention, deriving from a quirk of fate, would send events spiralling on a collision course that reeked of disaster!

It was on the cards. Sooner or later, Ronnie Callaghan, as prophesied by Siddie, would eventually blow! As of now, a blend of hatred and overwhelming vengeance had run its designer course. Putting it mildly, he was having a shit day.

Dismantling his stall that particular afternoon, Siddie

pleaded with Ronnie's sanity. 'What are yer trying to prove already?'

'Prove? Huh, justice for Mickey will do for a start! And me? I don't need a bleedin' excuse.'

How do you reason with a man like Ronnie Callaghan? Fully aware of the frame of mind he was in, even though the signs were all there, stemming from the moment he put his foot in the market that morning, Siddie was at a loss to break him down. As a lifelong friend, he should have known better. From a personal point of view, he'd witnessed Ronnie's latest change in temperament only once before, and that had happened way back, as kids on the street. It concerned a life-changing altercation between Ronnie and Rossetti. According to Siddie's reckoning, the incident occurred, 'Some thirty years ago… and now,' he reminded himself, 'it's turned a complete circle!'

Siddie grasped his hand, before Ronnie decided to leave. Words were all he had to offer. 'I fully realize and understand what you have to do. Nothing I say or do will change your mind. Just promise me that you won't put yerself in any unnecessary danger, my friend.'

'I'm sorry too, Siddie. But I have to do this to make things right! I know yer understand. I'll be in touch.' Again, they shook hands warmly.

'Mazel tov, my friend, take care already.' Turning on his heel, Siddie walked away, resembling a broken man.

★

The atmosphere in his flat was bad enough. Arriving home some twenty minutes after leaving Siddie, Ronnie slammed the front door behind him. Mickey happened to be in the lounge, and called out. There was no expected response.

'Uhm, who's upset him, I wonder?'

Just then, Ronnie put his head round the door. 'Sorry, mate, few things on me mind. Have yer eaten yet?'

Mickey straightaway picked up on an air of vagueness in his manner. His body appeared to be saying one thing, while his mind veered off on a tangent. 'Er, no, I thought I'd wait for you. Maybe a takeaway... yeah?'

Declining his offer, Ronnie headed for the shower. 'Don't wait for me, son, you carry on... do yer own thing,' he shouted. 'I'll give it a miss tonight if yer don't mind?'

Mickey shook his head, pondering for a minute. 'He's coming down with something, and it ain't bloody illness!'

He never did get his meal. Twenty minutes later, showered and prepared, they left the flat together. The mood in the car was getting to Mickey. *A word... a sign... contact... Anything!* He was almost willing Ronnie to confide in him. Under the circumstances, he went for low key. As the car pulled up outside of the gym, Mickey felt compelled to confront him.

'D'ye realize you haven't said a word since we left the flat? We need to talk about it; something is bothering yer.'

'That noticeable, eh? Believe me when I say it's a long story, mate. Besides, I ain't got the time right nah.'

'I don't buy that! There must be something I can do?'

Ronnie appeared adamant when replying. 'Thanks, but no thanks, Mickey! What I've got in mind is all down to me alone. Yer gonna have to trust me on this one.' A serious look registered on his face; pursing his lips, he continued. 'Trouble is, I need to go missing for an hour or two. So you carry on, and I'll catch yer later.'

At this point, Mickey felt completely sidetracked, wishing he hadn't opened his mouth. This wasn't the same Ronnie Callaghan he'd come to admire and trust.

'What could be more important than the gym? You owe

me that much,' he demanded. The offer of a one-to-one debate wasn't forthcoming.

Ronnie threw him a desperate look. 'Some other time, son. I've really got to go.'

Angry and deflated, he got out of the car, and leant on the door. 'This business, or whatever it is, must be bloody damn important to yer?' His last-minute ditch attempt to break Ronnie down… vanished as Ronnie slammed the car into gear. Mickey took the hint by closing the car door, as it pulled away, leaving him feeling completely demoralized. Instinctively, his arm dropped down to one side, as if to retrieve his kit bag. Added frustration kicked in followed by utter dismay. Looking around, there wasn't a sign of it anywhere.

'Shit,' he exclaimed. 'I don't believe this is happening. I must have left it in the car boot.' Feeling at odds with himself made him feel totally inadequate. Stepping out into the road, he could just make out the tail lights of the car in the distance. Purely by chance, an empty cab swung into view, and in doing so gave him a vital option. He literally threw himself in front of the car, causing the driver to swerve violently, before finally screeching to a complete standstill!

Mickey lost no time getting in. 'Sorry about that, mate, but I need to catch that car up in front.'

'Christ almighty, mate! You could have fooled me!' he retorted. 'And here's me thinking you had a bleedin' death wish.'

Mickey breathed a sigh of relief. 'Like I said, sorry, but I really do need to catch that car.'

Slowly but surely, the erratic jigsaw pieces resembling the day's events were now falling into place. The cabbie could never have known that his no-nonsense reply to Mickey's suicidal actions would have so much bearing in an hour's time. But then, life itself is one big open jigsaw, you might wish to say. Problem! This particular one had a cast of exclusive players, and not one of them was aware of what the others were doing. So two down and two to go to complete a quartet of intrigue!

★

Fifty yards or so from Slatteries, Rossetti leaned forwards, enabling him to peer through the windscreen of his car, looking for any sign of life. Stationary and lost in the shadow of a derelict warehouse gave him ample cover. The clock on his dashboard said 7 pm. The light reflecting from Winters' office seemed dimmer than usual, although it was enough to send his pulse racing with expectancy. Craning his body further forwards created a shift in weight to the side of his jacket pocket. The .38 Cobra Colt nestling inside was also on the move. As a result, the tautness of his suit material clearly defined the weapon, small as it was. Placing an open hand over it, Rossetti caressed it in a sickly manner, allowing his evil perversion to manifest.

Squinting hard, he suddenly became aware of the door to Slatteries opening up, bringing his sicko lust to a premature ending. Two figures emerged, and made their way to a nearby stationary car. Within minutes they were gone, swallowed up by the misty gloom of the night. Satisfied that they were long gone, he quickly emerged from the car; in one hand he was holding a gallon can of petrol! Warily, he approached the door to Slatteries, the ongoing light from the office becoming a beacon of salvation to assist his heinous motives.

'So far, so good,' he muttered under his breath. Negotiating the door proved to be the least of his problems. With scrutiny, it appeared to be unlocked, enabling him to slip inside unobserved.

Apart from a temperamental strip light, visibility was low. He should worry. He was on home ground, and he welcomed the darkness. He could almost feel himself sweating, as body tension set in. Placing the can down, he released his top shirt button. For the time being, his discomfort gave way to the passionate feel of the .38 Cobra, as he withdrew it from the depth of his pocket. By now, his vision had become accustomed to the alien light, enabling him to focus on the door to Winters' office. As images went, this particular door represented everything that stood between him and the invincible top rung that he'd craved.

In a few minutes' time, it would all be over! *The reigning king is dead! … Long live the king!* Adjusting the safety catch on the gun, a wave of anti-climactic force engulfed his body.

'You lucky bastard, Winters, you're gonna get yours quickly. Me!? I've had to suffer poxy months for this moment. You're going to rot in hell and back again!'

As he ranted his insidious intentions, a car pulled up a short distance away from Slatteries. An alien figure got out, and furtively made his way across the car park. Pausing briefly, he glanced across to where a red Mercedes saloon car was parked. Registering a look of ingrained menace, he doggedly strode towards the door. He noted that it had been unusually left ajar.

And so it starts!

The suddenness of it all was never in doubt. Winters' facial expression became a fixture of total shock and stark terror as Rossetti forced the office door open, brandishing the shooter in his direction.

'You!? … You! … I…' Choking on fear, his words failed to materialize. In seconds, his useless frame morphed into a spineless wreck. Again, the intimidating shooter beckoned him forwards. Exiting his chair, he fell to his knees, grovelling and convulsing at Rossetti's feet.

'Kiss 'em! ... I said fucking kiss 'em!' Rossetti screamed. He lowered the weapon, and the snub of the barrel met his wet forehead, as Winters looked upwards in a submission of terror. Mercy, it seemed, had been erased from the script. 'That wasn't so bad... was it? Yer getting the fucking hang of it nah.' The moment had got to Rossetti, as he savoured the pathetic figure of Winters performing at the top end of degradation. For a split second, he got careless, by allowing his concentration to lapse. Easing off, he glanced backwards over his shoulder, as if anticipating an uninvited guest. In doing so, it gave Winters a lifeline to turn the situation around. There was no reason for him to think otherwise. He knew his death was imminent the moment Rossetti broke through the door. A faint chance to break the mould came to him on a welcome plate.

Gripping Rossetti's ankles tightly and yanking at the same time, he managed to roll over onto his side. The impetus took Rossetti completely by surprise, throwing him off balance in the process and forcing him to crash down onto his back. For a small man, Winters seemed to have inherited the strength of two men, as he desperately lunged for the handgun in Rossetti's grasp. But then, he was fighting for his miserable life! Managing to secure a joint hold on the shooter, the two bodies thrashed about wildly on the floor. First one way and then the other. Without any prompting, their life-threatening struggle ceased abruptly, as if in animation, leaving their faces inches away from each other. A recipe of pleasure and death wavered between the two bodies for a second or two, almost as if they were awaiting a major decision, hovering in the background. When it finally came, it produced a slightly muffled climax, as the .38 Cobra exploded into life.

Winters gave out a sickly and despairing look of agony; his mouth fell open wide as he involuntarily wretched. A trickle of blood welled from out one corner of his mouth. His eyes rolled heavily as he uttered his last dying word.

'Why?!'

His chest rose, releasing a surge of blood to gush from out of his mouth, in turn becoming frothy caused by the last remaining air in his body, stemming from his pre-determined death. His grip on Rossetti loosened, and he fell backwards in a heap via the floor, on his one-way ticket presumably to hell! After disengaging himself, Rossetti stood up, and straddled his legs apart over his defunct corpse. His lust for revenge appeared more prominent than ever. The residue of evil left in him came by way of his mouth.

'Can yer hear me, Winters? I know yer not fucking dead yet!' he screamed.

By now, Winters' body could be seen knocking on the gates of hell. Although it didn't appear to have made any impression on his show of deranged verbal madness.

'Didn't I tell yer?' Rossetti continued to rant. 'There's a bonus as well!'

Winters' lifeless form jerked spasmodically from the force of four more bullets ripping into his body. A stunned silence followed, and just as quickly it was all over!

The sharp reality became a distant nightmare, formed by a shadow in the light invading his space. In an instant, he spun round pointing the shooter. Framed in the doorway of the office stood none other than Ronnie Callaghan! The wheel of destiny had finally turned full circle. Everything that had become rotten and festered over the years now lay at Rossetti's feet! Ronnie broke the spell before his nemesis could make a move. He indicated towards the blood-soaked corpse of Winters, now looking grotesque in death.

'Says it all. You've dug yer own grave again. This time for good. Looks like the old bill have saved me the grief.'

'You'll never get the satisfaction, Callaghan. I always knew it would come down to this in the end. I've got one more poxy bullet left, yer bastard, and it's got your fucking name on it!'

Instinctively, Ronnie's body stiffened as Rossetti prepared to fire. In a split second, an outside force emerged from out of the gloom. The alien body threw him completely off his feet, allowing him to fall sideways in the process. At the same time, Rossetti pulled the trigger. Ronnie fortunately hit the floor; at the same time his redeemer landed on top of him. Allowing for the speed of events, his faculties hadn't deserted him. Even as he hit the floor an inner instinct was telling him that the figure belonged to Mickey Gibbons, no less!

With little time to think, there was barely time to talk.

'God in heaven. What the hell are you doing 'ere?' shouted Ronnie.

'Same cause as you, I reckon. You're forgetting what the asshole did to me!

ARRRRRGH! Mind my shoulder, I think I've been hit.'

'You're getting to be a bloody habit, Mickey. C'mon, let's get the hell out of 'ere.'

That was as far as they got. The incensed figure of Rossetti emerged from the shadows, and stood over them. Powerless to defend himself, Ronnie had no answer to Rossetti's frenzied attack that followed. The butt of the handgun contacted the side of his head with sickening force. Not content with that, he used it to continue pistol whipping Ronnie. And then he vanished.

The high octane smell from petrol fumes filled his nostrils and lungs, as Mickey continued to shake some life into his inert form. 'Ronnie! ... Ronnie! ... For Christ's sake, wake up.'

Stirring, Ronnie's eyes flickered open, and the fumes did the rest. From a distance, they made out Rossetti pouring a ring of petrol around them from a can, dispersing what remained into the office. The two rose shakily to their feet, looking on in despair while Rossetti produced a lighter from his pocket. Laughing hideously, he torched a discarded newspaper and calmly threw it onto the trail of petrol. There came a sudden rush of air, as the vapour pre-ignited the petrol, sending the flames on their unstoppable journey of destruction.

The trail grew even longer as if drawn by a magnet. By now, the pair found themselves completely surrounded by flames. Worse still was to follow. The flames were no longer relying on the fuel. Instead, they appeared to devour whatever stood in their way.

Fully awake, Ronnie went into survival mode. 'I've seen enough, we need to get out of this hellhole. Try to get some help. I need to find Rossetti. By now, smoke was becoming more than an issue. Fortunately, they managed to breach the wall of fire. Ronnie spotted the door and virtually pushed Mickey through it; he then turned his attention on Rossetti. He didn't have to look too hard. From out of a lung-wrenching barrier of thick smoke, he loomed large and menacing.

In his hand, he wielded a heavy iron bar. The two circled each other, oblivious of what was happening around them. The well-worn adage 'Be first' ran riot in his mind. Ronnie didn't hesitate. But this time Rossetti beat him to it!

Lunging forwards gripping the bar, he swung it wildly at shoulder height, screaming like a maniac as he did so. Acting on instinct, Ronnie neatly sidestepped his murderous attempt. Dropping down to waist level, he drove a short left hook to Rossetti's solar plexus. His body arched over, while his face contorted in pain. Fighting for breath caused his arms to drop, revealing his stricken features. In an instant, a feeling of déjà vu came into force. Nobody that day had been on hand to tell Ronnie Callaghan, 'Think before you act!' You see a bit of meat, you hit it! That was street lore; it worked for him some thirty years ago, and it was about to work again. 'Be first' once again came back to haunt him. This time around, his timing was never in doubt, as he threw a textbook looping right hand, delivered directly from the shoulder. Sucker that he was, Rossetti didn't even see the punch delivered. It caught him flush on the chin, sending him reeling backwards, through a ceiling-high wall of flames, which, by now, had become impassable.

The stench arising from the acrid smoke was fast becoming harder to deal with. He began to feel disorientated; shaking his head, he swiftly looked around for a possible escape route.

'Over here, Ronnie! Bloody well move it.'

Turning around, he spotted Mickey Gibbons through the smoke, screaming away at him from the door. He didn't need a second bidding. Minutes later, they were both outside, leaning on each other for support. In the distance, the sound of wailing fire engines could be heard over the crackling of flames. The pair needed to get some distance between themselves and the fire, due to the heat rapidly intensifying. The inferno itself had now taken full control within the building. Within minutes, Slatteries, as a whole, had now been consumed from end to end, forcing them back even further to take refuge alongside the road.

Ronnie felt aware of Mickey shaking his shoulder and at the same time pointing towards the direction of the office window. At first glance, silhouetted within the framework appeared to be the outline figure of a person, arms outstretched, as if resembling a crucifix. Through runny, bleared eyes, Ronnie strained to catch a second glimpse. Could it have been his imagination? Or were the arms of the apparition beating away at the glass in a desperate attempt to break out?

If so, then the ironwork security grille covering the window did nothing to aid his cause. Rapidly advancing flames were now creating shadows to spring up from behind the terminal backdrop, and then the figure vanished, swallowed up by perplexity!

Totally mystified, Ronnie shook his head. Turning to Mickey, he said, 'I honestly don't know what to make of that! … Do you?'

Mickey hadn't even been listening to him, engrossed as he was watching a couple more appliances pulling in, followed by an ambulance and a squad car.

'God! I'd forgotten,' Ronnie exclaimed. As before, his reasoning had once again fallen on deaf ears. Then it finally hit him! 'Rossetti! … Of course! … It has to be.' To satisfy his curiosity, he looked across in the direction of the window again. Apart from the dense smoke billowing out through the broken glass, he realized he was wasting his time.

His immediate dilemma came to an abrupt halt. He became aware of a figure next to him, shouting. 'Would you know if there's anybody in there?'

'Two people as—' For reasons of his own, Ronnie checked himself before continuing. '…far as I'm aware.'

'God help 'em!' came back the reply. Grim-faced, the fire chief strode away shouting out orders.

EPILOGUE

To all intents and purposes, it appeared to be over and done with! As before, a sense of normality slowly began to make its mark. For some, life would never be the same again. Two days later, after wrestling with his conscience, Ronnie decided on a one-man pilgrimage, his intention being to visit Docklands. Grim-faced, hands clasped behind his back, he stood in silence, surveying what was left of Slatteries. The remaining stench of acrid smoke hung like a perpetual shroud, incorporating a vast area of brick rubble and distorted steel girders, infilled with a carpet of inevitable ash.

What the hell am I doing here? he questioned himself with a ring of uncertainty. The point had been made, leaving time only to reveal his singular motive. Lingering for a further couple of minutes, he finally turned his back on the scene, walking away with a determined gait in his step. Opening the door to his car, he paused briefly for one last parting glance, knowing the time had come for new beginnings. His eyes momentarily closed, as a convulsive shudder swept over his body. The car park, he noted, was now littered with the remains of debris and burnt-out cars. He slowed down to avoid the shell of one in particular that lay in his path. Even in death, it still bore the hallmarks of a Mercedes. Winding the side window down, Ronnie looked long and hard at a section of undamaged coachwork that had caught his eye. No! He hadn't been mistaken; it was bright red!

'No! It couldn't be. Could it?' he said with uncertainty.

He'd seen enough for one day; booting the pedal, he roared away. It took a full week before Slatteries finally gave up the ghost, making way for the bulldozers to move in and raze it. But there was no disputing the fact that its past reputation would remain as an epitaph for some time to come. After a few years of wrangling, a consortium took the site on. It now comprised a ten-storey block of flats. Yes, time and people had moved on with a vengeance. Some more so than others, it seemed.

This particular day in the Docklands area would have been no more different than most days, as a whole. Although, one certain person had other views on the subject. A hunched figure shuffling down a side street could be seen heading towards the harbour basin. He was noticeable by the distinctive dragging movement associated with his left foot, which appeared to be twisted at an obscure angle to his leg, adding to his obvious discomfort, while his face and hands bore the worn scars arising from defunct skin tissue! Arriving at the harbour side, he made for a particular public house incorporating a housing reclaim development. Standing outside, he hesitated briefly, taking his time to look around, intent on checking out the locale. Glancing up at the sign hanging above the door caused his eyes to narrow. Shaking his head, he made his way inside. Ordering a large scotch, he attempted to make light conversation with the barman.

'Whatever happened to the Rat and Trap?' he asked scornfully.

A look of total surprise greeted his enquiry. 'You're obviously not local, mate; it was demolished bloody years ago!'

Downing his scotch, the stranger pointed towards the optic. 'You'd better make it another large one, mister. By the way, I'm looking for a room to rent. Got any ideas?'

The barman deliberated for a second or two before

replying. 'Will that be a short- or long-term stay?' replied the barman.

An icy silence came into play, and not before an overworked vein broke the surface, causing his patchy skin to noticeably redden on his face. He leaned on the bar for support, and his distorted mouth twisted, as if in torment.

'It'll be for as long as it takes!' he replied vehemently.

THE END... MAYBE?

GLOSSARY

ANTE – Money

BANGED UP – Taken into custody

BBBC – British Boxing Board of Control

BENT – False/illegal

BIG FELLOW/BIG BOY – Largest punchbag

BLOWN AWAY – Murdered/killed

BOTTLE – Bravado

BUBBLE – Bubble & squeak (Greek) slang

BUBULA – Darling/sweetheart

BUNGARIAN – Duel Bulgarian/Hungarian

CHARLIE – Cocaine/heroin

CHUTZPAH – Nerve/guts/daring/audacity

CONTRACT – Murder by arrangement

CRACK – Cocaine/heroin

FACE – Villain/somebody of note

FINGERED – Named/exposed

FIRM – Gang/team

FUNK – Chance/anticipation

GAFF – House/building

GIVING IT LARGE – Going for it

GORILLA – Minder/bouncer

GRAND – £1,000

GRIEF – Unwanted aggravation

HEIST – Robbery/hold-up

HITMAN – Paid assassin

HOLIDAY – Time spent in jail

KARZY – Toilet
KOSHER – Legal/true
MANOR – Area/locale
MEET – A specific date
MESHUGGENEH – Crazy man/woman
MONKEY – £500
MOODY – Unreal/plastic
MOUTHPIECE – Boxer's gum shield/spokesman
MULLERED – Killed
NIFTY – £50
NOBBINS – Appreciation money
OLD BILL – Police/law
PATCH – Designated area
PLASTIC GANGSTER – Only acting the part
PLOD – Policeman
PONY – £25
PUTZ – An idiot
RACKETS – Organised crime
SCAM – Complete rip-off
SCHMALTZ – Old world charm
SCHMUCK – Idiot/contemptible person
SHOOTER – Firearm
SHTUM – Keep quiet
SP – Ready information
SPOT – Job
STABLE – Boxers allied to one manager
SWEET – Butter up
THE DOGS – Best there is
THE SMOKE – London
TOOLED UP – Carrying a gun
TUG – Pulled over by the police
TUKHUS – Person's backside
VOLLEY – Call Up/Shout

THE FINGERLESS GLOVES

WAFFLE – Have a chat
WEDGE – Roll of banknotes
WEIGHED IN – Paid out/as on scales
WHEELS – Automobile
WINO – Alcoholic/drunkard

ACKNOWLEDGMENTS

I would like to thank my wife, Sheila, for all her support and tolerance throughout my writing career. I would also like to thank James Watson, once again, for his superior computer backup assistance, and his creative involvement designing the book cover graphics. To my mother, who introduced me to the bleeding business in the first place as a kid. Also, to anybody I have ever met, inside or outside of the ring, whilst I participated in the leather business over the years. To one and all, you have my greatest respect and admiration... keep punching! Last, but not least, grateful thanks to my publisher Troubador Ltd for services rendered.